The boyfriend trial

THE BOYFRIEND TRIAL

The Boyfriend Trial is a steamy college romance with strong language and mature themes. It is the second book in The Hookup Type series. For a full list of content warnings, please visit the author's website.

Proofreading by Sadie @DotTheIEdit

Character Art by Nina @croquith

Cover Illustration by Layla @designwithlayla

ISBN-13 (paperback): 979-8-9882216-4-7

ISBN-13 (eBook): 979-8-9882216-5-4

For every girl who saw themselves in Brooke Davis.
"You do not have to compromise. Not if you don't want to."

Jaxon's "Mace" Playlist

....

Because of You – Ne-Yo
One Dance – Drake
In the Morning – J. Cole
Somebody Like You – Keith Urban
T-Shirt – Thomas Rhett
Come and Get Your Love – Redbone
More Than That – Trey Songz
I Don't Want To Be – Gavin DeGraw
Heartbeats – José González
All My Life – K-Ci & JoJo
Hey Pretty Girl – Kip Moore
Lay It Down – Lloyd
Sex on Fire – Kings of Leon
Promiscuous – Nelly Furtado
Without Love – Cast of Hairspray

PROLOGUE

JAXON

VALENTINE'S DAY 2016

My Valentine's Day usually consisted of a girl (or two) who didn't want to be alone and an evening that required no effort on my end. It sounded shitty, but it was hard to scrap a routine that worked so well. It kept emotions out of a day that vomited red and pink hearts all over the fucking place, and since I didn't do relationships, it was an easy way to get laid and move on with the rest of my week.

Last year, a girl named Heather came over to my apartment. She ordered us a pizza, and then we hooked up for an hour before she left. This year, I sat across from Maci Lawson at Carl's Corner. Carl's Corner offered cheap beer, good wings, and a low-key crowd.

There was nowhere else I'd rather be.

When our waiter returned with another round of draft beer and set the giant mugs in front of us, he smiled as foam dripped over the tops of the glasses. I wasn't sure if he was pleased with how full the mugs were or if he thought Maci and I made a cute couple.

We weren't a couple, but the possibility didn't make me want to vomit.

Wait, what the fuck?

I slid Maci's frosted glass closer to her, watching her thumbs go to work on her phone screen. "Do you mind writing your book later?"

She leaned her elbows on the table, her blue eyes focused on whatever she was typing. She glanced up for a moment, and since I was doing a shitty job at *not* staring at her, she set her phone down. "I'm sorry. I had to email my professor back. You now have my full attention."

"Tell your professor to go get laid. It's Valentine's Day."

"Says the person ordering chicken wings at a dive bar," she snapped, sipping her beer. As much as she tried not to spill, a small puddle formed on the table in front of her.

I handed her a stack of napkins. "There's nothing wrong with getting some beer and wings with your best friend."

"Am I really your best friend?"

I shrugged as if the look on her face didn't tug on my heartstrings. "As far as females go, yeah."

She placed her hand over her heart. "You have such a way with words, Jaxon Hayes."

I also acted like it didn't drive me crazy when my full name rolled off her tongue. It brought me back to the night in her apartment when we almost hooked up—the night I said no, and she ran into my best friend and roommate, Bryson, the next day.

"Why do you have to email her all the time anyway?" I asked, trying to ignore the pull in my groin.

"She's got *a lot* of connections, and since I wanna teach at a university and design curriculum someday, I wanna make a good impression with someone who has."

"Just live in college forever, huh?"

She smirked. "It's a little more professional than that."

"You'll get there," I assured her. "You're one of the most driven and book-smart people I know."

Maci rolled her eyes and passed me a menu. "Thanks for adding book-smart in there."

"Are you forgetting about your car earlier this year?" I scanned the wing sauce options, and when I looked up from the menu, she was glaring at me.

"We all have flaws, Jaxon. Must we forget how you like the *delicacies* that come with the Cup O' Noodles?"

I shook my head. "I'll never forgive you for throwing those away."

"Freeze-dried vegetables should not exist," she exclaimed. "I stand by my choice."

The waiter appeared back at our table, and we placed our order. We handed him the menus, and he informed us that all tables received an ice cream sundae with their meals—complimentary of the holiday.

Maci eyed me playfully across the table, excited about the unexpected dessert offer.

Everything about my friendship with Maci was unexpected. When I met her at the beginning of the year, I never expected that we'd become friends. I never expected her to be the first girl I didn't want to risk losing by hooking up with her, and I sure as shit didn't expect her to still be hooking up with Bryson, the guy who was everything I warned her I would become the next morning.

I chuckled as she bobbed her head to the beat in the background. "Is this your jam?"

She pointed to the ceiling. "I can't believe they are playing this anthem!"

My eyes narrowed as the lyrics registered in my head. "Why does this song sound familiar?"

"It's the theme song of *One Tree Hill*! Gavin DeGraw?" Maci drained the rest of her beer, and the glass hit the table as the chorus picked up. She locked eyes with me and sang along to the lyrics.

I mouthed the final line of the chorus, and her smile grew wider.

"See! I knew you liked 'The Tree People,'" she quoted the title I made up for the show. "You know they actually shot the show in North Carolina?"

"I'm sure the state of North Carolina was honored to have them."

"Hey, I would want to know if I lived three hours away from Wilmington!"

Before I could say anything back, we were interrupted by our baskets of food.

"Is there anything else I can get you?" the waiter asked.

Maci pointed to her beer mug. "Could we get another round of these?"

The waiter returned with fresh drinks, napkins, and a small menu for the sundae that Maci snatched off the table.

"Order whatever you want," I insisted, taking a bite of one of my wings. In one swift motion, I worked the meat off the bone and tossed the remains into the basket. I couldn't tell if Maci was mortified or impressed.

Her mouth curved into a grin as she poked her fork into her boneless buffalo wings—or nuggets, as my dad called them. "Such a gentleman."

I pointed to my basket. "Do you want one? I have garlic parm and hot."

She leaned over the table to survey her options. "Garlic parm."

I slid a wing into her basket, and she picked it up, nibbling in the middle around the bone and dropping it to the side of her plate with at least half the chicken left on the wing. My mouth dropped and I zoned in on her bright blue eyes.

She halted her next forkful of buffalo nuggets. "What?"

"Maci Lawson, who *the fuck* taught you how to eat wings?" I asked sweetly.

She laughed with her fork still hanging in front of her mouth.

"Probably the same person who told you it was okay to order buffalo nuggets at a place that serves regular wings," I muttered.

Now she was laughing so hard she had to cover her mouth with her hand. I attempted to sip my beer but had to put the glass back down. Whenever she burst into hysterics, I usually lost it too.

"First of all"—she wiped her eyes—"how dare you insult boneless wings. And second . . . not everyone inhales their chicken like a roadside raccoon."

"A roadside raccoon!" I exclaimed, sending her into another fit of giggles.

Once she regained her composure she asked, "What was your worst Valentine's Day date?"

That was an easy question. "I don't have one."

"You've *never* had a bad Valentine's Day date?"

"I've never had a Valentine's Day *date*."

She stifled a smile. "Is this your first Valentine's Day date?"

I raised my eyebrows. "Is this a date?"

"I consider this to be therapy after Chase crash-landed in my living room."

Fuck. I forgot the reason we were here in the first place.

"Order this ice cream thing," I suggested, trying to keep her mind off the Chase drama.

Once Maci placed her order, the waiter returned with a giant goblet of ice cream covered in hot fudge and topped with a hefty dollop of whipped cream.

"Jesus," I said, taking the spoon she offered me.

"You work out." She waved my comment away and stuck her spoon in the middle of the sundae. "Live a little, Jax."

I took some ice cream from the edge of the bowl.

"You're avoiding where my spoon is touching," Maci noted, purposely taking some ice cream from my side.

I shrugged. "I'm weird about dairy!"

"You shared your ice cream with me after knowing me for five minutes!"

I smiled at the memory. "That was different. I got the last Blizzard, and we weren't eating out of the same container."

"Well, I hate to burst your bubble, but I snuck a bite out of that Oreo Blizzard I gave you."

My smile faded. "You're lying."

"I guess you'll never know."

After I talked Maci into letting me pay the bill, we drove the fifteen minutes back to Bowling Green's campus. I pulled into the parking lot of her building, stopping in front of the stairs that led up to her apartment.

"Thank you for today," she said with a soft smile. "Best Valentine's Day date ever."

I gave her hand a light squeeze. "Anytime, Mace."

If someone had told me I'd be spending Valentine's Day driving home with my mind racing around a girl I couldn't have, I would've told them to fuck off. It would be so easy to follow her upstairs and pick up where we stopped back in

October—so easy to put my instincts first and set aside all of the emotions for later.

For a sliver of a second, I pictured it.

I pictured myself as the guy who could give her everything she wanted—everything she deserved out of a relationship. I was already the guy she trusted to take care of things—to take care of *her*.

Could it really be that different?

For the first time in my life, I muttered a word I never allowed in my vocabulary.

Boyfriend.

"Fuck me," I mumbled as Maci waved from the top of her stairs.

Boyfriend?

Fuck, I liked this girl.

Chapter One

MACI

May 2016

There were so many moments at Bowling Green State University that I wanted to bottle up and take with me. I knew one day, I'd look back on my time in college and recognize it as a blur. I would remember the people I met and feeling invincible because the laughter never seemed to stop.

Once I had a house to manage and a job in the real world, I'd rely on songs and trinkets to bring me back to moments like this—cleaning my apartment with my roommate, Katie, while we shared a bottle of Moscato and sang to her Drunk Betch playlist.

"One Dance" by Drake came through the TV right as I was about to start the vacuum. I held off on the final cleaning task and grabbed my wine instead, giving in to the catchy lyrics.

"Yes, girl," Katie sang, popping up from the kitchen floor. "How is Drake going to release this banger right before we leave the college bars?"

"It's criminal, actually," I said, glancing around at the memories that covered the walls.

A soft pang bounced through my stomach—another reminder that this was our last night on campus. It was hard to believe how much had happened since Katie and I moved into our apartment. It seemed like yesterday we were talking about Katie's casual relationship with Tyler and my conquest to find a hookup for junior year.

"What's criminal is how long this pizza is taking to get here." Katie threw her phone down on the coffee table. "What are you thinking about? You have ten minutes until the guys get here, so any last-minute items we haven't covered"—she gestured for me to come closer—"give them to me."

"Just remembering all of the craziness of this year, that's all. We started with just the two of us, and now we're ending it with four."

"We said we'd save the sappy shit for tomorrow," Katie warned before taking the seat next to me on the couch.

"And this isn't sappy! It's happy, actually. Because of your cooking, we now have two boyfriends who can't seem to find their way back to their own apartment."

Katie chuckled into her wine glass. "Girl, don't blame my Pinterest board of recipes. This all happened because you met a boy at Dairy Queen."

"All because they were out of cotton candy," I muttered fondly.

Katie's smile began to taper, and her eyes narrowed. "Sometimes I look back on the girl from the beginning of the year, and I don't even recognize her. It's like a version of myself that didn't know what she was doing."

I swallowed, unsure what to say. "Do you wanna talk about it?"

"Nope," she stated proudly. "What's done is done. I'm here, and I'm present, and the past is the past. I wouldn't be where I am now if I hadn't experienced the trainwreck."

A trainwreck was one word for it. I wasn't sure how else someone described an abusive ex-boyfriend who tried to break into their apartment.

"Since you're exempt from the sappy shit this evening, I'll leave you with this." I leaned forward to squeeze her hand. "You're one of the smartest people I know. Try not to let one memory trickle into everything you're making moving forward. We can't simmer on something we aren't proud of. Life's too short."

"Hmm. I like that. Who said that?"

I scoffed, getting up to retrieve the bottle of wine from the counter. "Me!"

"First Morgan Freeman and now Emily Dickinson. Who else can you channel into your life advice without their permission?"

"Emily Dickinson!" I exclaimed, barely holding it together at her choice of famous poets. "You know what, I do think that was one of the last lines of her poems." I fanned the words in front of me. "Life's too short, don't simmer."

Katie raised her glass. "Don't simmer."

We clinked our drinks together, and I delivered another tough question. "Are you nervous to be away from Connor for three months?"

"Eww. We're choosing that route, huh?" Katie cocked her head and sighed. "I'm not nervous, but I'm bummed. It'll be weird not having him down the street."

It was wild to think an entire world could exist outside of Bowling Green. College was a lifestyle, and it only took a few days in the real world to realize how different it was from everything else.

"Why do you ask?" Katie prompted. "Are you nervous to be away from Jaxon?"

My eyes flew up from the counter, and when they met Katie's, a pained expression washed over her face.

She winced. "You're hesitating."

"I'm really not meaning to," I said through a breathy laugh. "I'm not nervous. I trust Jaxon."

"Then, what's the problem?"

It was a loaded question, and we were running out of time before Jaxon and Connor walked through the door.

"The problem is that I'm the girl who is in love with the boy who said the words too soon," I admitted. "I'm also the idiot who provided my boyfriend—who doesn't do relationships—an option to trial-run our relationship."

"Life's too short, don't simmer." Katie shrugged as if her answer would hoist me over my mental blocks. "When are you going to actually take your own advice? We already threw Morgan Freeman's Fun Dip quote out the fucking window. Do we need to do the same thing to poor Emily?"

I held up my hands. "Okay, I'm done! You're right—well, actually, *I'm* right."

"No more," Katie stated, joining me at the counter. "No more worrying about things that happened this year. In three months, we'll be laughing about all of the nonsense that happened over the summer."

Even when I knew everything would be fine, I always let that sprinkle of doubt take over every positive feeling I had moving forward. It must've been delightful, living a life where you didn't overthink every possible outcome.

"If anything, I'm surprised you aren't nervous to meet Jaxon's mom," Katie murmured. "That's what I'd be tripping over."

I glared at her as a round of knocking came from the front door.

"Kidding!" Katie cackled, resting a reassuring hand on my shoulder. "Imagine the girls Jaxon dragged in and out of that house. You'll be like a breath of fresh air!"

Chapter Two

Jaxon

The boxes of Pisanello's Pizza in my hands were getting hot, and I was about to knock again before the front door of Maci's apartment flew open, and Katie's giant grin greeted us on the other side.

"My favorite person *and* the food? I would've answered the door sooner!"

"Connor is right here, Katie." I smiled, shoving the pizza boxes into her arms. "Don't be so obvious with how much you like having me over."

She rolled her eyes right before Connor leaned in to kiss her. I let the two of them have their reunion while my eyes scanned the living room for *my* favorite person.

"Mace?" I leaned into her doorframe just in time to catch a glimpse of the small of her back. My shirt fell to the middle of her thighs, completely covering her ass. I needed to give her smaller shirts to wear.

"I smelled like bleach," she said, giggling as she closed the space between us.

When she wrapped her arms around my neck, I cupped her chin and kissed her. I gripped her doorframe harder with my free hand so it wouldn't slip under her shirt and try to back her up to the bed. I was already on edge with the idea of leaving her for a month. I didn't need any more temptations.

Maci scrunched her nose. "Is the pizza here?"

"Yeah." I laughed at how easily food took over her senses. "Pizza guy handed it to me on our way up."

"And he just gave it to you?" She slid past me into the hallway. "You could've been anyone!"

"I know, right?" Katie added. "I said the same thing."

"I asked if it was for Maci, and the guy said yes. I told him you were my girlfriend and offered to take it." I pulled a paper plate from the top of the fridge. "Do you want me to escort him next time?"

"I thought it was cute," Connor added, excusing himself to the living room. Katie followed behind him, whispering something in his ear that caused him to pull her closer.

I lowered my voice so only Maci could hear me. "Did you wear that shirt on purpose?"

"Maybe." She bit into her pizza, slowly licking the sauce from her thumb. "You told me you wanted to talk about something, and whenever you need to talk, you require some prompting."

My jaw went slack when she repeated the teasing motion with her thumb. "So you're baiting me with sex by wearing my shirt?"

"I consider it motivation." She stood on her toes to kiss the side of my neck.

The small gesture sent butterflies into my stomach. I didn't even know I fucking had butterflies until I discovered how Maci's mouth felt against my skin. Now, I had an infestation of the fuckers.

She peered up at me with innocent blue eyes. "I can wait, Jaxon Hayes. I'm just not sure if you can."

"Whatever you say, pretty girl." I grabbed a box of pizza and a beer from the case on the counter. "I've got all night."

We settled into our usual seats on the couch while Connor and Katie stayed cocooned together in the recliner. Once everyone had their controller and a drink ready, Connor started the countdown.

"3 . . . 2 . . . 1 . . . go!"

We all cracked open our beers and chugged.

Our favorite drinking game to play on the GameCube included MarioKart and rules that required you to finish your drink before beginning the race. It was called Drunk Driving, and it wasn't until the mind-numbing tune of Rainbow Road played in the background that I realized how quickly four beers could rush to my head.

I tried not to fly off the glowing track while Katie cackled uncontrollably from the floor. The last race grew so intense that she needed her own space.

"Katie, if you don't shut the fuck up, I'm gonna smack you with this controller," Maci threatened, trying to keep her laughter under control.

"I'm sorry!" She inhaled dramatically, wiping away a few tears. "Connor is just so bad at this."

"Fuck, Mace," I muttered as my car spun out of control. For the third time in this series, her annoying little turtle character jumped up and down after crossing the finish line.

Maci stood up and began collecting the empty cans on the floor. "I'm not making it through another round, guys. It's already midnight, and let's face it, I don't have any competition."

Connor scoffed and tossed a pillow in Maci's direction.

Everyone slowly started cleaning up the area around them. Calling it a night meant putting an official end to my junior year of college.

My stomach sank as I thought of the nine-hour drive I had tomorrow to get home to Charlotte. I was excited to go home and see my family. Even though part of me would always exist there, I couldn't help but feel like a piece of me was staying in Ohio.

The fuck? What the fuck did that mean?

I watched Maci pull four bottles of water from the fridge. She twirled her finger in the air and gestured toward the hall, mouthing, "Ready?"

I nodded. I was ready to have Maci in her bedroom the moment I walked in.

Katie turned around and pointed a finger at Maci. "Sappy shit for tomorrow!"

Maci rolled her eyes, lacing her fingers with mine so she could pull me into her room and close the door behind us.

"Do we have sappy shit to talk about tomorrow?" I teased, tossing my shirt in her hamper. It was tighter than the one she was wearing, and I wanted her to have another one to take with her when she left tomorrow.

Her eyes lingered on my bare chest. "Katie and I do."

I sat on the edge of her bed. "Come here."

She shot me a warning glance, taking a few steps forward and judging the space between us carefully. Her blue eyes had a slight gloss to them, and she hadn't had enough to drink for alcohol to be the reason why.

"I just want to talk to you," I said, pulling her into my lap. "What's in your head?"

"Noth—" She sighed, and a grin of defeat crept into her right dimple. "I'm gonna miss you, Jaxon Hayes."

"I'm gonna miss you too, baby. I feel like I just got you."

Her eyes narrowed. "You've known me since August."

"But you've only been my girlfriend since March." I gripped her hips, and she giggled.

She traced my jawline with her fingers. "What was that you said?"

"Are you gonna smile every time I say the word *girlfriend*? You act like you haven't heard it before."

"Oh, I've heard it," she reassured me. "It just sounds better coming from you."

"That's some cute shit." I shifted us so we were lying next to each other on the bed. If she wanted me to wait to touch her until I told her my news, I'd play along. "I wasn't joking when I told you I wanted to fly you out to me."

"I know you weren't." She tucked her hair behind her ears and bit the inside of her cheek.

I hated being the one to make Maci nervous, and I knew her too well to ignore her signs. "Talk to me, baby."

"Is this what you wanted to talk about? There isn't anything else?"

"Yeah." I smiled as my head hit the pillow. "What else would there be?"

"I wasn't sure if this trial period would make it through the summer," she admitted softly.

Her words felt like bullets to my chest. "Mace—"

"This is why I didn't want to say it! I didn't want to make you mad or think I was crazy, but I don't want to lie to you either."

"I'm not mad," I stated calmly. "And I don't ever want you to feel like you need to lie to me about something. I understand where you're coming from."

Her face fell, and I grabbed her hand, immediately regretting my choice of words.

"I understand because you're trusting me to be something I've never been before," I explained. "I want you to come see me for a few weeks."

Her eyes widened. "A few weeks?"

"Is that okay?"

She pursed her lips and scooted closer to me. "I have a summer class I might have to do a few things for."

"Of course. Anything else?"

"Will your job let you take that much time off?"

I shrugged off her question. "It's contract work. I'll only have a few projects to work on while you're there."

She wrapped her arms around my neck. "I'd hardly call building houses a *project*."

"I've worked for Koll Construction before," I said, dipping my mouth to kiss the sensitive skin behind her ear. "First job in high school, actually." My mouth traveled down her jawline until my lips brushed hers. "Good friends with the owner."

"Your mom wouldn't care?"

I kissed her. "Nope."

"I thought you had to fly to Cali to work with your dad—"

"Save your follow-up questions, and let me kiss you, dammit." I rolled so I was on top of her, fighting against another fit of giggles rising from her gorgeous mouth. "We talked about what we needed to talk about."

"You had me all hyped up to play this waiting game with you!" She smacked my chest as my hands made their way up her shirt.

"Oh, I lost the moment I saw you, Mace." I kissed her again, nipping softly on her bottom lip with my teeth. "I've wanted you since October, and if I have to talk to get that from you, I'll lose every fuckin' time."

Chapter Three

MACI

May 2016

After listening to the Miley Cyrus' *Bangerz* album for the second time, I figured it was time to give Miley a break. I was ten minutes from my childhood home in Columbus, Ohio, and I didn't want to be recovering from another performance of "We Can't Stop" when I walked in to greet the family.

The closer I got to my destination, the more I craved the comforting bubble of my tiny college apartment. I still felt Jaxon's arms around my shoulders when he said, "I'll miss you, Mace." His husky goodbye got me every time, and no matter how hard I tried, it always made the tears threaten to fall.

It was terrifying—feeling so strongly about someone and giving them the power to make you crumble in just a few seconds.

As if my goodbye to Jaxon wasn't hard enough, I also had to leave Katie. She became my soulmate in the dorms, and the separation left a different kind of heartache.

I pulled into the driveway next to Chase's pickup truck. Regardless of the mixed emotions I had being back in Columbus, I was excited to see my snarky older brother.

Maybe it would be good to be home—at least for a little while.

As soon as I reunited with our living room that hadn't been redecorated since the early 2000s, my long to-do list became irrelevant. Chase sat at the dining room table with my mom, both of them with cups of coffee and some sort of breakfast pastry that would be tossed out in a few days because no one bothered to eat it.

Chase paused his story and smiled. "I thought you wouldn't be home until later!"

"Campus is a ghost town. Once Jaxon and Katie left, there was no reason to stay." I wrapped my arms around his waist and pulled him in for a hug. "Nice to see you, Sheesh."

Mom wasted no time dissecting my last sentence. "Who's Jaxon?"

I took the empty seat at the table. "Jaxon's my boyfriend."

"Wait, is this the guy who helped her with her car?" Mom grazed Chase's forearm. "Is that the guy you said she had a thing for when you visited in February?"

"Glad to see you two have been chatting," I murmured, making my way to the coffee maker for a much-needed cup. "To answer your question, Mom, yes. At least we're trialing it to see how it goes."

Chase spun around in his chair. "Trialing? What the fuck does that—"

"Language, please!" Mom scolded.

"Forget that detail," I added quickly. The hazelnut creamer in the fridge provided another reminder of my trial boyfriend. "We've been dating since March, and I really like him."

Chase mimicked my innocent expression right before he sipped his coffee. He knew I couldn't hold a poker face to save my life, and I probably had "I said I love you way too fucking soon!" plastered on my forehead.

Cue the spotlight, the helicopter reporting for Channel 5 News, and one of those obnoxious signs that people on the street used to sell mattresses. It wasn't hard to figure out that there was more to the story. I just didn't have it in me to start my summer off with such a serious conversation.

"Just be careful, honey," Mom pressed gently. "The last guy you brought home from BG was . . . *questionable*."

"Questionable?" Chase scoffed. "That's an understatement."

I rolled my eyes. "Really, Chase?"

Chase held up his hands in defeat, acknowledging the point I wasn't saying out loud. I didn't believe in judging someone by their worst mistake, and my brother was no different. I'd never use something he did in the past as ammo to hurt him.

I squeezed his hand as I reunited with my seat at the table. My mom's gaze still lingered as I searched my brain for a topic change.

"Isaac, was it?" she muttered.

"Jaxon is nothing like Isaac," I said, chuckling at the thought of the two of them standing next to each other.

"I like Jaxon," Chase assured me, directing his opinion toward our mom.

I'd never considered my mom to be a positive person. She was someone who Chase and I always strived to impress but always fell short. She wasn't mean or hurtful, at least not in the ways most people meant to be. Mom stared at a sunny seven-day forecast and focused on the one day that had a chance of rain. No matter how many good test grades I brought home or soccer trophies Chase presented, there was always the speck of negative in the rearview that clouded the rest of her vision.

Over time, I learned it was easier to look past my relationship with my mom instead of fighting against it. It caused too many arguments between us in high school, and once I left for college, I realized I was better off without the stress.

Mom leaned forward on her elbows and smiled. "Go ahead and tell me about him then."

I started the story of how I met Jaxon from the beginning, setting the scene at Myles Dairy Queen. I decided to give them the censored version, keeping the lenses my family viewed me through as clean and innocent as possible. I was positive that no mother wanted to hear about her daughter's journey of self-discovery—especially when that journey included casual sex and a chlamydia mishap.

She shook her head, and I couldn't tell if she was disappointed or still processing. With a quick quirk of her eyebrow, I had my answer.

"Do I need to remind you that you offered him *dinner* after he fixed my car? You didn't even know him!" I shrugged, getting up from the table. "You still don't!"

Chase quickly followed my lead. It was only a matter of time before she started digging into him and his problems.

I felt him following me down the hallway. "Why do I come home again?"

"Because it's *home*," Chase stressed, leaning into my doorframe. He peered down the hall to make sure Mom was still in the kitchen. "Dad—"

"Let me guess." I sighed, cracking open one of my windows. "Dad hasn't been home in a while because of work and that's why she's . . . *extra* cheerful?"

Chase shot me a sympathetic grin. "I offered you a place to stay in Pittsburgh."

"I know," I said calmly. "I just wanted to come see them for a few days and let them push me there instead of me leaving willingly. Normal shit, right?"

"I imagine it's hard for them to work on their relationship when the only two things they have in common are in this room."

"Touché." I plopped down on my bed, in desperate need of a subject change.

"Just know my door is open," he said with a smug grin. "Even after you graduate."

I smiled back. "Want to help me unpack my car? I'll reimburse you with ice cream."

"Graeter's?"

I grabbed my keys from my bag. "I mean, it's no Myles Dairy Queen, but it will do."

Chapter Four

JAXON

THE VOICE OF MY best friend, Bryson Kennedy, came through my speakers as another round of horns sounded around me. "Why don't you ever fly? That's a far-ass drive for you."

The trip from Bowling Green to Charlotte was a far-ass drive, and it sucked every time.

I dragged my hands down my face, forgetting he wasn't actually in the car to see my response. "I like having my car on campus."

"Once you get settled you should come down and see me for a week. Summers in Miami are *wild*, bro. We can roll through the bars and find some sloppy bit—"

My lips formed a hard line as he worked through the rest of that sentence.

His cocky voice returned. "You're still on that trial, right?"

I laughed. "Fuck you, Kennedy."

Even though I was still learning how this whole boyfriend role worked, it seemed like an excellent step in the right direction to deny a trip down to Miami to party with drunk broads.

"Is Maci still coming to see you for a while?"

I veered off the highway and started the last few miles home. "I gotta figure out flights and shit for her, but yeah, I'd like her to."

"Might hit a record for your dry spell. What is your record? Like two weeks?"

"This conversation just gets better and better."

His cackling returned. "I'm not taking shots at your girl! I'm just stating a fact."

Bryson and I had an unspoken agreement when it came to Maci, but there was nothing in that agreement that stopped him from giving me shit about being in a relationship.

I hung up with Bryson as I pulled up to our gate. I punched in my code and parked behind my mom's Range Rover. I was surprised to see the driveway empty. It was almost five o'clock, and no one messed with Evelyn Hayes and her dinner plans.

The foyer was uncomfortably quiet. I dropped my bags near the staircase, expecting my mom to peek her head around the corner from the kitchen. When I passed the breakfast counter and found the dining room empty too, I started to worry.

"Ma!" I shouted, my voice bouncing off every corner in the house.

"Can I help you, sir?"

I spun around, prepared to square up with the small, unintimidating voice behind me.

A woman with bright red hair who couldn't have been much older than me stepped out of the den. A tight black dress stopped right above her knees, and she hugged a clipboard to her chest to cover any possible cleavage. A trail of freckles ran across her cheekbones and over her nose. She narrowed her light brown eyes, and I realized I was taking way too long to respond.

"Evelyn Hayes, is she home?" I asked, remembering that I was the one who lived here. "Wait—who are you?"

She giggled, opening the door to the deck. "She's out by the pool."

I slid past her, shielding my eyes from the sun as she shut the door behind me. I turned my hat around and spotted Mom in one of the lounge chairs, wearing a swimsuit and what looked like one of my dad's white dress shirts.

I'd never understand women's fashion.

She looked up from her binder, and I smiled. Her mouth fell open as tears threatened to escape from her dark green eyes.

"Hey, Ma," I said, giving her a kiss on the head. "Don't get up, I'll come to you." I lowered myself onto the chair next to her so she didn't strain herself, and she wrapped her free arm around my neck, pulling me in for a hug.

She cupped my face with her hand and gave my chin a squeeze like she did when I was little. "Hi, baby. How was the drive?"

"Crap. But"—I cocked my head toward the house—"when did we get a welcoming committee?"

"Oh, that's Lucy, my intern for the summer."

"Lucy," I echoed.

"Don't look at her, don't touch her, don't make her feel anything but welcome in this house, do you understand me?" Her warning made it sound like I was threatening Lucy with an eviction notice. "She's going to be spending a lot of time here, and she is off-limits."

Mom wasn't *completely* out of line. She had witnessed too many one-night stands walking out our front door.

"I'm going to have to look at her, Ma," I teased. "I can't be some weirdo that comes in and out of the house."

She shook her head. "Jaxon—"

"And I wouldn't do that to Maci."

My smile grew as her name left my mouth. I was giddy about my mom's reaction to the idea of me having my first girlfriend. This was the kind of sappy shit that happened in Maci's TV shows.

What the fuck is happening to me?

Mom placed her binder on her lap, giving me her full attention. Apparently, this was worth pausing whatever notes she was taking on page ten of her business proposal. "Who's Maci?"

I laced my fingers together and rested my elbows on my knees. "Maci . . . is my girlfriend. I've been dating her since St. Patrick's Day, and I really like her."

Mom smacked my arm. "Since *March*!"

"I know the news is a little delayed, but if it helps, you're the first one to know," I offered, stealing a sip from her drink on the end table. "Jesus, Ma, I didn't know I interrupted happy hour. What is this?"

"Sangria," she said, defending her fruity beverage, "and if I would've known you had news to share with me, I would've told you to bring me another glass."

So that's what sangria was supposed to taste like. All I had to go off of was Katie's Blood Orange Sangria and how I kissed Maci for the first time after a few glasses.

"Well, go on and get yourself some if you want to!" Mom exclaimed, waving me toward the house. "You must've known I would have questions!"

"Just save some of those questions for her when she comes to visit this summer."

Mom flipped a few pages in her binder and settled on her calendar. I was confident the woman would charter a plane to Maci's house if I couldn't make this trip happen in her timeframe. "When? How long? Would you stay here, or you guys could always spend a few days at the house in Topsail?"

Every time I tried to find a few weeks in my schedule, I ended up with a headache. Taking over Hayes Sports and Entertainment had been my plan since I could remember, and the closer I got to graduation and working under my dad, the more time I gave to the West Coast so I could start to learn the ropes.

I handed her back her drink and stood up. "I have to talk to Dad first."

"Your dad won't expect you to work if you're bringing someone home to meet us," she said, using a tone she reserved for when I was getting antsy. "You should coordinate with Alex! He was just talking about taking another trip here in June with Bella."

Alex.

Bella.

Engagement.

You're a dumbass.

Of course, Alex was planning on flying out here again in June. He told me a few months ago he was proposing to Bella on her birthday.

"You could celebrate the Fourth of July here," Mom suggested.

"You know what!" I exclaimed, bringing my hands together in defeat. "Do you mind jotting this agenda down on your calendar while I go get a drink?" I shouted over my shoulder as I walked toward the house. "I need a day and a half in Wilmington, too!"

"Don't be an ass," she yelled, chuckling as she held up her glass. "Bring me a refill, please!"

I passed through the den and saw Lucy at the breakfast counter.

She smiled politely when she saw me. "More sangria? The pitcher is in the fridge."

"Yeah," I said through a breathy laugh. "I'm Jaxon, by the way."

"I know." A hint of pink flooded her cheeks. "Your mom keeps a bunch of photos in her office. Plus, you have the same eyes."

I smiled at the comment I would never grow tired of. "So I've heard."

Chapter Five

MACI

The dreaded annual gynecologist visit.

I had nothing personal against Dr. Bell. She was one of the only people who could ask how many new sexual partners I'd had since our last visit and not require any kind of backstory. I tried not to look mortified when she added the tallies to my chart.

Two new sexual partners? No biggie.

Having to share that one partner was my trial boyfriend while the other partner was his roommate and best friend? It was a CW storyline in the making. Just cast me as the twenty-something year old who played the high school student, and my saga would fit right into the lineup.

Dr. Bell wasted no time when I mentioned switching birth controls. The shot was a great option for people who didn't want to deal with the daily dose situation, but I felt my body changing with the quarterly injections. I was tired of feeling on edge all the time. Regardless of the consequences, I needed to give the pill another try.

As I slumped into the couch with a heating pad on my uterus, I was regretting my decision to put my mental health first. My only companion was a TV tray stocked with ibuprofen, a bowl of half-eaten chicken noodle soup, and a hot tea. All that was missing was my glass half-empty perspective that it would all be over soon.

Why were these our only options as women? We had to choose between a birth control that fucked up our nervous system or one that hated our ovaries when it was that time of the month.

"Still in the same spot, huh, kiddo?"

I heard Dad's smile all the way from the kitchen. He arrived back home the same day my mom conveniently had to go help my Aunt Monica move into her new house.

"Until you have a uterus, you can't comment on how I choose to suffer," I muttered, flipping through streaming services until I spotted my comfort show. I hit play on *One Tree Hill*, and a wave of relief hit my poor, unfortunate soul.

"I'm going to run to the store." Dad grabbed the umbrella out of the closet. "Do you need anything? Maybe something to eat other than soup?"

"I mean, if you're offering to get me a Philly from Penn Station I'm not going to argue."

"You got it," he said, flashing me one last smile before he walked out the door.

As one man left my company, another one popped up on my phone screen. A picture of me and Jaxon brought a much needed smile to my face. He had his arms wrapped around my shoulders as I took the picture, and his eyes were squeezed shut as he planted a kiss on my temple. I wanted nothing more than to sink into his chest and sleep away my misery.

I cleared my throat so I didn't sound like a total frog. "Hey, Jax."

"Hey, pretty girl. Can you FaceTime?"

"Oh, absolutely not," I said, looking around at the evidence of my PMS. "Not in these conditions."

"*Conditions?* What conditions are you battling that I don't know about? Are you sick?"

"Well, technically you haven't had to deal with these conditions since I've been on the shot. I got my period two days ago and it's been . . . *lovely*."

"Yeah, I'm calling you."

"I'm a hot mess," I warned.

He scoffed. "And you're probably still gorgeous. We both know I won't be avoiding you once a month so let's just get this over with."

I rolled my eyes when the video request appeared on the screen. I checked my appearance as the call rang, flattening the staticky mess toward the back of my head. The lighting helped tone down the redness in my skin, and as usual, I'd depend on my blue eyes to take the lead.

When I answered the call, Jaxon met me with a toothy grin.

I rested my head against the cushion. "Happy?"

"Ecstatic. And see? I still find you beautiful—lookin' all cuddly and shit."

I laughed weakly at his compliment. "Are you heading home from the gym?"

"Yeah." He ran a hand through his hair, loosening up his curls. He'd get it cut soon. Jaxon hated being hot, and the sweat was driving him crazy. "But I finally figured out the dates for you to come out here. Are you ready for them?"

I sat up a little taller in my couch cave. "Yes!"

"June 27th to July 7th."

I pulled up my calendar app and swiped through the dates. "That's almost two weeks."

"I wanted you here for three weeks, four weeks, shit, the rest of the summer. But with me flying out to Cali and working for Koll Construction, that's the best I can do."

"And your parents don't care?"

Just the idea of asking my parents if Jaxon could come stay with us for a weekend left a bad taste in my mouth. He'd witness firsthand how they managed to never be in the house at the same time. A week and a half was a long time to be around someone's family.

Then I came to the harsh realization that maybe it only felt like a long time because I was picturing my own.

Jaxon threw his gym bag in the trunk and climbed into his driver's seat. He placed me on the dash and took a long sip of whatever cloudy green liquid was in his shaker bottle. "Mace, my mom already has a dinner planned and my dad booked a flight home. This might be the most exciting news I've ever shared with them."

Jesus, no pressure.

I began to sweat through all of my layers. Katie's comment, "You'd be like a breath of fresh air!", returned to the forefront of my headspace.

"Mace?"

I hadn't realized I looked down.

"I don't need an answer right now," he said, his mouth lifting into an adorable half-smile. "But could you try to let me know soon?"

What the fuck was I doing? Jaxon was asking me to come to North Carolina, and I was dragging out my response.

I opened up a new event in my calendar. "I'll put the dates in my phone."

"Phew," he exclaimed before starting his car. "Had me nervous there for a second."

"You? Nervous?" I giggled, bringing my knees to my chest. "Why?"

"Because I already bought your tickets," he admitted, picking me up from the dash. "I miss you, Mace, and I hope you feel better. I'll text you when I get home, okay?"

"I miss you too," I said, quickly adding, "oh, and *please* respond to Jared's messages on Instagram. Ever since I told him I haven't seen *Guardians of the Galaxy* he has been bullying me with memes from *The Avengers*. He said since you don't respond, he sends them to me instead."

Jaxon sucked his teeth. "I'm afraid I can't help you with that. Once Jared places you in the meme category, you're on your own."

I was honored to reach a stage in my friendship with Jared that I didn't know I wanted.

Once I hung up with Jaxon, I pulled up my messages with Jared. I shook my head, laughing as I typed out a response to the meme he sent twenty minutes ago.

Maci

> Where can I stream this movie? I'm waving the white flag.

Jared

> FINALLY

> Pull up this website and use my code. I have the digital copy you can stream!

Following Jared's instructions, I ran into my room to get my laptop. I clicked play on the movie, snuggling into the couch as the flashy Marvel introduction took over the screen. I wasn't sure why I was so tired, but I fell asleep dreaming of being on a beach with Jaxon, with Redbone's "Come and Get Your Love" playing in the background.

JAXON

June 2016

My least favorite part about traveling back and forth between Charlotte and Los Angelas wasn't the time change or the obnoxious traffic on the California freeway. It was the amount of time I had on an airplane alone with my thoughts.

Why were all songs about love and sex? There was nothing more agonizing than being alone with the two words that had nagged at me since I left campus a few weeks ago.

Maci's face became the album cover for every love song I listened to. I missed her so much that I started catching glimpses of her in other people. Any female who had blue eyes or brown hair instantly drew my attention. I felt like a fucking squirrel with how many times I darted my head around the fucking airport.

Fucking squirrels and fucking airports.

What could I say? Apparently, I got angry when I was horny.

I stared out the window, watching the clouds and trying to ignore Bryson's cackle as it echoed through my memory. Our last conversation played through my head as the number of days in my dry spell continued to climb.

I officially went a month without having sex, and the universe was doing everything it could to throw it in my face. The reminders of who I was a few months ago were *constant*, and I was starting to take it personal.

A few months ago, my mom's warning about Lucy would have been necessary. Now there was only one girl I would've bent over the kitchen counter.

None of the messages that flooded my inbox mattered. My eyes didn't wander, and my mind never went there. There were no parts of me that even considered another female's attention.

Before I slept with Maci, I never understood how someone could want to be with the same person over and over again. Suddenly, everything about my script changed. I cared about the setting and how I spoke. I appreciated the details and the choreography of how I moved with her. I paid attention to who watched and floated in and out of a scene when we were together. There was no one else I wanted in my story. It was just her.

Love and sex—the two words that came to mind when I thought of my girlfriend, yet I could only say one of them out loud. I could sing "Sex on Fire" by Kings of Leon for the entire first-class cabin, and it wouldn't phase me in the slightest. It wouldn't be good, but it would be a lot less scary than saying "I love you" back.

I knew I cared about Maci, and that I wanted to be with her. I just wasn't sure what all of that meant yet.

The wheels touched down, making me pause The Weeknd as we rolled into Los Angeles.

Once I stepped out of the terminal, I pulled my hat from my bookbag and slid on my aviators. It wasn't hard to find Alex and his red Mustang. The guy had a weakness for loud engines and stickshifts, and like any asshole with a car they liked to show off, he completely blocked the first lane just waiting for me to get in.

I tried to relax as Alex weaved in and out of traffic, reminding myself that he made this drive at least six times a month. I'd have to get used to the hustle and bustle of a city that never seemed to sleep. A year from now, I'd be thirty days into my new address, spending long days at Hayes Sports and Entertainment and traveling to meetings so my dad wouldn't have to.

It was too loud to try and talk while we were on the highway, so I waited until Alex pulled off onto the exit for Dad's office.

"Is Bella working today?" I asked.

He nodded. "She'll be off in a few hours. She's excited to see you."

"She acts like it's been a while," I teased. "You guys were just at the house last week."

"She hates the travel," he admitted with a shrug. "She wants what all of us want—everyone and everything in the same location, but also having the best of both homes."

I completely understood Bella's way of thinking. The first time I came to visit Dad's new office, I fell in love with California. The sun, the energy, the scene—it was just a different vibe than the Carolina coast. But as much as I loved it out here, nothing would ever beat home.

Hayes Sports and Entertainment was a glass building that shot up to the sky. Dad's office was on the top floor, and I couldn't even name any of the offices that rented below it.

"Speaking of *location*," I said as we pulled through the gate that surrounded the property. "You're still planning on proposing, right? You mentioned doing it at our house, but I wasn't sure if you changed your mind."

Alex parked in one of Dad's reserved spots and glanced nervously at the area around us. Bella wasn't hiding out in the bushes, so I wasn't sure what his deal was. Maybe this was what happened when you were about to become the H-word.

"I never pictured you as a *husband*," I added, "but the anxiety I've heard that comes with marriage seems to suit you."

Alex reached across my lap and tugged on the glove compartment. He pulled a blue box from underneath a pile of papers.

"Are you insane?" I exclaimed, unable to hide my laughter. "Do you just drive around with that in your car all of the time? It's *worth* more than your fucking car."

Alex smiled proudly at his shiny investment. "Only because she wanted the blue diamonds on the side."

"Do you even know what those blue diamonds are called?"

Alex shrugged. "You don't need to know the names of everything as long as you can afford them."

"You sound like an arrogant asshole," I said, chuckling because Alex was anything but arrogant.

My dad didn't keep Alex on his marketing team because he was his son. Alex was damn good at his job, with multiple companies in his inbox every day asking for his services. He liked having nice things, but you'd never know the guy had money.

We got out of the car, and Alex handed me the box so I could get another look. It looked even better than the first time he showed it to me. Warmth flooded my chest as I pictured the ring on Bella's finger. She had always been family—the sister I never asked for. It would be nice to make everything official.

"I'm proposing at the birthday dinner Mom is throwing her," Alex quietly explained as we entered the lobby. "You're still the only one who knows, and I want to keep it that way. If I tell Ma what I'm planning she will go all Evelyn Hayes Catering on me and have the whole staff there to run the show."

I couldn't disagree with that statement. Any chance our mother had to create an event binder she took it. The woman was a sucker for colorful tabs and laminated files.

I pushed the button on the elevator for the top floor and handed Alex back his ring.

"I figured you could mention it to Maci so she isn't completely blindsided," he suggested. "You're still flying her in for a few weeks?"

"A little over a week. It's all I could get between work and coming out here."

The doors opened, allowing a few people to get off before we boarded the elevator.

"Good," Alex stated cheerfully. "Bella won't suspect a thing. She'll be so thrown off by you inviting a girl home that me proposing won't even cross her mind."

I laughed. "That simple, huh? Still confident that she'll say yes?"

His eyes narrowed. "You know, I never saw myself as a husband until I pictured Bella being someone else's wife. She's always been my girl, and even if she didn't say yes, I'd still be with her." The elevator dinged and the doors flew open. "Now shut up and smile."

Dad's secretary, Helen, grinned proudly over her computer monitor at the sight of Alex and me leaving the elevator. His staff was always excited to see us when we visited, and it was hard not to feel happy in a room surrounded by gorgeous floor-to-ceiling windows with a beautiful view of the city.

I led us down the hall and talked quietly over my shoulder. "Smile at who—Helen? I always smile at Helen."

"As delightful as Helen is, I wasn't talking about her." Alex patted me on the back and opened the door that had Reed Hayes CEO plastered on the front of it. "I was talking about your future view."

Dad's focused expression relaxed as Alex and I took the chairs across from his desk. Sunlight poured in from the glass behind him, and the seating area to the right was armed with SportsCenter, a minibar, and a table filled with appetizers.

"Perfect timing!" Dad exclaimed. "I was just about to break for some lunch. I want you to look these over, J." He pulled me in for a hug and handed me a manilla folder. "There is a young man out at Florida State University, and I'd love to hear your thoughts."

My jaw went slack as the weight of the folder rested in my hand. Dad squeezed my shoulder as the shared understanding of what was happening passed between us. It was the first potential client I was taking a look at before he did, and the first step I was taking as someone who would join him after I graduated.

His attention shifted to Alex who was making himself at home on the massive burgundy L-shaped couch. "I'm gonna need that report for June early this month."

Alex stuffed another eggroll in his mouth. "You'll get it."

Dad's hearty chuckle filled the room, making my chest swell with pride. My dad was living proof that with hard work and determination, you could have everything you ever dreamed of.

Hayes Sports and Entertainment was his legacy—our family's legacy—and I owed him everything to continue in his footsteps.

My mouth curved into an involuntary grin as I took in the view of the city skyline. The sun, the energy, the scene—it was *definitely* a different vibe than the Carolina coast.

Chapter Seven

MACI

June 2016

When I flew out to North Carolina next week, I anticipated nice weather and getting sunburnt at least once while I was there.

I anticipated Jaxon's family having questions about our relationship.

What I didn't anticipate? Jaxon having my preferred toiletries on hand when I landed. I could get by with a trial size package of Q-tips, but a trial size bottle of shampoo that would stop my hair from frizzing in the humidity? No thank you.

Like any good woman on a mission, I wandered aimlessly through the aisles of Target, allowing the red cart to guide me. Of course, having Katie on the phone lifted my spirits since I was slowly spiraling into the depths of hairspray hell.

"This one adds lift, this one has color protection, and this one fights humidity. Where the fuck is the can that does all of this shit?" I whisper-exclaimed, demanding the shiny black bottles in front of me to pipe up and offer some sympathy for my petty problems. "Why are these our only options as women? Don't get me started on shampoo."

"Whyyy am I here right now?" Katie whined. "Why are we doing this?"

"Bitch, you called me," I said, laughing as I settled on the bottle that would hopefully save my curls.

"Geez. You're right I'm losing it."

"Or you're just horny," I muttered, smiling sweetly as an elderly couple passed me. Once they cleared the vitamin aisle, I continued. "I reheated the same cup of coffee five times in the microwave yesterday. Five times! All because I was replaying the last time Jaxon and I had sex."

"You don't have a microwave that beeps when you leave something in it?"

"What part of my parents haven't remodeled since the 90s are you not getting? That reminds me, I need condoms."

"You sound like a fucking squirrel right now." Katie laughed. "Did you even go into the store with a list? What exactly are you getting?"

"Essentials." I snagged a box of Trojans and tossed them in the cart, quickly adding a second box to the pile.

"Essentials," Katie echoed before letting out a hefty sigh.

"You know as cheerful as this call has been so far you're acting extra *lovely* today," I noted sweetly, emphasizing the word we both used to call each other bitchy to their face. "When is Connor arriving again? Someone sounds like they're *simmering*, and I'd like to channel my original life line if she could make it to the phone."

"Two days!" Katie's irritated scream forced me to pull the phone away from my ear.

I threw a ChapStick and a shiny clear lip-gloss into the cart for good measure. The summer air wasn't kind to lips that hadn't been kissed in a month.

Cue the poetic lines of a girl in a dry spell.

I rolled my eyes. "So I can call you back on Wednesday and you'll be in a better mood? Or should I wait until Thursday to give you a full forty-eight hours to bang it out of your system?"

"Make it Friday just to be safe," she murmured.

"Noted. Did you get that email about our apartment? I thought our security deposit was good until we moved out. Is that a yearly thing?"

"I already took care of it. I'm surprised they sent you an email in the first place. The guy still calls you Marci when you call to complain about the deadbolt sticking."

"I just don't know what I'll do next year when I'm not calling Frank from maintenance about my key," I said fondly as the elderly couple from before was approaching. My Trojans were completely exposed, so like any normal person would do, I grabbed a gift bag from the end of the aisle to throw overtop of them.

"The end of an era," Katie mimicked my endearing tone. "Speaking of end, I got my one night class moved! So I won't be on campus until eight on Thursdays."

"That class interfered with weekly dinner plans, and we couldn't have that."

Katie laughed. "That's what I included in my request to have my schedule changed."

Part of me wouldn't be surprised if she did. Thursday had been our dinner night with Jaxon and Connor since Jaxon and I met in journalism.

"Now if only I could get out of student teaching and have a normal spring semester," I whined, passing the last few aisles before self-checkout. "It could be worse. At least my placement is only a half hour away."

"You don't have to go to your placement until November, right? That isn't horrible."

"It's not!" I added quickly. "It's just . . ."

"The end of an era?" Katie offered sadly, prompting a pathetical chuckle from the both of us.

I approached the checkout and ignored the unflattering image in the camera above. There was nothing more humbling than watching yourself on a security screen. I plucked the Trojans from the bottom of the cart and waved them over the scanner. To my complete and utter horror, the service light dinged, and a judgmental female voice alerted everyone around me that I needed the assistance of an employee.

I pressed my lips into a hard line. "Katie, I have to go."

Correction. There was nothing more humbling than a sixteen year old Target employee price checking the boxes of condoms you tried to conceal under a giftbag, all for the couple you concealed them for in the first place to catch you buying them anyway.

Chapter Eight

JAXON

June 2016

Every part of my body hurt, and it wasn't the kind of hurt that I loved after a good workout. It was the kind of pain that throbbed throughout your body after manual labor—the kind of pain you got paid to endure.

After two days of working for Koll Construction installing kitchen cabinets and tearing a bathroom down to the studs, the last thing I wanted to do was go through my room and give it a deep clean. Maci would be here in a week, and right now my room made it seem like I was a cluttered mess.

I almost sorted through my first pile of clothes when I couldn't take it anymore. The vibrations in my pocket from the group text I had with Bryson, Jared and Connor was driving me crazy.

Pictures and videos of Bryson flooded the feed, and I wasn't surprised when the last video included two topless women and a strip tease from a third in the background.

Bryson

Spring break location?!

Connor

How many times do I need to ask to be removed from this group chat?

Jaxon

We've had this group chat since we moved in last year

Connor

But can't Bryson send shit like this to just the three of you?!

Bryson

No bitch.

Jared sent a meme of Chris Evans laughing as Captain America. Maci wasn't kidding. He really was on an Avengers kick.

Connor

I hate all of you.

Jared

Just a few more weeks until I can see that gorgeous face in person!

Connor

I'm flattered.

Jared

Idk why you would be. I was talking about Katie.

An hour into organizing my laundry, and I was still working through my unmatched socks.

"Fuck it," I murmured, tossing the sad single socks back in the laundry basket. I'd rather buy a new pack tomorrow than try and guess what black socks were supposed to be together.

My closet was officially full, and my room started to feel like my own again. It was no longer taken over by clothes, empty Gatorade bottles, clutter brought in from my Jeep, or disheveled scraps of paper. It was a place I could host my girlfriend in, and the thought of her being here in person made me excited all over again.

I went to fall back on my bed before I remembered I still had socks and boxers to put in my dresser. I opened the top drawer, and all of my excitement was quickly replaced with the lingering anxiety that came whenever I saw John Krane's name.

For the second time this year, I pulled a letter from my birth father out of the top drawer of my dresser. There were no reasons to keep putting off the attempted communication. I guess I couldn't label it as "attempted" since I'd read the damn thing five times. It had been five years since his last letter, and I honestly thought something happened to him. I was still deciding how it made me feel to discover he was sitting in a Florida prison.

John wanted to see me. He didn't state why or when or where. I mean, the where wasn't hard. It wasn't like I could suggest a public place for us to get coffee. I'd have to go to him. I'd have to get on a plane and go through the visiting process and sit across from him and—

I tossed the letter on the floor, letting my arm drape over my face. I hated this shit.

If there was one thing I learned growing up, it was that the more you gave to people, the more they could take. The more you told them, the more they could use your words against you. I kept a small circle, and I preferred it that way. Only a handful of my friends knew about the personal shit, and the last person I told anything to was partying on a yacht somewhere in Miami.

Bryson met Alex and my parents before our sophomore year. By some crazy coincidence, I had Evelyn's eyes, but Reed and I looked nothing alike. It wasn't hard to tell that we were a blended family. In typical Bryson fashion, he had the nosey questions, and I had the honest answers. After a five-minute explanation, he asked if I wanted Campus Pol-lyeyes, and we went about our day.

That interaction was two years ago, and it was the last time I even thought of my birth parents until Mom handed me a letter in January.

My chest started to hurt, and that was my cue to start moving. I slipped on a cut-off T-shirt and shorts and made my way down to the garage. If I didn't run some of this off, I'd start to waste away in it.

I was about to slip on my left shoe when I heard Mom's voice from the kitchen. "J?"

I threw my head back. Caught by the woman who gave me the home gym in the first place. "Yeah, Ma?"

"Come here and try this, please. I need an opinion."

That was a lie. Lucy sat across from Mom at the breakfast counter and could've taste tested whatever red sauce Mom had bubbling in the pot.

Maybe Lucy was allergic to tomatoes. Maybe Lucy was worried she'd get red sauce on her nice white shirt. Maybe I would learn something about Lucy if she didn't ignore me like I was the fucking plague.

Mom handed me a small spoon, and I dipped it into the pot. I knew better than to test anywhere near the bulk amount, so I backed away and took my sample.

She sprinkled some more oregano into the pan. "You went to the gym earlier this morning. Going on another jog?"

I smirked. "We both know that sauce doesn't need more oregano."

She rolled her eyes and turned off the burner. "It's just the three of us for dinner tonight, and I'd like to have it together."

Lucy looked up from her screen. "Oh, Mrs. Hayes, I—"

"Lucy, how many times must I tell you to call me Evelyn?" Mom smiled and reached over the counter to slide Lucy's computer out of the way. "I'd love for you to stay so we can work on a few more items, and I promise Jaxon doesn't bite."

Lucy tucked her red hair behind her ears.

"There's only one girl I bite," I said with a cocky grin, "but she won't be here until Monday."

Mom smacked my bicep. "Jaxon Reed!"

Okay, maybe it wasn't a *complete* mystery why Lucy avoided me.

Mom shot me a warning glance, and I bit my cheek so I wouldn't laugh. I lost all self-control when I noticed Lucy hiding an amused grin behind her hand.

"Don't mind him, Lucy." Mom reached behind her and opened a box of pasta. "This will be ready in twenty minutes. I figured we could watch a few episodes of your show. Lucy helped me book that place for you next week!"

I shifted my focus to my new red-headed best friend. "You watch The Tree People?"

Lucy nodded. "I've seen the entire series twice."

"I have some questions for you, Lucy." I took the empty barstool next to her and smiled when she didn't look away. "And there's something you might be able to help me with if you're interested."

Chapter Nine

MACI

June 2016

The month of June was a painful circle of Hell I desperately wanted to escape. It was a never-ending time warp of exams, my parents dodging each other in the living room, and phone calls with my two lifelines—Katie and Jaxon.

Life was moving slowly for Katie too. Since we no longer shared a living space we couldn't vent with a comfort show in the background. We'd pop a bottle of Moscato, laugh about stories from the past, and I'd benefit from Katie's love of cooking. It would be unbearably hot when we moved back into the apartment, and the only window in our living room would be open with a giant fan in front of it. The air would be warm but we'd pretend like it made a difference. We'd walk around in sports bras and shorts and have to shower again before we tried to go to sleep.

I got excited just thinking about my return to Bowling Green. Unfortunately, that reunion was still seven weeks away.

My statistics class was taking more time than I cared to admit. I never had trouble with words—they poured out of me with ease whenever I had to write papers or complete discussion boards. I preferred a thirty-page essay instead of a multiple-choice exam that asked me about data and binomial coefficients.

What the *actual fuck* was a binomial coefficient?

This was my punishment for leaving my last exam for the night before my flight to Charlotte. I figured it would be a good distraction from all of the overthinking I was prepared to do—a nice appetizer for the main course of anxiety that consisted of flipping through scenarios that probably wouldn't happen and preparing for conversations I probably wouldn't have.

I tapped my pen on the arm of my desk chair, as I utilized my last free point question and moved on to question thirty-three. If I answered too many questions wrong, the test would close automatically to let me know I failed. Since I had two questions left, my hopes were high. I hit submit on the exam and prayed to the gods of binomial coefficients to grace me with a seventy percent.

"Fuck yes!" I exclaimed, falling back into my chair.

I propped my phone on my desk and angled it to face my bed. I hit Jaxon's contact photo, and before I could pull my suitcase out from under my bed, a loud whooshing sound let me know he answered the call.

"Give me two seconds!" I yelled, hoisting my carry-on onto the bed. "I'm getting my shit together."

"You're fine!" he yelled back. "I'm just getting home."

Ah, yes. My boyfriend the housemaker.

I imagined Jaxon in a hard hat, wearing nothing but a toy-filled toolbelt. I added Construction Worker Jaxon to the file where I kept Auto Repair Jaxon. I had never been the fantasy type before, but that mindset was changing.

When I looked up, Jaxon was shaking his head. He wore the same look of disappointment my dad made when I told him I'd only need two hours at the airport instead of four. "You still haven't packed anything?"

I placed my hands on my hips. "All expert packers wait until last minute to put it all together. It's just an unspoken way of travel."

"Says who?"

I reached into my closet and started pulling tank tops off my hangers. I didn't need to look to know that he was smiling. "No one. I just made that up."

"Don't forget a swimsuit," Jaxon suggested. "Preferably one with the least amount of fabric."

I chuckled, tossing my blue bikini into the pile. I would be a fool to leave myself with one option so I added my red bikini as a backup. Tank tops, shorts, a few dresses, sandals . . . I did a quick run through a mental list I should've written down and started throwing clothes into the open luggage.

"My mom keeps the house cold, so bring some sweatpants," Jaxon shouted.

"Jaxon, if you keep interrupting my thought process I'm going to have to call you back."

"Here I was just trying to catch you before I went to Vince's," he teased. "How'd your test go?"

"Good!" I exclaimed. "I passed and that's all that matters."

"Told you it would be fine."

"Yeah, yeah, yeah," I murmured. "Are you going out tonight?"

Jaxon fell onto his bed with his arm slung above his head. He let out a deep breath, and I could tell by the hint of gloss in his eyes that he was exhausted. "I'm just meeting Vince and Ian for a drink at their place before they go out tonight. They're meeting some people we went to high school with downtown."

"Where is *out* in Charlotte? Is it anything like the bars in BG?"

"Not at all. A lot more city and *a lot* more expensive. One of the bars Ian mentioned for tonight only does bottle service."

"Geez." I scoffed. "Strip club?"

He chuckled at my question. "Nah, baby. Unless you'll be there, no strip clubs for me tonight."

I held up two hoodies, trying to decide if they were the same shade of black. "You know I wouldn't care, right?"

"Do boyfriends get to go to strip clubs?" His voice shot up a few octaves. "Is that a trial perk?"

I swear I needed someone who flagged shit before it flew out of my mouth. It was no surprise that "boyfriend trial" and "I wouldn't care if you went to a strip club" were generated in the same trap.

Fantasy Seeking Maci just stood by and shook her head. She'd never get to come out and play if I was pushing strip clubs.

I rolled my eyes. "I think it's a look-but-don't-touch kind of thing."

Jaxon's contagious laugh floated from the phone. As much as I tried to keep a straight face, I was a sucker for the sound and the lips it came from.

I needed to get a few rounds of self-service in tonight before I boarded the plane tomorrow. There was no way I could sit through family introductions and pretend like I wasn't aching for Jaxon to touch me. It would be the type of performance people won awards for.

Jaxon sighed. "Vince is calling me now. He's probably wondering where I am since I said I left fifteen minutes ago."

"Why did you tell him you left when you didn't?"

"Because I'd rather talk to you," he said, his voice raspy from relaxing further into his mattress.

Yes. A *lot* of self-service.

"You'll have me in front of you soon," I offered. "Go have fun and I'll text you tomorrow."

As soon as Jaxon hung up, the room grew eerily quiet. I pulled up my music and hit shuffle on Katie's Drunk Betch playlist. "Crazy in Love" by Beyoncé joined me and my overfilled suitcase.

"Really?" I demanded, annoyed at the irony of the song choice.

As if I needed another reminder about the words I said and couldn't take back.

Chapter Ten

JAXON

JUNE 2016

WHEN I WAS IN middle school, my dad sat me down and we discussed strategies for how I could prepare for football tryouts. He gave me running drills and emailed the coaches for some plays that I could memorize. He also offered to throw with me every day after school to practice. He always stepped in to encourage me when he noticed I was nervous about something.

Even though Dad traveled a lot for work, his presence never lacked from my childhood. He was always there when I needed him.

My mom, however, had a different approach. When she noticed me getting antsy, she found things around the house she *really* needed my help with. The week before my epic middle school football tryouts, there wasn't a loose screw in the entire house. She had a knack for creating projects, and I wasn't embarrassed to admit that her distraction tactic still worked on me.

When I woke up, ready to count down the minutes until I picked Maci up from the airport, Mom pulled out a list of items that needed my attention. While she worked on her menu for tonight's dinner, I hovered over the breakfast counter, fixing a fan that suddenly seemed "unstable" for her to cook under.

"Does Maci like fish?" she asked without looking up from a blue binder. She flipped a few pages before returning to the page she started on. "Never mind, this isn't a fish type of event."

"What exactly constitutes a *fish type* of event?"

"Not this," she murmured. "We could always do sushi. I could have Lucy run to the store and pick up some salmon from the market."

I peered down at her and smiled. "I thought this wasn't a fish type of event."

She waved away my comment. "Different type of fish, J. Sushi presents a much more casual vibe than garlic-parmesan-crusted salmon."

I lowered myself so I was sitting on the counter. "Turn that on and see if it's . . . *stable*." I shot her a playful smirk before I closed my toolbox.

She mirrored my expression and flipped the switch behind her. "Much better. See?"

"Oh, yes." I laughed. "Much better."

As soon as my feet hit the ground, Bella's voice floated in from the foyer. "What's much better?"

Bella entered the kitchen with Alex close behind her. Her blonde hair was pulled back into a ponytail and and her wide blue eyes made it seem like she hadn't just arrived from a four hour flight.

She noticed the toolbox on the counter and her smile fell into a sympathetic smirk. "I see someone needed some distractions this afternoon. Nervous?"

Mom chuckled into her binder as Alex bypassed the entire conversation so he could lay on the couch.

"No," I deadpanned. "I'm not nervous."

Bella crossed the room for a hug. "It's okay to be nervous. This is a massive step for you."

"Bella," Mom warned playfully.

I pulled away to look at both of them. "A *massive* step, huh?"

Bella's face sharpened into a serious scowl. "Yes! This is the first time you'll be bringing a girl into this house without sneaking her out the next morning."

I opened my mouth to protest, but Alex's annoying cackling from the living room didn't strengthen my case. Bella practically lived with us when she was in high school, giving her a front row seat to the start of my dickhead ways. Looking back, I wasn't necessarily proud of the way I treated the women I slept with, but none of them ever did anything they didn't want to do.

Mom started chasing girls down our stairs when I was fourteen, and she wasted no time making sure I understood the difference between silence and consent. Even though she wasn't a fan of my heightened sex drive, she never shamed me for it. The sneaking around part was what always tipped her over the edge, but that only added to the thrill of not getting caught.

Since I was young and stupid, I wasn't super successful.

"Get all of this shit out now," I said. "Maci knows who I was before I started dating her, but I don't want her to have a play by play of how I was a douchebag."

"And she's smart, right?" Bella sat at the breakfast counter, innocently resting her head in her hand. "Like she'll be able to hold a conversation and not just eye-fuck you from the other side of the table?"

"Bella!" Mom scolded, smacking her the way she would me or Alex.

Seriously. The older sister I never asked for.

"She's very smart," I insisted proudly over another round of Alex's cackling. He still hadn't gotten off the couch, but he had no reason to intervene. Bella's heckling was enough for the both of them. "She's going to school to be a teacher, and eventually wants to work at a college."

Mom stopped chopping in case I said anything else she could swoon over. As soon as I started talking about Maci, she'd come flying from the other side of the house to hear whatever words I was offering. Poor Lucy would have calves of steel when Evelyn Hayes was finished with her.

Bella grabbed my hand. "You know I'm only messing with you because I love you, right?"

I rolled my eyes, reaching into the pocket of my shorts to check the nonstop vibrations coming from the group text with the guys.

Only it wasn't a group text.

It was my alarm.

It was two o'clock, and Maci was landing in Charlotte in thirty minutes. My heart started racing, and before I knew it, I was practically jogging to the stairs.

"Wait, where are you going?" Mom yelled.

I lowered my head so I could peer into the kitchen from the top of the stairs. "To change really quick. I've gotta go get my girl in like five minutes."

I threw on some jeans, a black V-neck, and my BGSU hat. I was moving so fast that I almost dropped my bottle of cologne before I sprayed a few pumps.

Did I need more deodorant? I hadn't broken a sweat all day, and suddenly I felt like I needed a shower.

Was I nervous?

Why the fuck was I nervous? Maybe Bella wasn't messing with me.

Did people scramble around this much when they were nervous?

The endless sea of questions continued as I walked out the front door, leaving Alex asleep on the couch and my mom and Bella with giant smiles plastered on their faces.

Chapter Eleven

MACI

June 2016

Last year, when Jaxon mentioned his mom would be so excited to meet me that she would fly me out first class, I thought he was kidding.

To my delightful surprise, my ride to Charlotte came with third row seating and complimentary champagne and snacks. If I weren't meeting Jaxon's family for the first time, I would've thrown myself into bottomless mimosas and an endless supply of those small cinnamon cookies they offered.

Since I could blink and miss the Columbus airport, it took me a second to figure out where I needed to go. I pulled out my phone and smiled at my text from Jaxon.

Jaxon

Let me know when you're past baggage claim! I'll keep circling around until I hear from you

It was too hard for me to navigate and text at the same time, so I popped in my headphones and called him.

"Hey!" he exclaimed. "Where are you?"

I scanned the signs above me. "I'm almost out of the concourse. What gate do you want me to meet you at?"

"Doesn't matter. Just pick one and let me know the number."

I caught a whiff of coffee and followed my nose to Starbucks. The motherland of caffeine was calling to me, and if it weren't for Jaxon's breathy laugh in my ear, I would've gone willingly.

"I'm so excited to see you, baby. What are you wearing?"

"Plane clothes." I laughed. "Sorry if you were expecting lingerie."

"Are you in leggings or shorts? Since we'll have a full house, my mom already turned the air down twice today."

"Leggings." I rounded the corner and looked again at the signage. "I'm about to pass through the security checkpoint, so I shouldn't be much longer. I took your packing advice and brought extra sweatpants, too."

"Did you pack any of my hoodies?"

Once I claimed a spot in the lobby near the window, I propped my luggage next to me and watched the endless streams of cars as they flew by. It was warmer with the sun coming in through the glass, so I slipped off my sweatshirt jacket and hung it over the handle.

"No, I didn't." I chuckled at the idea of trying to shove anything else in my suitcase. "I'm in front of the last gate, by the way. Are you close?"

"I like how that jacket falls off your shoulder," he said, his voice growing louder. "And I'd say I'm pretty close."

I pulled my headphones from my ears and slowly turned around.

Jaxon stood a few feet in front of me, grinning as he lowered the phone from his ear and slid it in the pocket of his jeans. "Hi, pretty girl."

Suddenly, nothing else in the room existed. The crowds of people, the airline workers taking tickets behind the counter, the security officers walking back and forth—everything disappeared as soon as Jaxon entered my vision.

He was exactly how I remembered him. His shirt hugged his chest and showcased the definition in his arms and shoulders. His green eyes popped against his tan skin, and as if his presence alone didn't make me feral, a backward hat covered his dark hair.

If it were long enough to run my fingers through it, I'd lose my fucking mind. For a guy who claimed that he didn't know anything about being a boyfriend, he sure knew how to catch me off guard.

I swallowed around the lump in my throat, unable to stop my voice from wavering. "Hi."

No sooner than the word fell from my lips, he stepped forward so I could throw my arms around his neck. He cupped the backs of my thighs and lifted me off of the ground, pulling me against him as I tried to soak in the sensation of being in his arms again. The familiar scent of his cologne enveloped me in a hug held together by muscles and his need to feel me close to him. He was warm and sensual and everything I missed after spending seven weeks away from him.

"I missed you so fucking much, Mace," he murmured, his breath hot against the sensitive skin behind my ear.

Goosebumps covered my freshly shaved legs as his hands slid over my hips, tracing familiar lines up my back until my feet touched the ground. Before I could say anything else, he took my face in his hands and kissed me.

Heat coursed through my veins as I reunited with the movements of his mouth, his tongue lightly grazing my bottom lip until I allowed him all the way in. I understood why so many kissing scenes took place in an airport. There was something about getting lost in the dozens of different background noises while still feeling like you were one of two people in the room.

A small groan settled in the back of Jaxon's throat. He planted another soft kiss on my mouth before kissing my forehead. His gaze lingered on my face, almost like he was trying to memorize my features and his mouth curved into an adorable grin.

I was completely and utterly fucked, and since I couldn't say the words I really wanted to say, I whispered, "I missed you too."

Jaxon took my luggage and led me to the parking garage. Walking toward his Jeep was like coming back to a piece of the past that housed so many moments I shared with Jaxon—the little touches after every drop-off, all of the last kisses before I went upstairs, and a secluded backseat that served us well when neither of us could wait any longer.

I pictured my hands on the headrest and wondered if my grip left an imprint yet. My stomach tightened as the familiar ache settled between my legs.

Jaxon turned to take my bookbag from me and stopped when he read through my shitty poker face.

"What?" I asked, innocently clasping my hands behind my back.

The corners of his mouth twitched upward. "You better stop thinking about what you're thinking about."

I walked around to the passenger side and slid into my post. Before I could buckle my seatbelt, Jaxon climbed into the driver's seat and angled my face so I could look at him.

"What?" I laughed as he handed me his phone for the music.

He leaned forward, brushing his lips against mine. "Don't *what* me. Stop thinking about what you're thinking about, and stop looking at me like that. The last thing I want to do after not being able to touch you for seven weeks is fuck you in my backseat. I want the time, and I want the space." His thumb skimmed my bottom lip. "Those thoughts in your head? Save them. I want you thinking about how much I want you while we play house for a little while."

I wasn't sure when his hand started to linger near the base of my throat, but I leaned away to gather the strength I needed to get through this stupid car ride.

"I can do that," I lied, tossing any weaknesses I had in the trunk with my overpacked suitcase. I plugged in his phone and scrolled through his playlists. "Now prep me again for who is all going to be th—excuse me, what is Mace Playlist?"

Jaxon looked over his shoulder to steer us out of the garage. His hand gripped the back of my headrest, and I stared out the window to hide my eye roll. I couldn't ignore how much I wanted him even if I tried. All that was missing from this reunion were gray sweatpants and the three little words I was hoping he'd eventually say.

"Just songs that make me think of you." He answered like he hadn't made my heart skip a beat. He rested his hand on my upper thigh and brushed his thumb along the thin fabric of my leggings.

"I have a playlist?"

He selected a song from his phone. "This one especially reminds me of you."

I laughed as "T-Shirt" by Thomas Rhett drifted into the cabin. I continued down the list of songs and queued "Somebody Like You" by Keith Urban next. If Jaxon were embracing his country side, I'd continue to feed it.

"You and that damn car on College Drive," he said, smiling as he slipped on his aviators.

"It was an easy mistake," I protested playfully. "And look at us now! All because of an oil change. Who knows what could've happened if I would've just—"

"Read!" he exclaimed, squeezing my thigh. "I didn't think I could find someone so chaotic and fucking adorable at the same time. Now that you know about my secret playlist, what were you asking me before?"

Ah, yes. Before, my heart stuttered.

"Who's going to be there tonight?" I asked. "You mentioned your parents, but was Alex able to fly in?"

"With Bella, yeah. You're not nervous, are you?"

"Maybe a little?" I admitted, placing the phone on my lap. I cracked the window for some air and helped myself to the extra pair of sunglasses Jaxon kept in the glove compartment. Even though it was summertime back in Columbus, nothing beat the feeling of a breeze that carried traces of salt and sand.

He shifted his hand from my thigh to my forearm, tracing lines along my wrist before he laced his fingers with mine. "You have nothing to be nervous about, sweetheart."

Jaxon merged off the highway, and as the meeting-the-parents nerves subsided, a fresh set made an appearance when we pulled down a street with houses bigger than the education building on Bowling Green's campus.

I knew Jaxon's parents were well off. They both owned successful businesses and were big names in the entertainment and event planning industries. I wasn't sure what I expected when I saw where Jaxon was from, but it never crossed my mind that he lived in a gated community with his own personal code to pull into his driveway.

The house was beautiful. A roundabout driveway curved into a four-car garage with a basketball hoop positioned on the side. Stone the color of sand covered the exterior, while a dark wood accentuated the window frames and both front doors. Gorgeous greenery extended around the flower beds and toward the sides of the house. It was a scene that belonged on a beach. All that was missing was the shoreline in the background, and I wouldn't have been surprised if it was hiding in the backyard.

Jaxon typed in a code at the gate and I made sure my mouth was closed when he turned to face me. He scoffed at the bright red Mustang parked in front of the garage and pulled behind a shiny black Range Rover.

"Every time he comes here, the bitch takes my spot," he murmured.

I relaxed my shoulders and fell back into my seat.

"Ready?" he asked, flashing me a boyish grin. He was excited to bring me inside, and his eager expression made me feel foolish for being nervous in the first place.

It didn't matter if we were in North Carolina or Bowling Green or somewhere that required a passport. I was with Jaxon, and I was halfway convinced that I would follow him anywhere he wanted me to go.

Chapter Twelve

JAXON

June 2016

Maci gasped, taking a few steps toward the giant window taking up the back wall of my room. "Is that your yard?"

I stifled a grin at the sight of her in my room. "Part of it. You can't see the deck from up here, and it cuts off half the pool." I approached her from behind and wrapped my arms around her waist, pulling her close to my chest. "The only way someone can look in is from the rose garden over there."

She followed my gaze and smiled. "It's beautiful. Are you a secret gardener, too?"

I kissed her temple. "Nah. That's all my mom."

A comfortable silence filled the room, and I squeezed her tighter. I wanted to remember what this felt like—having Maci in my arms after being away from her while she was mine.

She spoke over her shoulder. "You said that people *can't* see up here?"

"Ahhh," I exclaimed, chuckling as I retreated back to the dresser. "Come on. Let's go downstairs."

Her laughter turned into an agonizing whine. "It was worth a try. How do I look? Should I change into something else before I meet everyone?"

I shook my head. "You look beautiful."

And she did. I could've brought Maci downstairs in a paper bag, and she would've been perfect.

"I'm in leggings and a tank top," she protested.

"My mom and Bella will be wearing the same thing. It's pretty casual here. I promise."

I led her downstairs and through the kitchen, trying to put as much space between us and my bed as possible. My mom got notifications on her phone when our gate opened, so she knew I was here. If I didn't appear with Maci soon, she'd become a dangerous one-woman search party I didn't want to be found by.

We stepped down into the den, and Maci pulled back her hand. "Wait."

I recognized the playful spark in her blue eyes. The right corner of her mouth lifted into a slight smile, and when her gaze traveled up my chest and finally met mine, I blew out a breath I didn't realize I was holding.

That look lit a fire inside me. That look would convince me to do anything she wanted.

She threw her arms around my neck, stood on her toes, and kissed me. I grabbed her hips and pulled her against me, her fingers tightening around the hair at the base of my neck. They curled under my hat, knocking it to the floor as her mouth opened up for me. She tasted even better than she did at the airport—sweet and needy and ready. If I slipped my hand down the front of her leggings, I knew exactly what I would find.

I could've teased her, got her going only to send her outside wanting more. Instead, I kept my hands on her hips, tightening my grip when her teeth grazed my bottom lip. She was good, but she was overconfident for someone who wasn't playing on the home field.

She sucked softly on my lip, bringing it into her mouth along with my last drop of self-will. "There," she whispered, her heated gaze replaced with an innocent smirk. "Now I'm ready."

"I bet you are," I murmured, adjusting my jeans so I didn't greet my family cock first.

We stepped onto the deck as Alex was in the middle of telling a story. He was full of animation with his hands out in front of him, with Bella clasping her stomach and my dad chuckling into his glass of whiskey.

Mom eyed me over the brim of her wine glass, waiting for me to make introductions. She was a woman on a mission, and her mission was to finally make conversation with the first girl I ever invited home.

I rested my free hand on Alex's shoulder, making him pause mid-sentence.

"Everyone, this is Maci," I said, slipping my arm around her waist. I purposely grazed her lower back with my hand, stifling a chuckle when she flinched at my touch. "Mace, this is my brother, Alex."

Alex offered her a charming smile. "Hi, Maci."

I continued the introductions around the table. "This is Bella, Alex's girlfriend, and older sister I didn't ask for."

Bella shrugged. "He says that with love."

"Of course I do." I scoffed while Maci and Bella shared a laugh. "This beautiful woman right here is my mom, Evelyn."

Mom stood up and held out her arms. "Maci."

Maci smiled as my mom pulled her in for a hug. A warmth flared in my chest watching them interact.

"It's so nice to meet you," Maci said. "Jaxon has told me so many things about you."

"Well, damn." Alex's voice drifted from the other end of the table. Mom shot him a warning glance, but his cocky grin had already surfaced. "He didn't tell you anything about me?"

I chimed in before Maci could answer. "Don't be a dick."

"Jaxon!" Mom scolded, smacking my dad on his shoulder. He looked taken aback by his punishment for laughing, causing the rest of us to join in. "What was that? Two minutes before one of them dropped a word?"

"A word," Dad echoed, still chuckling when he held out his hand for Maci to shake. "Pleasure to meet you, Maci."

"Jaxon's told me a lot about you too, Mr. Hayes," Maci teased, peeking over her shoulder to raise her eyebrows at Alex.

"All good things I hope," Dad said with an amused grin, "and please call me Reed."

I pulled out Maci's chair and we settled into the two remaining seats at the table. Bella offered us wine while Alex finished his story. Mom moved effortlessly around the table, prepping the space before she brought out trays of sushi, homemade potstickers, and some sort of soup I didn't recognize.

"This is what sangria is supposed to taste like," I whispered as Maci reached for her drink.

She laughed. "Yeah, that's really good. Poor Katie."

I leaned closer, letting my hand slip under the table so I could to brush my thumb along her thigh. Her shoulders relaxed at my touch. She was nervous, but based on the reactions from the table, she had no reason to be.

Dad reached behind him to refill his whiskey glass. "So, Maci, Jaxon tells us you're going to school for teaching? High school, right?"

"High school English," she answered proudly. "I'd love to work for a university as an instructional designer or even a curriculum director, but I think a few years in the classroom will give me the experience I need to take that step. There are a lot of people in education right now who have never taught, and unfortunately, it shows."

"So you'll be licensed to teach in Ohio, but could you eventually move to a university outside of Ohio?"

"As long as I carry the required licensing for that state, I can go anywhere! I'll get the Ohio license first because it makes the most sense, but I plan on adding a few more states as well."

"I'd love to go back and teach at Brown," Bella added. Her dimple dug into her right cheek, and when the coast was clear, she looked at me and mouthed, "Thank you."

I rolled my eyes, sending her a "You're welcome" for not lying about the fact that Maci could hold a conversation. Over the years, Bella held numerous conversations with random broads I brought back to the house. I paid them no attention if they were still here the morning after because that would imply I wanted them to hang around. Bella was too polite to ignore them, and eventually, she knew more about the women I slept with than I did.

Fuck. I really was an asshole.

"Brown!" Maci gushed. "Ugh, I hear their campus is *gorgeous* in the fall."

"It is! If you ever apply to teach there, I'd love to give you a tour. I'm always looking for reasons to visit."

While my heart swelled at Bella's offer, my stomach sank at the thought of Maci being across the country. It was the first time the plans I had laid out for my future slapped me in the face. Next year, I'd be in California, and next year, Maci would be—

"California has some amazing colleges, Maci," Mom added innocently.

"Ma," I groaned, resting my forehead in my hand. We'd been here for twenty minutes, and my mom was already thirty steps ahead. I needed Alex to pop the question so she could focus on his wedding instead of mentally preparing for mine.

Maci chuckled along with the rest of the table. "Yes, I've heard that California has some impressive schools."

About an hour later, the sun started to set behind the tree line. A soft breeze drifted through the yard as everyone recovered from another award-winning dinner delivered by Evelyn Hayes.

I lost count of how often Maci laughed at one of Alex's comments or Bella's smart remarks. My parents divided questions between them, asking about Maci's family, where she was from, and why she chose to go to Bowling Green State University for school.

I hadn't been nervous to introduce Maci to my family—I was nervous that a change would shift in my mindset.

"Hey," Maci lowered her voice so only I could hear her. Her blue eyes had a slight gloss thanks to a third bottle of sangria being passed around the table. "Are you okay?"

I reached down and grasped the leg of her chair, tugging it toward me and opening my arm so she could lean into my chest. No one batted an eye at the interaction, as if it were the most natural position they had ever seen me in.

I ran my fingers over the goosebumps on her shoulders and brushed my lips against her temple. "Never better, baby."

Chapter Thirteen

MACI

June 2016

When Evelyn appeared with a banana pudding cake topped with cookies and whipped cream, I thought my stomach was going to explode. She was a woman after my heart, with her endless stream of homemade food that would put any item I had ever eaten to shame.

Later when I provided the SparkNotes version of the evening to Katie, I would leave out Jaxon's comment about the sangria. Hearing I loved another woman's cooking would be hard enough.

As distracted as I was by Jaxon's mindless tracing along my shoulder and bicep, I couldn't take my eyes off his parents. The same word came to mind when I first saw Jaxon—*pretty*.

Reed didn't look a day over thirty-five, and he couldn't go a full minute without smiling. His eyes had beautiful gold undertones that popped against his brown skin, and for a man whose name took over most of the sports and entertainment industry, there wasn't a single wrinkle in his calm expression. When he wasn't focused on the conversation at the table, his eyes always drifted back to Evelyn.

I knew right away that Evelyn was someone who didn't take anyone's shit. I loved her immediately. Delicate facial features softened her piercing green eyes, and I adored how they were the same shade as Jaxon's. She could garden, run a successful business, and manage a household while rocking a red lip. If this woman ran for president tomorrow, she'd have my vote.

It was refreshing to see a couple whose love you could feel from across the table. Meanwhile, I had parents at home who planned out times in the living room so they could avoid each other.

Jaxon reached for a dessert plate. "Did you want a piece of this?"

My stomach groaned in protest. "A small one, please."

"Is there more in the fridge?" Bella asked, smacking Alex's hand away from the dollops of whipped cream. "I'm gonna head to bed, but I'll want some tomorrow."

Evelyn nodded and rested her hand on Reed's. "We aren't far behind you."

Bella waited for Alex to load his plate with cake before they said goodnight to the table. My eyes started to close at the mention of sleep. After an afternoon of traveling and fueling myself into a food coma, I felt the exhaustion kick in.

We said goodnight to his parents and helped put the leftovers in the kitchen.

Once we reached the top of the stairs, Jaxon pointed down the hall opposite his room. "Alex's room is down there on the end, and there is a spare bedroom that no one uses next to it. The bathroom is across the hall from my room."

"Oh, perfect. Do you care if I shower really quick? I want to wash the airplane off of me."

Jaxon opened the closet next to the bathroom and pulled out a towel. "I got one of those spongey things you like. It's sitting in the basket on the sink."

I tried not to laugh. "A loofah?"

"Yeah." He kissed my forehead before backing into his room. "That. Want one of my shirts for when you get out?"

"I prefer not to run into any of your family members without pants, so toss me some shorts."

"No one is going to run into you. Alex and Bella won't be leaving his bedroom anytime soon," he added suggestively, tossing me a shirt.

As the warm water ran down my back, I got to work lathering my legs. I would forever be jealous of the women who could shave and have smooth skin for at least twenty-four hours. I'd never know what it was like to be a chosen one. I found a razor among my basket of goodies on the counter and did a quick, yet careful, glide check.

Things didn't bother Jaxon the way they bothered my last boyfriend. Jaxon didn't care about morning breath or stubble or how sweaty I was after cleaning all day with Katie. He only cared about me. I hadn't decided if that was incredibly sweet or made me even more terrified by my feelings for him.

When I opened the door to Jaxon's room, he stood with his back facing me. My eyes traveled down the muscles that framed his spine, settling on the waistband of his jeans. I meant to announce my presence, but the words caught in my throat.

Just as I closed the door behind me, he saw me in the window and turned around. The last lingering traces of sunlight rested on his chiseled chest, making its way up his forearm and highlighting the hues of green in his eyes as he walked toward me.

The muscles in my stomach tightened as his fingers traced the dips in my hips, trailing over my belly button until his thumbs found the sensitive skin under my breasts. My body was on fire, begging me to react on instinct instead of trying to keep it together.

"Did you lock the door?" he murmured, his voice raspy.

I nodded, clenching my thighs to try to ease the ache between my legs. It was his voice, the lighting, and the gorgeous view from his window. It was how soft his bed looked and how warm his skin was against mine. His room was one giant cocktail of temptation, and I came armed with ten fucking straws.

He kissed my cheek, brushing his lips against my jawline. I was betrayed by a small moan, prompting a low laugh that danced softly against my neck. I knew what he was doing, and it was working. I left all of my self-control in the shower with my loofah.

"Good," he whispered. "Watch a movie with me."

"Let's do that after."

"After what?"

I ran my hands through his curls and gripped them with my fingers. A soft groan fell from his mouth, vibrating against my chest as he pressed his erection to the flimsy material of my boyshorts.

I tugged on his bottom lip with my teeth. "Is that even a question?"

His mouth collided with mine, and I tightened my grip around his neck as he placed me on the bed behind us. My clothes hit the floor in all directions, and my fingers found their familiar place in his hair as his tongue swept down my neck and over my chest. He took my nipple in his mouth and teased the sensitive skin.

"Jaxon," I begged. "Please, I want—"

"Patience, pretty girl." He looked up at me through thick lashes, laying me down on the bed before he kissed me. I could've come apart just feeling his weight on top of me again. His warm skin pressed against me with his hands trailing up and down my sides. I tightened my grip on his hair and ground my hips into his erection, looking for relief as he continued to tease me.

"I told you I need time," he warned, making his way to my mouth. "And from my understanding, I have a few days." He kissed me slowly as he reached his hand past my panty line, gently stroking my clit. "I missed this. I missed how ready you are when you want me. I missed the noises you make when I do this." He slid a finger inside me and curled it toward my naval, my sighs turning to whimpers at his touch. "I missed how you arch your back when I kiss you here." He nipped and kissed the side of my neck near my shoulder, my body responding just like he said it would. "I missed the first woman I've ever wanted to memorize. I missed you, Mace."

The pressure began to build in my core. He pulled out his finger, shifting his attention to my throbbing clit as he stared down at me with a heated gaze and slack jaw. I squirmed with need, begging him to go faster and return his fingers to the sweet spot inside me.

"You want me to fuck you with my fingers, pretty girl?" He used his free hand to pull at my bottom lip with his thumb. "Make you remember what it feels like to come all over my hand?"

I nodded with a shaky breath.

Jaxon answered with a hungry grin, pulling back to crawl off the bed and remove his jeans. "Show me what you did when you missed me," he demanded softly. "When I wasn't there to touch you, what did you do, baby?"

"I thought of you."

He raised an eyebrow in question. "With just your hands?"

"Yeah," I said, smiling shyly. I was grateful the sun decided to disappear. We had just enough light, but he couldn't see the color rushing to my cheeks. But as he bent down to smile against my lips before he kissed me, I realized that factor didn't matter. He could tell in my voice I was unsure.

"I'll do something about that," he assured me, deepening our kiss as he moved my hand between my legs.

I closed my eyes, instinctively moving my hips to match the rhythm of my fingers, sighing against his lips as the pressure started building again. My stomach dipped as my palm rubbed against my clit, and I pumped harder. I was close, and it wouldn't be long before I toppled over the edge.

Jaxon pressed his forehead to mine, his hand grazing my stomach as he stroked himself. "I could come just watching you, Mace. Tell me what you're thinking about."

"Your tongue."

I shuddered when I felt him lick up my neck before planting a kiss under my ear. "This tongue?"

The simple touch was all I needed to coax my body to the breaking point. I groaned, chasing the high as I bucked my hips and arched my back. I gripped the pillow behind me and just as I was about to cry out, Jaxon grabbed my wrist and brought my fingers to his mouth. He sucked them slowly as he pulled me to the edge of the bed, dropping to his knees so he could dip his face between my legs.

His cocky grin resurfaced. "I also missed how good you taste."

His lips brushed against my clit, and my head fell back. He was killing me. It was a long, deranged kind of torture that would undoubtedly be the death of me.

I thought being away from him was hard. That was nothing compared to having him in front of me and not *having* him.

When his tongue lapped eagerly against my center, I couldn't take it anymore. My hands shot to his head, my fingers tugging on his curls as I moaned his name. With every move of my hips, Jaxon pressed harder against me, throwing my legs over his shoulders so I couldn't move away.

"Jaxon," I begged, trying to keep my voice down.

He crawled over me, kissing me while his erection teased the sensitive skin between my legs. The sensation was incredible, and when I wrapped my legs around his back, he sat up, bringing me with him.

"Turn around," he instructed.

I followed his lead, kneeling in front of him as he pressed my back to his stomach. I expected him to push me forward, fuck me from behind so we could take what we both needed. But when nothing came, I shifted slightly to watch him plant soft kisses up my neck. With one arm draped over my shoulder to tease my nipple, his other wrapped around my hip, allowing his fingers to reunite with my clit.

I reached down and took his cock in my hand, stroking him slowly against my entrance. I teased the tip, and a groan fell from his mouth, vibrating against my back. My fingers dug into his neck as he pushed inside me, letting me adjust to the angle before he rocked his hips again to repeat the sweet motion.

"Fuck, Mace," he murmured, his next thrust much more eager than the first few.

His arms tightened around me. My heart hammered against my chest as he filled me over and over again. I had never felt this close to him—with his mouth against my ear, catching every sound he made and every murmur that fell from his lips. He kept our movements slow, his hands working in perfect sync in a position I didn't know could feel so sensual.

He moved his hand from my breast and angled my face so he could kiss me, pumping harder as my tongue moved eagerly against his. As much as I loved him this way, I wanted him to go harder. My walls started pulsing around him, and I clenched the muscles in my stomach as his fingers moved faster. My legs shook at the sensation, and before I knew it, he was claiming my mouth with his to keep my voice down. I clawed his neck so I wouldn't fall forward as my entire body trembled with an orgasm that dominated every cell in my body.

As if he had read my mind, he shifted my hips so my hands hit the mattress. I gripped the sheets as he slammed into me, adjusting slightly so he could hit the sweet spot I needed to come undone one more time.

"Come for me, pretty girl," he said, digging his nails into my ass.

I licked the pad of my index finger and reached between my legs. With a few quick movements, I felt another wave, wetting the sheets and everything between us.

Jaxon's groan filled the room as I collapsed onto the mattress. Tired and spent, he rolled to the side to keep his weight off of me, resting his arm above his head while his other lingered on my skin.

I chuckled. "Sorry about the bed."

"I'm not," he said through a breathy laugh, kissing me again. "I have more sheets in my closet. Let me get a towel."

While I cleaned myself up, Jaxon reached up to the top shelf of his closet for more sheets. I was admiring the muscles in his back when alarm bells sounded in my head.

This clean-up was different, and I was an idiot.

We hadn't used a condom.

Fuck.

"Fuck," I echoed my solitary thought into the universe.

Jaxon looked over his shoulder. "Fuck?"

I stared at him with the towel in my hand. "We didn't use a condom."

He ran a hand through his air and sighed. "Fuck."

"Everything just happened so fast and—wait." My eyes narrowed. "What is the reason for *your* fuck?"

His jaw went slack as he looked at the white sheets in his hands. My heartbeat thumped behind my ears. My mind raced in twenty different directions, all of them heading to a giant caution sign that read, "BOYFRIEND TRIAL."

I trusted Jaxon, but the look on his face left an uneasy feeling in my stomach. This would be the second time I sat on a bed with wet sheets, waiting for clarification from the man who caused me to make them that way.

"The reason for my *fuck*"—an amused smile replaced his uneasy expression—"is because you just started a new birth control. One that you have to take every day."

My shoulders relaxed at his obvious statement. "Okay?"

"And I have a girlfriend who mentioned how nice it would be to have a microwave that reminds her she has a cup of coffee in there." He sat next to me on the bed, tossing the towel in the hamper so he could grab my hand. "Were you expecting me to say something else?"

"No," I answered quickly, squeezing his hand. "Nothing else."

His eyes trailed down to our joined hands. "I got tested back in May, not because I was worried that something would show up, but because I wanted to feel like I was starting over with you. That this was going to be . . . you know my past . . . fuck, you've seen how I was—"

I watched him battle whatever thoughts were running through his head, and my heart sank. I knew about the past versions of Jaxon, but the only version that mattered was the one sitting in front of me.

He ran a hand through his curls, looking defeated. "I wouldn't blame you for not trusting me, but just in case it crossed your mind, there hasn't been anyone else, sweetheart."

"It did cross my mind," I admitted softly, "for about a millisecond. But Jaxon, I wouldn't be with you if I didn't trust you."

I almost regretted the words, but we promised each other honesty when we made this official in March. All of the miscommunication from last year got us nowhere, and it almost drove us apart.

He squeezed my hand back. "I care about you a lot, Mace."

"I know." I smiled reassuringly. "I care about you a lot, too."

The corners of his mouth dug into his cheeks as he tried not to smirk. He would never throw my premature "I love you" in my face, but we couldn't ignore that I said it.

I scanned the bed for my shirt. "I'm going to rinse off really quick—"

"Wait, wait, wait," Jaxon said, pulling me to him. "So, about the no condom thing . . ."

I smacked his chest and pushed him away. "Change the sheets, Jax."

"I'm just saying," he added with a boyish grin. "You got a clean bill of health shortly after I did."

Heat rose to my cheeks as his tongue grazed the center of his top lip.

I knew that look, and I swore I heard the sound of judgmental cackling from the Trojans in my suitcase.

Chapter Fourteen

JAXON

June 2016

Even though we spent all day yesterday locked away in my room, Maci and I didn't do a ton of talking. I never mentioned Alex's proposal, and she didn't hint at having any questions after meeting my parents. We were busy making up for lost time, and neither of us seemed bothered by that taking priority.

In exchange for leaving my bed only for snacks, water, and slices of my mom's banana pudding cake, I let her talk me into a Harry Potter marathon. I had nothing against the Wizarding World, but ever since our slip with the condom, I wanted to spend all of my time inside her. Maci was right about it just happening—but when I dug into her stash of Trojans, she let me get two thrusts in before she told me I could take it off if I wanted to.

No matter how many rounds we finished yesterday, I always asked if she was sure. I wanted her to know that just because it happened by accident didn't mean I expected it to be the new normal. I loved the feeling of being close to her, and it added a whole new level to what I already thought was special.

Was *special* the right word? Since "different" made it sound bad, I'd stick with special. I just knew a lot of fucking feelings were involved.

We both showered and washed off yesterday's activities before we headed downstairs.

"Ma?" I yelled as we entered an empty kitchen.

"Ew, Jaxon, why are you yelling?" Bella whined from the table.

"Well, happy birthday, Bella." I flashed her a smile and poured Maci some juice. "Where is everyone? And why do you look so bothered?"

She dragged her hands down her face. "Thank you, and I'm not. I'm just tired of staring at this computer screen. I've been up since five trying to figure out this meeting for our new client, and they are beyond unpleasant." She sighed, closing her eyes as she rested her head in her hand. "This is officially the most stressful day I've had this year."

"Did you wanna get out of the house for some birthday brunch?" Maci offered. "Jaxon and I were going to go to—"

"Nope," I interjected, ignoring Bella's scowl. I wanted to tell Maci about Alex's proposal, and I couldn't have Bella sitting across the table. "Just us. I want you all to myself for a little bit longer."

Maci gasped at my response, and before she could speak, Bella picked up on my urgent tone.

"Thank you for the offer," she said sweetly. "I should be done in a few hours, and then I plan to wine and dine with Evelyn by the pool until dinner tonight. You two enjoy your afternoon."

About twenty minutes later, we had a table outside at my favorite breakfast place. We were the only people on the patio, and the way the sun hit Maci's blue eyes when she looked up from the menu made me smile every time.

"Will I regret getting both caramel and peanut butter on my waffles?" She scrunched her nose and restarted her scanning. "Or maybe I should just do those chocolate strawberry crepes—"

"Mace." I plucked her menu from her hands. "You've read the same page ten times. Order them both."

She eyed me suspiciously and slid both our menus to the side.

After the waitress returned and took our order, Maci crossed her arms and leaned her elbows on the table. "Is something bugging you? Care to tell me why Bella couldn't come with us even though it's her *birthday*?" Her eyes narrowed. "Hips hurt?"

I scoffed, unable to replay anything from yesterday, or else I'd get hard under the table. "My hips are fine. You're the one who told me you were a little sore this morning."

"I am, and I'm not ashamed of it. Who knew Ron Weasley said, 'bloody hell' so many times throughout the series?"

"Who knew there were eight Harry Potter movies," I murmured, taking a sip of my mimosa.

She shrugged. "It was your rule."

"And you didn't think to warn me!"

"Listen, when your boyfriend offers you an orgasm for every time Ron Weasley says 'bloody hell,' you don't turn away the opportunity." Maci threw in a British accent for the phrase, causing me to choke on my drink. She giggled while I wiped my party foul from the table.

I lifted my hat and ran a hand through my hair. "So, about this morning—"

Maci coaxed me to continue. "Go on."

"Bella couldn't come with us because I wanted to tell you that Alex is going to propose to her at dinner."

"What!" she exclaimed, unable to hide her excitement. "That's amazing!"

"I've been the only one who's known for months. It feels good to tell someone about it."

"Months? When did Alex tell you?"

"March," I said, smiling at the memory. "It was a few days after Port Clinton, and as soon as he told me I'd get a plus one, I knew exactly who I wanted to bring with me."

"That's a long trial period, Jaxon Hayes," she teased.

I grabbed her hand. "Not really. When she says yes, Alex wants to get married in December. He's been in love with her for years. He doesn't want to wait any longer than he has to."

"I love that," she said softly, running her thumb over my fingers. "Find your person and make them yours."

"He makes it sound pretty easy, doesn't he?" I chuckled before I took a deep breath. I hated changing the topic so quickly, but I wanted to get it over with. "Mace, I'm sure you have questions about my family."

"I do," she answered fondly, "but probably not the questions you think I have."

I had the summarized version ready to go in my head this morning, and suddenly, I was drawing a blank. Every single time I had to talk about my past with someone, I was reminded of the consequences that came with trusting them.

But this wasn't just *someone*. This was Maci, and I wanted to let her in.

"Hey," she prompted, forcing me to keep eye contact. "You don't owe me anything you don't want to share."

"No, it's okay." I offered her a reassuring grin. "I just don't talk about this with people, that's all."

Her smile wavered slightly. I needed to get better with my deliveries.

"But you're not *people*, Mace. My past is a little dicey, but long story short, Reed and Evelyn adopted me when I was four. I have no idea where my birth mom is, and my birth father is in a prison down in Florida."

The waitress returned with our food and refilled my mimosa.

Maci poked at the strawberries on her crepes as a comfortable silence settled over the table. "And Alex?"

"Alex is my half-brother. Reed is Alex's biological father."

Maci grinned as she took a bite of her waffles. "You have the same cocky smirk after you say something that's only meant for one person to hear." She snagged some caramel off her bottom lip with her tongue, drawing my focus to her mouth.

I cleared my throat. "Yeah, I've been told that."

"You said your parents got together when Alex was two," she stated, remembering our conversation before winter break.

I took a bite of bacon and admired how adorable she looked while she worked through the timeline in her head.

"So, Reed and your birth mom weren't together long, then?"

I shook my head. "They weren't together at all. Karina got wrapped up with John shortly after that, and Reed filed for custody of Alex the same day he applied for graduation. John is my birth father."

"Graduation?" Her eyes widened. "Wow."

"Yeah," I said with a hefty sigh and finished the last of my mimosa. "Told you it's a little dicey."

"How long were you with . . . John and Karina for?"

"Honestly?" I leaned back in my chair and rested my hands behind my head. "I don't really know. When Alex was six,

Karina called Reed from an unknown number, asking to see Alex. She was on something—whatever John had her taking at the time. She went on and on about how she was going to turn her life around for her two sons. When Reed asked her about me, she didn't know much. She couldn't even remember when I was taken from John's home." I rested my elbows on the table and shrugged my shoulders. "Evelyn did some digging and found out where I was. I'm convinced that woman can find anything she puts her mind to."

Maci averted her gaze to the street and let out a shaky breath. This wasn't at all where I wanted this conversation to go.

"Baby, I didn't tell you this to make you sad," I said.

"I just don't know what to say, I guess," she offered softly.

"Well, I know this—" I pulled her hand to my mouth and kissed her fingers. "I couldn't have asked for better people to be my parents. And I got to grow up with Alex, even though he's a pain in the ass sometimes."

That earned me a giggle. "Thank you."

"For what?"

"For trusting me," she said, sounding more like herself.

"You're not people," I reminded her, stealing a strawberry from her plate and popping it in my mouth.

I knew my theft would make her pick up her fork again. I hid my satisfaction when our conversation shifted to Jared's incessant Avenger memes, and she was close to clearing her plate. It felt good to share my past with Maci, but I didn't want it to take away from our time together while she was here. Part of me was tempted to tell her about the letter from John and get it all out of the way in one sweep. The other part of me dusted around the topic once I caught her sneaking cash to the waitress for the meal.

I cocked my head. "I told you I was paying for everything while you were here."

"Bloody hell," she said, her British accent returning. "It's the least I can do for all of that hip work you did yesterday."

Chapter Fifteen

MACI

June 2016

When Jaxon told me he was helping Koll Construction with a few houses this summer, I never imagined the three-story mansions we drove by on the way to his barber. The lots offered amazing lake views and a wide spread of land with gorgeous greenery and stone fixtures. I couldn't believe people lived like this. There were beautiful beaches almost four hours away, but lakeside living existed right in their backyard.

We rolled up to the barbershop, and a pathetic pit formed in my stomach.

Jaxon laughed at my disgusted expression when I rounded the front of his Jeep. "It's just hair, Mace. I let you get a few tugs in, but I can't keep it long like this in the summer. The heat kills me."

"I just won't survive the loss if I witness it first-hand," I argued. The thought of his soft curls hitting the floor only deepened my frown lines.

"Well, fortunately, you won't have to." He pointed across the road. "See that store over there?"

I scanned my options and landed on the small white building in the center of the strip. "The nail salon?"

"You said last night you should've gotten a pedicure. Go get one while I get my haircut, and meet me at that store when you're done."

I followed his hand to the bright pink building a few doors down. "Loca Lovers? That sounds like a horribly written Hallmark card."

Jaxon cupped my chin and kissed me. "Go relax, and I'll see you in about an hour."

Jaxon watched me cross the street and, I left him with a final wave before I turned and went inside. I was hit with a troubling wave of cold air, and immediately crossed my arms over my chest. The last thing I wanted to do was meet my nail technician nipples first.

A woman approached the desk with a charming smile. Her bright red curls were piled in a bun on top of her head, while a few pieces hung down to frame her porcelain features. "What are you in for, hun?"

I smiled politely back. "A pedicure. I know it's last minute so I understand if—"

"Are you Maci?"

I blinked a few times before answering. "Yes."

"You're right on time." She grabbed a pen and pushed a clipboard across the counter. "Go ahead and sign here confirming your slot."

"My slot?" I scanned the line of names and read the note next to mine.

"I couldn't stop laughing when Jaxon called and tried to make a *feet appointment*. I thought Evelyn was going to keel over in the background just listening to him try and figure out what the hell he was calling for."

"I can only imagine how flustered he sounded," I said, laughing. "I'm so sorry, I didn't ask for your name."

"Oh, no apologies necessary, hun." She gestured for me to follow her to the spa chairs. "My name is Viv, and Evelyn and I go way back. Go ahead and take the seat at the end while

I get everything. Did you want something to drink? I've got water, tea, wine, champagne—"

"Champagne?" I repeated, settling into the chair.

Viv raised an eyebrow. "Champagne?"

I shrugged. "Why not."

She smiled before heading into the back room.

The massaging chair started its ripples of relaxation over my shoulders and down my back. I wanted to close my eyes and enjoy the first moment I had to myself since I arrived, but my thoughts wouldn't let me. My mind was racing with everything Jaxon told me over brunch.

My phone buzzed in my lap, and Katie's name lit up my screen. It was as if she could sense that my pot was simmering. "Hi, Katie."

"Are you alone?" she asked, practically panting.

"I am until Viv returns with my champagne." I scanned the empty salon, growing more concerned with the sounds Katie was making. "Uhm . . . are *you* alone?"

There was a soft rustling, followed by a giggle. "I'm hiding."

I lowered my voice as if I were right next to her. "From who?"

"From Connor."

"Okay," I reprimanded. "If this is some sort of hide-and-seek foreplay you're calling me from—"

"No!" she exclaimed, keeping her voice down. "No foreplay, I promise. We haven't had much of that this entire trip."

I winced at the thought. "Really?"

"Really," she emphasized. "I'm hiding in the garage for a second to catch my breath. I don't know what to do, Mace."

Viv returned with a glass of champagne and a basket of pedicure essentials. I gestured to the phone and apologized for being on it. I hated being the person who was having a conversation in front of someone, but Viv waved it off and motioned for me to dip my feet in the bubbling water.

Katie continued with her hide-and-seek saga. "Everything was fine when it was just the two of us here! But it's like as soon as his family got back from their camping trip, Connor turned into a completely different person."

I sipped my champagne. "How so?"

Viv handed me a book and instructed me to pick a color. She sat on a stool in front of me and added, "I have some more in the back if those don't work."

I nodded, placing Katie on my lap and putting her on speaker.

"He turns into this needy little boy," she spat, prompting a chuckle from Viv and I. "He's making me hate his family when, really, they aren't the ones at fault here. He suddenly doesn't know how to clean up after himself or buy groceries or do anything remotely independent. Did you know he puts his dishes in the sink for his mom to *load* the dishwasher?"

"Maybe his mom has a specific way she loads the dishwasher?" I offered. I handed Viv the book of colors and whispered, "I'll go with red."

"I *think* it's all a load of crap, actually. Yesterday he left a spoon still covered in peanut butter in the sink, and I had to stop myself from scolding him in front of his mom. He could've at least licked it clean before he placed it in there. I've had a front-row seat to the tongue work, and I know he can do better than that."

My eyes shot up to Viv, who was turned away so she could laugh without disturbing the conversation.

I muted Katie and took her off speaker to offer Viv an apology. "I'm so sorry."

Viv put her hand to her chest. "Oh my gosh, don't be. Can you turn her up?"

I laughed along with Viv and put Katie back on speaker.

"I'm just annoyed that I've been away from Connor for so long and now that I finally get to see him—" She sighed, her humor leaving the conversation. "He also told his parents that he was looking at a few houses about an hour away from them."

Now I understood the source of Katie's frustration. "Katie, we both know this isn't about Connor's family or peanut butter spoons. Have you guys talked about graduation? Has Connor always planned to stay in Michigan?"

"We've talked a little, but it's still so early. I have to submit job applications and hear back from recruiters. All of that takes time."

Two days ago Evelyn Hayes reminded me of the amazing schools in California and all of the internship applications I sent out after winter break. Regardless of what I decided, Jaxon was headed for the West Coast, and I was waiting to hear back from program directors. "Talk to me about this foreplay thing. Has he not wanted to do anything?"

"Not since his parents got home a few days ago. It's bullshit!"

"Maybe he just wants to respect his parents' house?"

"Yeah, right. Has Jaxon been respecting *his* parents' house? Or can you still walk—"

"Oookay!" I exclaimed, removing Katie from Viv's earshot for the second time. She shook her head as she started on the polish. "I can't really discuss that now."

I could only imagine the report Viv was going to provide Evelyn. I just hoped there would be no mentions of foreplay or peanut butter spoons.

Chapter Sixteen

JAXON

June 2016

Loca Lovers was a hole-in-the-wall shop of costumes, props, sex toys, and lingerie. It was my first time being in the store, and a giant wave of satisfaction hit me when I saw Maci scanning a wall of colorful vibrators.

I bent down to whisper in her ear. "Find something?"

"Oh my god!" she exclaimed, quickly turning around. She swatted my chest when she realized it was me. She scoffed, running her hand through my short hair. "Oh my god."

"It'll grow back." I smiled, turning her around to face the wall. "But seriously, did you find something?"

"*Find something*? You mean you expect me to buy something here?"

"Well, technically, I will be." I grazed my hand across her lower back and turned her toward the smaller vibrating options. "I asked you what you used when I wasn't around, remember?"

She eyed me cautiously. "Yes."

"And I said I'd do something about that," I reminded her, drawing her attention to a bright purple wand with a rabbit.

"You want to—" She lowered her voice. "You want to buy me a *vibrator*?"

I stifled a laugh at her reaction. "Why are you saying that like it's a bad thing? Honestly, I'm surprised you don't have one. Don't girls have drawers of this shit?"

Maci picked up a hot pink item that came with a remote. "Not all girls have drawers, Jaxon."

"Well, let's start one."

She crossed her arms in front of her chest and peered around the store. "It won't bother you?"

Fuck. Was she pissed about this?

"Is it okay that I brought you here?" I asked. "If this makes you feel some type of way, Mace, I'm—"

"*I* don't feel some type of way," she reassured me with a grin. "I guess I'm just surprised you're okay with me having something that isn't you."

"Why wouldn't I be?"

"Well, the last one wasn't," she murmured.

"The last, what?" I stepped toward her as her eyes scanned a small box labeled, "The Red Bullet."

"My last . . . *boyfriend*."

Boyfriend. Her *ex*-boyfriend. I was about to experience what it felt like to hear about the ex.

"What about him?" I prompted casually, letting her know it wasn't awkward to mention. "He didn't like sex stores?"

"He didn't like anything that wasn't him. Katie joked about getting me something for my birthday, and he pretty much lost his mind."

I sucked my teeth. "Huh."

Maci averted her eyes from The Red Bullet. "What?"

"Nothing," I said, smirking at the thought of being insecure about a guest star. "Just sounds like he was nervous you might *enjoy* something more than him."

A slight pink flooded Maci's cheeks, and I remembered that I wasn't the only one who had items from their past they hadn't shared. I knew about a few of Maci's relationships, but not enough about them to recall details. The one I knew the most about was Bryson, and we never made their hookup a topic of conversation.

"You know what," she stated, pulling The Red Bullet from the rack. "Why not?"

"You don't have to get anything if you don't want to—"

"No, I do," she insisted, handing me her choice. She grabbed my free hand and pulled me toward the register.

The device couldn't have been longer than my finger, and my mind went wild with ideas. This was travel-size, pocket-size . . . all of the sizes that made it easy to use when the rest of the world wouldn't notice.

Before I got too excited, I searched her blue eyes for any signs of hesitation. "You sure? You don't have to get anything if you don't want to."

Her heated gaze stopped me in my tracks as we approached the register. It was the same look she gave me right before we went outside to meet my parents. Suddenly, my mouth was dry, and I had to swallow to remind myself that we were still in the store.

"Would *you* prefer something else?" she asked in a low voice. "If I'm signing up for a group project, I'm open to other things."

I shook my head, unable to hide my satisfaction. Every time I threw something new at Maci, there was a small part of me that feared she wouldn't trust me enough to want to catch it. I kept waiting for her to remember things she'd witnessed back at BG, back when I was out doing fuck knows what and treating broads like they were something instead of someone.

It was like a cog clicked in my head. I didn't want to be someone Maci had to drum up excuses for when there shouldn't have been any. I wanted to meet her expectations, to give her everything I knew she deserved the moment I had feelings for her.

Back at the house, an eerie silence fell over the kitchen when Maci and I entered. Mom was making homemade pizza, and when Maci offered to help with the salad, I darted upstairs to find Alex.

We were an hour away from his big moment, and when I saw him typing away at his computer, I tried not to look too surprised. Part of me expected to find him in shambles—stumbling over the words he had written on a piece of paper or pacing frantically around the room like the Roadrunner. Instead, he looked as if it were just another Wednesday and that he wasn't about to change the course of his entire life.

Alex smiled, patting me on the shoulder as he slipped past me and into the hallway. "Relax, J. I'm the one with the ring, remember?"

Before I knew it, we were all seated around the table outside. Maci rested her hand on my thigh, slowing the anxious bouncing of my foot, and reassuring me that our conversation from this morning was locked away in a safe space. It was the familiar calm that swept over me the moment after I slept with her for the first time.

There was no panic. There was nothing scary about letting her flip through the chapters I tried to leave out of my story because I wanted her to read them.

When Alex dropped down to one knee a few minutes later, Bella's hand flew to her mouth, and tears pooled in the corners of her eyes.

Alex grabbed her hand and smiled. "Bella, I had my first kiss with you when I was twelve years old on the back of a boat. Mr. Welsh caught us, and you were scared my mom wasn't going to let me see you anymore."

Bella chuckled, swiping quickly at her tears so she could regain focus. Mom's quiet scoff was pushed aside by her inability to control her emotions at the scene unfolding in front of her.

"I knew at twelve years old that I met the person I wanted to spend the rest of my life with," Alex continued. "I knew when we got into high school and you got your first boyfriend. I knew when you got accepted at Brown. Every single step you took to come back into my life, I knew, and when I somehow got lucky enough to make you my girlfriend, there was no doubt in my mind that I wanted to make you my wife." Alex pulled the bright blue box from his pocket, opening it with his finger to reveal the ring. "Marry me, Bella. Marry me, and—"

"Yes!" Bella exclaimed, dropping to Alex's level so she could kiss him. "Yes, of course I will marry you."

"Damn, woman." Alex laughed. "You can't even let me finish the sentence?"

Everyone burst into applause. Mom smacked Alex on the shoulder, silently scolding him for keeping a secret from her before she gave Bella a hug.

Maci squeezed my hand and smiled. "Find your person and make them yours."

"Yeah," I said through a shaky breath. "Sounds pretty fucking easy."

I watched Maci smile down at the ring like she had known Bella for years. They gushed over the way the sun hit the stones, and a warmth ignited in my chest. It was the kind of warmth that came with a serene sense of gratitude. It was the terrifying feeling that for once in your life, everything was how it was supposed to be.

Chapter Seventeen

MACI

June 2016

After an evening of wine and Evelyn's homemade pizza, I was excited to wake up with no plans. My head was pounding after a night of drinking wine with Bella to celebrate her engagement. I guess there was a difference between the Moscato that Katie and I lived off of in BG and the bottles that Evelyn kept in the cabinet.

"Mace," Jaxon murmured, his lips traveling up my jaw and settling behind my ear. "We have to get up soon."

So much for not having plans.

"Why?" I whined, rolling onto my side to avoid any temptation. I didn't have the energy. My legs were still sore from last night's round fueled by wine and whiskey.

Jaxon kissed my temple and pulled me close to his chest. "My mom made waffles," he said, trying to tempt me. "I can smell the cinnamon from up here."

"Waffles, huh?" I ran my thumbs across his cheekbones. The slight gloss to his eyes hinted that I wasn't alone in the recovery process this morning.

When we got downstairs, Alex and Bella sat at the kitchen table while Evelyn wiped down the counters. The smell of cinnamon, bacon, and coffee swirled through the air, and it took my body a moment to decide if it was hungry or nauseous. My stomach growled as I took the seat next to Bella.

"I'll get you a plate," Jaxon said, chuckling at my uneasy expression. He knew there was a chance I wouldn't eat a single thing he was about to get me.

"It's so strange," Bella muttered, taking a sip of her coffee.

I stared at the ring on her finger and gained a new appreciation for sapphires. "What's strange?"

Her blue eyes widened and her jaw went slack. "He's just *so* nice to you!"

I leaned my face into my hand and laughed.

Alex kept his focus on Jaxon. "Was he nice to you when you first met him?"

Jaxon placed my plate in front of me and sighed. "Yo."

"I'm sorry, I just have so many questions." Alex shifted his attention to me. "You like *know him,* know him, right? I'm just curious if he was nice when you guys first met."

I bit into a piece of bacon. "What do you mean by know him?"

Jaxon interjected. "She knew me when I was a dog."

"Jaxon!" Evelyn shouted from behind the counter.

Alex raised his eyebrows in question, waiting for confirmation.

I lowered my voice to avert Evelyn's ears. "I knew him when he was a dog."

"Lucky her," Bella said under her breath, getting a laugh from Evelyn in the kitchen.

It didn't matter if I was barely audible. The woman heard everything that happened in this house.

"But he was nice to you in the beginning too?" Alex asked.

"Jaxon's always been nice to me. When we first met, I didn't think I'd ever see him again, and he was nice. He even gave me his ice cream."

Jaxon's mouth curved into a small smile.

"You just accepted ice cream from some guy you just met?" Bella pondered, quickly adding, "Totally not judging!"

I chuckled at her transparency. "We switched our order. He got the last of what I wanted, so he offered me half."

"So trading ice cream with a stranger . . ." Alex nodded slowly. "That's kind of gross."

"You take my ice cream all the time!" Bella argued.

"Yeah, but you're my girl. Back then, Jaxon was just some dog at Bowling Green."

Everyone at the table laughed. It was nice being included in something as simple as breakfast conversation. A morning like this would never happen at my house. Even though we were just talking, it was too loud.

I finished two more bites of bacon and half of my waffle before Jaxon helped himself to the half he knew I wouldn't eat. Just as he cleared his plate, I felt a gentle hand on my shoulder.

Evelyn stood behind my chair. "Don't mind, Alex, Maci. He probably won't admit what he used to do to Bella when he first had a crush on her."

"We were kids!" Alex exclaimed.

"See, I'm nice." Jaxon walked to the sink to drain the rest of his orange juice. "I won't rat out the bullshit you used to pull."

Before Alex could counter again, Jaxon met my gaze. "I'm gonna shower really quick, and I want you to pack a bag for the weekend. There's a place I wanna show you."

I eyed him quizzically, and he ignored my silent pleading. I watched him walk out of the kitchen, averting my gaze from how well his basketball shorts hugged his ass since his mother was in the same room.

Bella shook her head. "Why do guys never tell you what to include for a trip?"

Evelyn sat down at the table with a fresh cup of coffee. "Reed used to do that to me all the time in college. I never knew if I should pack for a date or just a night in. It drove me crazy."

"Neither of you would happen to have any hints for me, would you?" I asked, trying not to sound completely lame.

Evelyn pursed her lips. She wouldn't crack under my pleading.

Bella leaned her elbows on the table. "I'm not saying a thing."

I sighed in defeat and walked my plate to the dishwasher.

As I left the kitchen, I heard Bella murmur, "Casual day clothes will be fine. Maybe pack a sundress, and make sure you bring a swimsuit."

Since all I had was my suitcase, I borrowed a gym bag from Jaxon's closet and went to work. I had no idea if we were stopping on the way to the destination, so I followed Bella's advice and slipped on my red sundress, pairing it with Converse in case I had to walk. I knew it would be too hot for makeup, so I fashioned a messy bun and thanked my lucky stars for making it look messy enough on my first try.

The sunshine was brutal on my eyes, causing me to sneeze just as I slid into the passenger seat of Jaxon's Jeep. I borrowed his extra pair of aviators and watched him settle behind the wheel. He adjusted his hat, using the motion as an excuse to let his eyes linger on my upper thigh. His tongue grazed the center of his top lip and he smiled.

"So no clues or anything for me, huh?" I asked, trying to pivot his focus. I grabbed his phone and hit continue on my playlist. "Oh, god. This is on the playlist too?"

"Hell yeah, it is!" Jaxon turned up the volume as "Lay it Down" by Lloyd played through the speakers. He rested his hand on my thigh, dragging his thumb along the sensitive skin. "Get ready, sweetheart. We've got about a three-hour drive."

"And does this drive include a performance?" I asked, laughing as Lloyd's familiar high-pitched voice flooded the cabin.

"Of course it does." Jaxon turned the music up again and belted the lyrics of the chorus. I tried to contain my laughter, but when hip movement followed the out-of-tune cover attempt, I couldn't help myself.

Once the song ended and I finally caught my breath, I said, "Oh, sweetie. I mean I'm thrilled, but you're no Lloyd."

"I might not be Lloyd, but I think I can pull off some J. Cole."

I winced out the window as the next song played. "Okay, but why is 'In the Morning' on this playlist?"

A smirk crept into his dimple. "Maci Lawson, you know *exactly* why this song is on your playlist."

Chapter Eighteen

JAXON

June 2016

Car karaoke kept Maci's attention for two hours, but I knew once the slow tempo of "More Than That" by Trey Songz started, she would lose to exhaustion.

We were getting closer to our final destination, and since guessing could only get me so far, I had to pull up my GPS app. Since we weren't technically aiming for my family's beach house in Topsail, I had to get an exact location.

The familiar highway signs appeared, and I knew I needed to veer south. From there, it was only a half hour until we reached the locations Lucy mapped out for me. Trying to find places in a sea of shit called Pinterest was one of the seven layers of hell, and Lucy was better equipped to navigate it.

My ringtone sounded through the speakers, and I quickly switched it to handheld mode so it wouldn't wake Maci. "What's up, Jared?"

Jared blew out a steady breath, followed by a loud crash. "Why isn't Maci answering my texts?"

"Probably because she's sleeping next to me," I murmured, admiring how adorable she looked with her knees curled into her chest. "Wait, why are you texting her?"

"First of all, I text Maci all the time. I'm seeing Stacy tonight, and I need to know what movie—"

"Wait, Stacy . . . as in your leech of an ex, Stacy?"

"She's not *that* leechy . . ."

"First of all, *leechy* isn't a thing," I said, making a mental note to remember that for Bryson later. "Second of all, if you're just using her for sex why do you care what your evening looks like?"

Jared scoffed as I merged onto the last stretch of highway. "Damn. You really are dating Maci. You sound just like her."

I rolled my eyes. "I'll make sure she messages you back."

"Preferably before nine, please."

"Is that east coast time, or . . ."

Jared laughed. "Shut the fuck up and just have her text me back."

As soon as Jared hung up, Maci sat up slowly in her seat. She adjusted her dress and rubbed her eyes until they were squinting at me, the sun aligning perfectly with her bright blue gaze.

"Was I asleep for long?" she murmured, helping herself to a sip of my Monster. She scrunched her nose in disgust.

I rested my hand on her knee and grinned. "I tried not to get too offended when you dozed off instead of requesting an encore."

She stared out the window as we passed another sign. "How much longer until we get there?"

I signaled into the right lane and didn't answer. If she didn't guess after seeing the next sign, I earned the right to question her TV show choices for the rest of our lives.

The rest of *our lives*? Yeah, I just thought that.

Fuck me.

Maci's mouth was still hanging open when we slowed onto the ramp.

I raised my eyebrows. "While you're thinking, why don't you answer Jared's text message. He needs your advice."

Maci pulled out her phone and sucked her teeth. "He needs a movie that will make his ex-girlfriend cry? What is wrong with your friends?"

I shrugged. "Kind of sounds like he's your friend, too."

"Well he is," she said confidently. "Somehow I've talked to Jared just as much as I've talked to Katie this summer. I like to think I'm the lady friend he's been lacking in his life."

"Don't call yourself his lady friend," I warned her playfully.

"Relax. I'm a harmless lady friend to Connor and Jared, and a friendly acquaintance to Bryson. I'll just send him the two movies that get me every time."

"*P.S. I Love You* and *Homeward Bound*?"

She smirked while she finished up her message to Jared. They were the same titles I would've recommended to him if I had let Jared finish his question.

"You brought me to Wilmington, North Carolina," Maci said slowly, taking in the small town streets around us. Her face shift into at least a dozen expressions as she realized where we would be spending our afternoon.

I patted her leg before giving it a squeeze. "Nah, pretty girl. I brought you to Tree Hill."

Chapter Nineteen

MACI

June 2016

It wasn't the L-word, but the gesture left me speechless.

The first time I brought this man into my living room I told him about my love for *One Tree Hill*—about my obsession with a show that was filmed only a few hours from where he grew up.

I sang him the theme song hundreds of times.

I made him sit through hours of episodes and my commentary.

It might not have been the L-word, but I knew for Jaxon Hayes, this meant *something*. He took me to the place that made my show come to life.

Something . . . yeah, something was pretty damn great.

Wilmington was a small coastal town that included streets filled with local eateries and shops. As Jaxon pulled into the parking lot of a small community college, I recognized the location that served as the high school in the show.

Jaxon presented me with a piece of notebook paper. It contained addresses and shop names, while the words "riverwalk," "table," and "bridge" were scribbled near the bottom.

I snatched the paper from his hand. "Jaxon, I don't know what to say."

He leaned closer, keeping a few inches of space between us. "Say where you want to start first. I've got every place we can visit on that piece of paper."

"Brooke's house?"

He smiled and planted a soft kiss on my lips. "Down to the red door."

I couldn't handle the obnoxious round of giggles that erupted in the Jeep. I wanted to pull him into the backseat and thank him before our tour even started. The only things stopping me were the cars surrounding us and the eagerness to start taking photos of locations I only saw through a screen.

I decided to take the driving tour first. Jaxon explained how Lucy helped him find the houses where the characters spent a lot of their time. For every stop we made, we got out to document the experience. Since I refused to be seen as a creepy tourist, we kept our distance and stuck to the street. I gushed over the homey touches of Lucas Scott's bedroom entrance and the pop of color Brooke's red door provided against the bright white structure. It was like I was rereading the story for the first time, but I was also rewriting it with the man I wanted placed in my future.

"Peyton's house was the last address on this list," Jaxon explained, crossing it off the list.

"I think I'm ready to see the Riverwalk," I said, pulling him in for another kiss. I lost track of how many times I kissed him since we arrived.

He pulled back and smiled. "I was hoping you would say that."

We returned to our parking spot at the college so we could walk to the center of town. Jaxon took my hand, pointing out the *One Tree Hill* posters and advertisements that hung in the windows of shops and restaurants. T-shirts and sweatshirts were laid out on tables, tempting fans as they passed by with the famous Keith Scott logo or popular lines from the show.

I was glad I wore Converse instead of my sandals. I didn't want anything to get in the way of this.

The Riverwalk was hard to miss. Wooden tables and benches replicated the setting for the famous Nathan and Haley scene, where Nathan presented a bracelet from a Cracker Jack box to Haley. It was a popular moment in the show, and it was hard to believe that it happened right where I was standing.

"This is so cool," I gushed, approaching the table slowly as if I were interrupting the episode. I leaned forward to read notes left on the wood by fans, who reassured me that this was where the famous exchange happened.

"Damn," Jaxon muttered.

I looked over my shoulder. "What?"

Jaxon wrapped his arms around my waist. "Just my favorite season, that's all."

I chuckled nervously at his heated gaze. "Summer?"

His teeth sank into his bottom lip while his eyes traveled down my chest. "Sundress."

Without warning, his hands cupped the backs of my thighs, lifting me so I sat on the table in front of him. He sat on the small wooden bench, staring up at me through dark lashes before placing his focus between my legs.

I averted my focus from the couple passing by on the street. "Jaxon, someone is going to see."

"No one's gonna see anything." His raspy voice ignited a small flame behind my naval. "It's just a guy admiring his girl."

He pulled something from his pocket and surveyed the area before showing it to me. It was The Red Bullet from Loca Lovers, but this time, it wasn't hidden with cute packaging or hanging up on a display shelf. It sat unused in the hand of the man who bought it for me in the first place.

I gasped. "You did not."

"Oh, I did," he said before he turned it on, and the tiny vibrations sounded. He pulled my ankles further apart, just enough so his hand could travel between my legs. "Don't look down, look at me."

"But—"

"Don't look down," he repeated sternly. "Look at me, Mace."

I swallowed, obeying while I waited for him to make contact. My breath hitched in my throat, and I gripped his shoulders, relishing in the new sensation as he moved the vibrator over my panties.

"Jaxon," I murmured, sounding more nervous than I intended to. If this was how it felt with some fabric in between, I couldn't imagine how it felt with nothing.

His green eyes grew darker as he rolled it side to side, paying attention to every movement of my thighs and the pressure from my hands. I couldn't have looked away even if I wanted to. A crowd of fans could've formed at the next table, and I wouldn't have noticed.

"How does that feel?" he prompted softly.

I bit my bottom lip, and a nervous laugh ripped through my chest. My body didn't know how to handle the speed at which the pressure was building. It was hard to stay sitting up. All I wanted to do was lie down and arch my back against the table.

"Look at me, Mace," Jaxon demanded playfully. His free hand innocently brushed the side of my breast, traveling down to grip my hip so he could pull me closer to him.

With every tiny movement, the sensation grew more intense. I slowly rocked my hips so it wouldn't draw attention, matching the speed of his teasing to the spots I needed him to hit.

He brought one of my hands to his mouth and kissed my fingers. "Tell me how this feels, pretty girl."

"It feels fucking amazing," I moaned, dropping my chin to my chest and holding onto his shoulders. My sighs turned to whimpers as my body shook, and the pleasure swept through every cell in my body. Everything was heightened by the fact that I couldn't scream Jaxon's name or pull him closer.

"Jaxon," I warned when the vibration became too intense.

Pulling his hand from under my dress, he cupped my chin and forced me to look at him. His mouth hung open in a satisfied grin, drawing in heavy breaths as he met me with a pleading gaze.

Jaxon placed The Red Bullet in my hand and closed my fingers around it. "Don't say I never gave you anything."

I was wrong before when I thought I was speechless. *Now*, I was fucking speechless.

I wondered if the bracelet that Nathan gave Haley ever lived up to something as naughty as The Red Bullet.

Chapter Twenty

Jaxon

July 2016

Every summer memory I had involved our family's house in Topsail Beach. I remembered when my parents bought the small three-bedroom house on stilts that overlooked a massive plot of untouched land. Alex and I would spend all day boogie boarding while our parents worked from the beach. We'd have small fires at night and hunt for crabs with flashlights. It was the perfect escape from our everyday life in Charlotte.

Then, one day, that untouched land became expansions and a wrap-around porch. The kitchen grew vaulted ceilings, and there was a second floor. Reed's agency took off, and our home away from home provided a fantastic place for Alex and me to cause trouble in high school. Small fires became bonfires, and boogie boarding was replaced with underage day drinking and bad decisions.

After our trip to Tree Hill, Maci and I spent the rest of the evening lounging around the beach house. I showed her how the moon and the stars lit up the sky over the darkness of the water, and in the morning, we watched the sun rise over the waves. I had many amazing memories in Topsail, but being here just the two of us, I realized I had a whole other bucket I couldn't wait to fill.

It was all new to me—the idea of wanting to create memories with someone. Maci made the quiet moments peaceful instead of turning up the volume that created chaos in my head. Silence wasn't so bad when you enjoyed the person you shared it with.

A few seconds after drifting into a dreamless sleep, I woke from a loud banging. It was July Fourth weekend, so it wasn't uncommon to hear fireworks going off up and down the coast. I rolled over to check the time and saw it was only two in the morning. Realizing how easy it was to move my arm, I looked over my shoulder.

Maci was gone, and I had been asleep since ten-thirty.

How long had she been gone for? If I hadn't heard her leave, would I have woken up if someone came into the house? Break-ins happened now and then in areas with rental properties, and Topsail was at it's peak for tourists. All it took was for one idiot to climb over the privacy fence and through one of the windows in the back.

I should've known better.

I slipped on some shorts and grabbed Alex's old bat from the closet. The house was quiet when I crept into the living room. The only light came from the small lamp on the end table, and a thick breeze wafted in from the back door. I followed the signs of life and found Maci sitting on the porch, nestled into one of the loveseats with her knees to her chest, peering out at the water.

My shoulders relaxed as I shifted from anxious to relieved. I went from being ready to beat someone senseless with the bat in my hand to feeling like an asshole for not waking up when she did.

I left the bat inside and spoke softly so I wouldn't scare her. "Mace?"

"Yeah?" she yelled before realizing I was standing a few feet away from her. "Sorry, I was kind of in a daze."

"You scared the shit out of me, baby. What are you doing out here?"

"I couldn't sleep and the house was too quiet. Out here at least I have the waves and random fireworks."

So they *were* fireworks. I let the thoughts of an imaginary intruder fizzle out with the sparks lighting up the sky.

"Go back to sleep," she said through a yawn. "I'll be back up in a little bit."

Maci looked so small and fragile curled up on the chair. Her blue eyes had a slight gloss to them, like she was debating something inside her head. There was no way I was leaving her out here by herself, so I went inside for a blanket and a Gatorade and took the seat next to her.

"What are you doing?" she asked playfully.

I pulled her legs into my lap and she helped me adjust the blanket. "If you're staying up, I'm staying up. You gonna tell me what's the matter?"

She took a deep breath and relaxed into my side. "Remember back in January when we weren't speaking?"

"Yeah . . ."

How could I fucking forget? I met a random girl for burgers right before I fucked her and lived the longest few weeks of my life without talking to my best friend.

"I'm not reliving the memories! I promise." Maci nervously tucked her hair behind her ears. "But during that time I applied to a few internships . . ."

I raised my eyebrows, prompting her to continue.

A tiny smirk slowly curved into her cheek. "And I passed the first round for three of them."

It felt like the wind had been knocked out of me. She had me thinking there was something else that happened that

I didn't know about, robbing me from a proud boyfriend moment.

I smiled. "Are you serious?"

"Santa Barbara, Tampa, and"—her eyes trailed back to the water—"New York."

I gave her thigh a light squeeze so she would look at me. "New York, huh?"

"*And* Santa Barbara and—"

"Yeah," I interjected gently. "But New York . . . that's the one you want, right?"

She winced, making both of us chuckle. "It's for curriculum at NYU."

"Why does it sound like you think you won't get it? You're brilliant, baby."

"So are hundreds of other education majors in the country," she murmured before stealing a sip of my Gatorade.

I shook my head. "Don't do that. Don't talk yourself down because you're nervous. It's okay to be nervous, but it's not okay to act like you wouldn't be an amazing choice." She settled into me again. "Why didn't you tell me you applied for these?"

Her eyes grew glossy again as she sank further into my side, and her voice was soft against another round of fireworks lighting up the sky. "I didn't think I'd get in. When I applied, I didn't have anything that might interfere with my choice."

And there it was. It was the same confession I had tumbling around in my head when I thought of leaving for California and leaving a piece of my heart on the other side of the country.

Piece of my heart?

What the fuck, Jaxon?

This was my punishment for letting Maci talk me into watching *P.S. I Love You* yesterday. I wasn't an interference. I'd support Maci wherever she wanted to go.

"Okay, maybe not *interfere*." She looked back at me and smiled. "I meant I wasn't expecting to have someone to miss other than Katie. California is pretty far from New York."

I brushed my lips against her temple and pulled her closer. "Yeah, it is."

"But chances are if I get one, it'll be Santa Barbara."

I chuckled at how quickly the words left her mouth. Change was an uncomfortable topic, and since we were already heading down a vulnerable road, I felt like she was opening a door for me.

"My birthfather asked me to come and see him," I whispered, barely recognizing my own voice. "He wrote to me in January, right before I came back to school."

"Wait, what? Why didn't you—"

I smirked while she caught the irony in her unfinished question.

"Shit," she murmured, furrowing her brow. "Are there any other items we need to catch up on? We promised to communicate."

"And we are," I protested, sensing her nerves channeling into overdrive. "I don't have anything else. I promise. I think part of me was still processing the fact that I even have to deal with this shit, so I wasn't sure how to say it."

"And how do you feel now?"

"Relieved," I admitted with a sigh. I met her gaze and smiled. "Relieved."

She smiled back. "Do you know what you're going to do?"

"I'm not sure. Part of me doesn't see the point."

"Closure, maybe?" She drew back from me. "I'm sorry, I said that so quickly and—"

"No." I laughed. "No, closure is a good reason."

She rested her head on my shoulder, and I knew what that transition meant. She would be asleep in fifteen minutes, regardless of if there were still fireworks. "Whenever you want to talk about your past, Jaxon, I want you to know that you can. Even if it just means you want me to listen."

"Can you remember that way of thinking next time you're keeping yourself up over something you need to tell me?" I murmured into her ear.

She giggled sleepily into my neck. Her warm breath on my skin usually got me going, but there was something different about this kind of intimacy. I was still learning how to feel exposed even though I was wearing layers. Physical intimacy was easy. Everything else . . . *fuck*.

That shit was brutal.

Chapter Twenty-One

MACI

August 2016

Nothing was more satisfying than falling into bed and not needing to move a single limb. You fell into the mattress, and the pillow was perfectly positioned. You sank into the pillowtop with the fan on high, and the blankets forming a perfect cocoon. You fell asleep with your mind ready to turn off for the day and recharge for whatever tomorrow may bring. You relaxed in the present and got excited for the future. The past blunders and negative images paused themselves so you could have a moment to feel at peace.

I might have been dramatizing my first night back in Bowling Green just a tad, but there was something magical about sleeping in our apartment again. With Katie across the hall and the train roaring outside my bedroom window, there was no way to describe the blissful return to a routine I desperately missed over the summer.

After our night with fireworks, my time with Jaxon in North Carolina went quickly. We spent one more night at his family's house in Topsail before we returned to Charlotte, where Evelyn made her famous Margherita flatbread pizza for us to share.

"I'll send you the colors when Alex and Bella decide, Maci," she had offered, pouring me a glass of red wine. "I know I always like to know the scheme before deciding what I wear to a wedding!"

"I can handle the colors, Ma," Jaxon murmured.

I smiled reassuringly at him. "That sounds great, Evelyn, thank you."

"We could even go shopping before if you want! I checked your school calendar, and it looks like your last day of exams is the ninth. That gives us a week to nail down some dresses."

At that point, my mouth hurt from smiling so much. I was flattered to be invited to the wedding, let alone for an extended stay during our winter break.

"Maci might want to spend some time with her own family," Jaxon protested calmly. "You've already invited her to stay for Christmas, and that's a week after the wedding."

Evelyn aimed the sweetest set of daggers in her son's direction. She almost cared that they stung when they hit the target. "Once you have to bring a suit out to California, you'll understand this way of thinking. You don't know what it's like traveling with formal wear."

Suddenly, one of Evelyn's daggers ricocheted off Jaxon's chest and into mine. I was beginning to hate my guttural reaction to the state of California.

Katie's worried squeal yanked me back to the present. "I found another one!"

My plush pillowtop experience had been replaced with a hefty dose of reality. An unwanted intruder had invaded our beloved apartment over the summer, and since the landlords were flooded with opening weekend move-ins, we were paying the price.

Ants.

Giant black ants had utilized our worn-down carpeting as a main road over the summer. Just when we thought we had snagged the last cadet in the squad, a backup brigade came an hour later. We were one can of Raid into this hot mess of a situation, and Katie's fear of anything that crawled wasn't helping.

"How are you a biology major? Aren't you supposed to love bugs and shit?" I murmured, shielding my eyes from the sunlight.

Katie's curly hair was piled neatly on her head, her dark brown eyes eager for me to take care of the insect issue. "How are you an education major? Aren't you supposed to love going to class and shit? Soak up all the knowledge this university has to offer?"

I popped my K-cup into the coffee maker and retrieved the hazelnut creamer from the fridge. "Touché, bitch. Hand me the can and a paper towel."

Katie and I spent the next thirty minutes spraying, squishing, and vacuuming the evidence of our unwanted visitors. Around ten, the sun was shining full force into our apartment, turning it into a hot box with no relief due to the lack of air conditioning.

Nothing beat the charm of the old apartment buildings in Bowling Green. It felt good to be home.

As soon as Katie dropped a cranberry-orange wax cube into the warmer, there was a knock on the door. I wiped away the sweat gathering at my hairline as my heart took off running.

When I opened the door, Jaxon's cocky grin greeted me on the other side. "Hey, pretty girl."

I averted my gaze from his dark green eyes to the Dairy Queen carrier in his hands. "You brought ice cream!"

"Ice cream?" Katie exclaimed, ditching her crockpot.

Bryson Kennedy slid past Jaxon as he stuck another spoonful of ice cream into his mouth.

"Aaand you brought Bryson!" I added cheerfully.

"Yay," Katie grumbled while Bryson made himself at home on the couch.

Jaxon pulled the carrier away before she could grab a Blizzard. "Ah, ah, ah," he teased, returning his attention to me. "Do you know *why* I brought ice cream?"

I rocked on my heels, trying not to laugh at Katie's impatient scoffs. The combination of waiting and Bryson sitting on our couch put her in danger of combustion. "Because it's, like, ninety degrees out?"

Jaxon handed us our ice cream, and Katie returned to her lonely crockpot. He pressed his lips together and shook his head. "We met a year ago today. I'll take a boyfriend point, please."

"*Boyfriend* point?" I raised my eyebrows and took a bite of the Cotton Candy treat. The popping candies were like traces of summer lingering on my tongue. "What do—"

Before I could probe for more details, Jaxon cupped the back of my head and kissed me. His tongue moved sweetly against mine, and I giggled against his lips when I heard the tiny explosions happening in his mouth. I was in high school again—making out with Pop Rocks and displaying a crazy amount of PDA in front of our best friends.

A familiar voice brought me back from the ninth grade. "Couldn't even make it in the door, huh?"

Jaxon pulled me aside so Connor's massive blond frame could join the small party forming in the living room. He shot me a playful grin as he moved quickly around us to get to Katie. She squealed when she saw him and threw her arms around his neck.

"Jared just got to that party, J," Bryson added nonchalantly from his seat on the couch. His eyes never left his phone screen. "Maci, could I snag a beer from the fridge?"

"Yeah, help yourself."

Jaxon kissed my forehead and followed Bryson. "Throw me one."

A can was tossed across the kitchen counter, and Katie turned up the Drunk Betch playlist. The apartment fell seamlessly into a scene we never left. Jaxon and Bryson set up the GameCube on the TV while Connor poured Katie a glass of wine. Bass bumped from a few house parties across the street, and another train roared loudly next to our living room window.

The air was sticky, and I was sweating through my sports bra. Bryson offered me a controller and shifted to the recliner so I could sit next to Jaxon. Jaxon rested his hand on my thigh, skimming his fingers between my legs and playing it off as if he were getting comfortable for our first round of MarioKart. "Fergalicious" by Fergie played next on the playlist, and Katie and I sang the lyrics flawlessly just as Bryson started our race.

Our last year at BG had officially begun.

———

Opening Weekend completely kicked my ass and didn't care that my first class was at nine on Monday morning. A low rumble of thunder sounded in the distance as I slid my laptop into my bookbag.

Lovely. Mother Nature didn't have to be a backstabbing bitch and mock my lingering hangover. I groaned when she answered with another round of thunder.

"Mace, I'm leaving!" Katie threatened from the kitchen.

Suddenly, my hangover didn't seem so scary. I grabbed my keys from the desk and prepared myself for Katie's wrath.

"Jaxon's walking me to my first class. I told you that yesterday, remember?"

Katie met me with an emotionless gaze. "How adorable of him. You might want to hide that hickey on your neck."

"What?" I screeched, darting into the bathroom to assess the damage.

"I'm sure your fellow future educators of America will appreciate the evidence of your happy relationship!"

I dabbed quickly at my neck with concealer and stared at my reflection. Of course, Katie forgot I wasn't coming with her to campus this morning. I had told her right after she had another hushed argument with Connor over the phone. They had been back and forth all weekend, conversing about where they would end up after graduation.

It was weird seeing the token Hallmark couple in this state. A year ago, location would've seemed like a small reason not to see someone. Chicago, Michigan, who cared? But with graduation inching closer every day, I understood the hurdle it presented.

It was terrifying to believe that we weren't always the artists in charge of the perfect picture in our heads, that someone or something could threaten all of the elements that created the canvas.

I heard Katie mumbling something in the living room. Right now, she needed advice or a distraction, and the logic rolling through my mind was pulling me into a dark hole of doubt that wasn't there when I woke up this morning.

I tossed my makeup under the sink and invited myself to Katie's monologue. "Okay, since my head is starting to sound like a depressing Taylor Swift lyric—and that is giving me *a lot* of credit—I—"

Katie stuck out her hand and dramatically fluffed out her curls. "I have a lab this morning, and I need to get my shit together."

"Oookay," I prompted slowly.

She sucked her teeth. "But Connor—"

"I told Jaxon about the internships I applied for." I shrugged, hoping my unplanned word vomit would provide the distraction that she needed.

Her eyebrows shot to the top of her head. "Really? How did it go?"

"He was happy for me." I smiled. "I mentioned how far New York was from California but said if I got one, it would probably be Santa Barbara. So I guess it kind of works out?"

Even through her muffled mental state, Katie offered me a supportive grin. "Look at you two communicating. Such a positive shift from last year. Lord."

"Hey, I'm working on communication this year!" I protested. "If I have to remind a hundred eighth graders every day to communicate their needs and ask questions, it would be hypocritical of me not to do the same."

"I love that for you. So, keeping with that mindset, let's backtrack a little, shall we?" Her voice shot up an octave. "What part of you being in the same state as him means it is *kind of* working out?"

I sighed. "Honestly?"

"Yes, that's a pillar of good communication," she teased.

I weighed my next words carefully. "If I'm in California with Jaxon, that means I didn't get the internship in New York."

There was a knock on the door, and we both knew the conversation was over. The topic of my confession was standing on the other side of the door, and I refused to add any more stress to the morning.

It wasn't even noon and we had a bitchy Mother Nature, Katie mumbling in the living room, and a hickey. Even without a drop of coffee in my system, my cup was already full.

Chapter Twenty-Two

JAXON

JUST WHEN I THOUGHT I might actually wake up to the sounds of birds outside my window, a loud crash echoed from the kitchen. I threw off my blankets, damp from sweat since I slept with the window open. September was just an extension of the fourth ring of hell. While the nights were cooler, the sun didn't take long to turn my bedroom into a sauna.

Bryson's loud laugh bounced down the hallway, followed by a trail of words I couldn't make out from Connor. My alarm went off, and I smacked the screen until the music halted.

Why the fuck had I stayed here last night? I knew I shouldn't have laid down after my last quiz. My routine of walking Maci to her classes in the morning, working out, making my own classes, and then balancing schoolwork with tasks from my dad was killing me. By the time Maci and I finished the day off with each other, I was exhausted.

My heart sank when I saw I had a missed call and a text from Maci.

Maci

> Get some sleep I'll be over tonight with Katie at 10 for Bryson's party.

Fuck. It was already nine o'clock.

I texted her back an apology and stripped my bedding so I could toss it into the hall. The conversation in the kitchen paused when my sheets hit the floor.

"How did I not know you were here?" Bryson demanded, peeking his head into my room. "Is Maci here?"

"Is she?" Jared yelled from his post on the bar stool. He could barely get another spoonful of cereal into his mouth before looking down the hall.

"No, she's not," I murmured, dragging my hands down my face. I scoffed at Bryson's eager grin. "What's it matter to you if she's here?" A sly smile crept into the corner of his mouth, and I shoved his shoulder. "You better watch how you answer that sentence."

Bryson's giddy energy slowly crept its way into my sleepy system. I knew he was amped up about tonight. We were going out for his birthday, and he was all about the party and the chaos.

"You inviting the girl who hit your truck?" Connor asked Jared, smiling into his Gatorade. He seemed happy this morning, so maybe the arguing with Katie was starting to subside. I wasn't sure how many more times I'd have to wait to leave Maci's bedroom because they were bickering in the living room.

It was fucking weird.

Connor's words quickly caught up to me. "Wait, some broad hit your *truck*?" My eyes widened. "Your *new* truck?"

Jared's spoon clanged against the bowl, and we all burst into hysterics.

"She's a really cool girl!" he protested lamely, causing us to laugh harder. He smiled. "Okay, she's cute as fuck, and it was a fender bender at the gas station. I can have it fixed."

"*You* can have it fixed?" I demanded, running a nervous hand through my hair. I pictured my Jeep in this situation and could've cried.

Bryson bumped my shoulder. "Bitch didn't even get the insurance."

"Don't call her that!" Jared warned, dumping his bowl into the sink.

Bryson scoffed. "I was talking about *you,* bitch!"

Connor excused himself to the couch because he couldn't stop laughing.

Once Jared was safe from the brutal wake-up call caused by Connor and Bryson, I lowered my voice and said, "I can take a look at your truck if you want me to. Is it running okay?"

Jared shook his head. "It was just a small fender bender. She didn't mean to do it. After it happened and I got out of the truck, she just looked so . . . so . . . ."

"Cute?" I offered. "Hot? Sexy as fuck?"

Jared blew out an exaggerated breath. "All of the above."

If Maci's car trouble had taught me anything last year, it was that you were completely fucked if even an ounce of feelings were involved.

I patted him sympathetically on the shoulder. "Good luck with that, man."

My phone buzzed in my pocket, and where I expected to see Maci's name on my screen, I saw my dad's. I left Jared with his thoughts and dipped back into my room, only to realize my bedding was still in the hallway.

Bryson started shouting "Shots!" from the living room, so I kicked my comforter out of the way and shut my door. "What's up, Dad?"

"I'm surprised you're up, J. Got a second?"

"It's almost nine-thirty," I countered.

"That kid I gave you the file for at FSU. Did you look at it?"

"Of course I did."

I poured over that file the moment my dad handed it to me in California. As soon as he mentioned a possible prospect for me to help with, I couldn't stay away.

"I have a meeting set up with his agent," he added eagerly. "He's free the Friday before Halloween. Think you can make it?"

I glanced at the calendar hanging above my desk.

Having a Friday meeting meant I would fly out Thursday and wouldn't be back until Sunday morning. I would miss the weekend that everyone went out to celebrate. It was the weekend with costumes and parties. It was the night Maci mentioned to me last week when she teased me about picking out my first couple's costume.

It was the first time I'd tell her that my work would have to take priority over something she was excited about, and unfortunately, it wouldn't be the last.

Chapter Twenty-Three

MACI

Halfway through the second Harry Potter movie, my cramps were finally under control.

Between my attempt to dissolve into the Hogwarts universe and Katie's frantic movements in the kitchen, we were a classic example of yin and yang energy. While she was being a productive Betty Crocker in the kitchen, I was putting down roots in the couch cushions.

"Mace, when are you going to get yourself together?" she exclaimed, tossing a rag into the sink. "Unless . . . wait, are you like, going to Bryson's looking like that?" Her raised eyebrow and pouted lip stated the obvious.

I looked like I was a day from starting my period.

I scoffed, staring down at Jaxon's hoodie and my boyshorts. "I just had chips and guacamole for dinner, Katie. Give a bloated bitch a break, okay?"

Once Katie pried me from the couch, it took us exactly an hour to look like we hadn't been sulking for the last five. I emerged from my bedroom wearing leggings and a low-cut tank top. While my new crop top was calling my name, I couldn't fathom wearing it in these conditions. That type of outfit was reserved for when I was at my highest confidence level.

Meanwhile, I about fell over when I witnessed Katie in black high-waisted jeans and a black long-sleeve crop top.

Her dark choice of eye makeup had me worried that maybe her last conversation with Connor hadn't gone as well as I had hoped, but her hairstyle contradicted that argument.

"So you've forgiven Connor?" I asked, draping my leather jacket over my arm.

Katie grabbed her set of keys off the hook and shrugged. "I'm undecided."

"But you have your hair in a perfectly imperfect ponytail," I challenged, earning me a small smirk from her stoic expression. I grabbed a bag of her baked goods and held open the front door. "You know neither of us can manage that hairstyle without a few tries."

Katie urged me forward, and my forearm thanked her. I was about to buckle under the weight of her brownie platter.

"You'll be happy to know that Connor and I have tabled all conversations about after graduation until I hear back about job offers. This year is already going by too fast, and neither of us wants to spend it worrying about things we can't change."

I knew she was telling the truth when the skin went soft around her eyes. "Don't tell me you're going to take your own advice and skip the *simmering*."

She shoved my shoulder, and we spent the five-minute drive to Falcon's Pointe singing "Closer" by the Chainsmokers. We had mastered the duet our first week on campus, and it provided the perfect dose of pep we needed to embrace Bryson's birthday shindig.

Katie opened the door to Jaxon's apartment, where I got a front row seat to Heather inserting herself into Jaxon's personal bubble. While I had nothing against the girl, I could be annoyed that no matter how clear Jaxon made it that he wasn't interested, she continued to shove herself in his direction.

Jaxon was finishing up a game of beer pong with Bryson when I noticed Heather's hand grazing his forearm. I placed my bag of desserts on the counter and watched him recoil at her touch. His scowl had gotten much better since he started dating me, but the disgust was evident. I knew it was killing him not to say the words whisking through his head.

"His poker face is kind of shitty, isn't it?" Jared noted, reaching his arm into the bag. He pulled out the plate of cookies, and his grin widened when he noticed the brownies hiding underneath.

"Depends on what it's for. Speaking of shitty . . ." I spun on my heels to face him. "How is the truck?"

Jared's smile fell flat, but he couldn't hold his serious gaze long enough for either of us to buy his annoyance. "She's supposed to meet us out tonight. I don't know if she'll actually come, but I hope she does." He shifted his weight from one foot to the other. "I actually wanna know what you think about her."

My heart swelled just a tad. Jared felt like the younger brother I never knew I wanted. I thought Chase provided enough drama for me to invest in. Jared was an endless book of side quests I couldn't wait to complete.

I smiled reassuringly. "Come find me when she shows up."

Jared's dimple rose into his cheek. "How do you know she'll show up?"

I handed him a cookie and stared into his baby blues. "The girl hit your car, and you probably flashed her that smile you're giving me now. Trust me, she'll show."

"Hey, pretty girl," Jaxon said as his lips grazed the back of my ear. He placed a soft kiss on my temple and pulled me closer. "Whatcha drinkin'?"

"Whatever drinks are on the house." I turned around and placed my hands on his chest. "I forgot my White Claws at the apartment."

Jaxon handed me his half-empty solo cup. "Rum and coke it is."

A few drinks into the evening, I was accepting friendly side hugs from Bryson and watching Jaxon encourage endless shots to honor his birthday celebration. I was grateful at how easy it was to be around Bryson and Jaxon at the same time. People could call it many things, but they couldn't call it awkward. Regardless of what happened last year, somehow, it all worked.

Just as I started to feel my head getting foggy, Connor sounded the alarms and announced that we'd be leaving in ten minutes. While the counter became crowded with people wanting one last shot, Jaxon grabbed my hand and led me out of the apartment and down the stairs.

I giggled drunkenly behind him, trying not to trip over my feet as we made it outside. "Jaxon, what are you doing?"

He smiled right before he kissed me. He took my face in his hands, and when his tongue slid past my lips, I placed my hands on his hips to steady myself.

The spark, the warmth, the madness of it all—everything was tied tight inside me, begging for a release. Jaxon got me high from just one kiss. He was the most dangerous type of fix.

"I realized I forgot to ask you something," he said, his voice raspy.

"And what is that?" I shivered as his fingers skimmed over my bare arms. All I wanted to do was relax into his touch and have him take me back upstairs. We could crawl into his bed, sink into the mattress, and not come up for air until tomorrow morning.

"I never formally asked you to be my date to Alex and Bella's wedding. Will you come with me?"

I was thankful for the drops of rain that started to fall between us. With the amount of booze I consumed this evening, his question threatened to make me cry. "Of course I will come with you Jaxon Hayes. I'd love nothing more."

Water dripped slowly down my forehead, running over my eyes and into my mouth. I pulled away from Jaxon and looked up at the sky. Dark clouds rolled overhead, and a strong gust of wind brought a welcomed chill to the humidity that had lingered over the last few days.

Drops turned to sheets of water, making it impossible to see past the edge of the parking lot. I attempted to pull us under the overhang of the building, but Jaxon didn't move. He angled my face with his hand and my breath caught in my throat.

He didn't do it on purpose, making me fall for him even harder with just a look. That's what made everything about relationships so scary. You fell unwillingly, knowing you were handing over the most fragile parts of yourself and trusting the other person not to break them.

"What's in your head?" he asked, stroking my cheek gently with his thumb. When I didn't answer, he shook his head and smiled. "It's just some summer rain, Mace."

"Just some summer rain," I echoed softly.

Right there in the last lingering traces of summer, I pulled Jaxon closer by the neckline of his shirt and kissed him, losing myself in the spark, the warmth and the madness of it all.

Chapter Twenty-Four

JAXON

September 2016

I was going to kill my roommates.

Maci stirred next to me, groaning at the shouting happening out in the kitchen.

"Ignore it," I murmured, pulling her to my chest and relaxing deeper into my pillow.

"I would," she murmured back. "But I think I hear a girl's voice, and now I'm curious."

"It's Bryson, Mace."

Whenever Bryson spent the night in his own bed, there was the chance of an unhappy broad leaving the next morning. It was like a scene from one of those obnoxious dating shows Maci and Katie got sucked into from time to time. I was just happy I was no longer a co-star.

"My SISTER, Kennedy? Are you *fucking* kidding me?"

Maci's blue eyes snapped open, and I knew she was about to combust. Bryson's cocky laugh rang throughout the apartment, and because I could picture the look on his face, I decided to enter the conversation for his safety.

Maci quickly followed me into the hallway—so quickly that I had to send her back into my room for a shirt so she wasn't greeting my roommates tits first. I double checked that I had shorts on before I entered the living room, where a bewildered Jared and a smirking Bryson stood with two girls I had never seen before.

The tiny redhead who was digging into her bag for a set of keys spoke first. "I'm leaving. Jared, don't talk to me for the rest of the day, and you"—her twisted scowl settled on Bryson—"just don't bother."

Her abrupt exit left us all in an uncomfortable silence. I strolled casually behind Bryson and pulled a Gatorade out of the fridge. I eyed him as I took a sip, but he continued to stare down at the counter. He seemed equally as baffled as the rest of us even though he orchestrated this morning's wake up call.

Maci let out a loud exhale, taking a step closer to the girl who was sitting on the couch. She extended her hand and smiled. "So you must be, Spencer, right?"

I sent a silent prayer up to the god of hookups that this broad's name was Spencer. My boy Jared couldn't take another hit right now.

This was the kind of shit that Connor and Katie were supposed to walk out to, not me and Maci. *They* were the parents of this shitshow, and this was a prime example of what happened when Mom and Dad were fighting.

The girl on the couch shook Maci's hand and tucked her blonde hair behind her ears. "It's nice to meet you . . ."

"Maci." Maci cleared her throat and gestured for Spencer to follow her into the kitchen. "Want some coffee?"

Jared dragged a hand down his face and stared out the window.

I looked between Bryson and Jared multiple times and neither of them budged. I was starting to get antsy. Finally I ran a hand through my hair and said, "So, can I just ask now, or—"

"No," Jared stated, and then to my surprise he laughed. "No, you cannot."

"Sister," Bryson grumbled to the kitchen floor.

I leaned closer because I wasn't sure I heard him correctly. "*Sister?*"

"Jared's sister," Bryson said calmly, and I looked away so I wouldn't laugh at his attempt to be serious. "The birthday broad from last night was Jared's sister."

I mimicked his puzzled expression. Jared might have mentioned his sister once or twice in conversation, but he never said anything about her being a student at Bowling Green.

Jared threw up his arms and started toward the counter. "I'm just gonna fucking kill you now."

"Stop!" Maci exclaimed, blocking the entrance to the kitchen. She didn't look intimidating at all with her hand clutching Connor's Michigan mug to her chest.

Her eyes locked on Jared's, and the lines in his forehead relaxed.

"Twenty-four hour pass," she said slowly. "In twenty-four hours, we can revisit this"—she waved her free hand around in the air before placing it on her hip—"*situation.*"

My shirt rode up her side, resting right above the lace of her boyshorts. Without meaning to, I suggestively licked my bottom lip. She caught the gesture and rolled her eyes.

"I have more Marvel questions for you," she added quickly. "Let's have some coffee."

The energy in the room began to shift back to normal when Jared retrieved a mug from the cabinet and murmured something to Spencer. She laughed, and Bryson took that as a sign to grab his gym bag by the front door.

I took a seat at one of the bar stools and watched Maci approach Bryson.

She lowered her voice. "Did you know?"

Bryson looked up from his phone. "Hmm?"

I hid my smile behind my hand. It was obvious Maci was talking to him, but it was a classic Bryson response when he was done talking about something.

"*Hmm?*" she echoed angrily. "The fuck do you mean *hmm?* Did. You. Know."

"No," Bryson admitted, throwing his bag over his shoulder. He knew I would lay him out flat if he ever took a tone with Maci, but there was no attitude or smart remark that followed his answer. "No, I didn't."

She searched his face for any weaknesses and let him pass.

Once Bryson closed the door behind him, Maci took the seat beside me and offered Jared an easygoing grin. I pulled her barstool closer to me, resting my arm on the back of the seat as she snuggled into my side.

"I'm Jaxon, by the way," I said, extending my hand to Spencer.

"By process of elimination, I assumed you were Jaxon," she said. "I met Connor and his girlfriend last night."

"And you already met Bryson," I joked, sneaking a sip of Maci's coffee before she could smack my chest.

Jared chuckled. "Nice, J."

"So my Marvel questions," Maci interjected before I could carry on with the subject she was trying to avoid. She'd get the real story later, but right now she was enjoying her meet and greet with the girl who hit Jared's truck and stole his attention. "I need to know. Does anything happen to the raccoon character? You know how I feel about animals dying in movies."

Jared's carefree stance returned as he settled into the conversation. He was completely captivated by everything Spencer had to say about the script and the soundtrack, and I knew it made him happy to see Maci trying to get to know her.

About twenty minutes later, Jared invited Spencer out to lunch, and I was grateful to have the empty apartment. I'd been fighting a hard-on for the last hour, and all I wanted to do was strip Maci out of my shirt and get her back into my bed.

"Jared's *sister?*" she exclaimed now that we had the room to talk openly.

I pulled her into my chest and shut my bedroom door behind us. "His sister," I repeated roughly, slipping my hands under her shirt. I captured her bottom lip between my teeth and she moaned. Throwing her hands around my neck, she fell back onto the mattress, pulling me on top of her.

I reached into the waistband of her boyshorts and she grabbed my wrist. "Now," she demanded between kisses. She took my cock in her hand and stroked it slowly. I wasn't even sure when I took my pants off. "I want you now."

I chuckled softly, pulling her panties to the side and easing myself inside her.

Her sighs turned to moans as I rocked my hips, taking my time so I could watch her expression shift with every thrust. She sat up so I could remove the remaining piece of clothing that lay between us. I rested my chest against her, pushing her into the mattress as my lips worked their way up the base of her throat. They traveled to the sensitive skin behind her ear, her temple, her cheek, until finally they melded with her mouth.

I slid my fingers between her legs as hers found my hair, the light tugging on my curls growing more intense as I sped up the movement of my hand and hips.

"I love waking up with you, Mace," I murmured, kissing her again as she dug her heels into the backs of my thighs. She arched her back, pressing herself closer and urging me to speed up with groans she didn't have to quiet.

"And I love fucking you," she panted, digging her nails into my neck.

That line.

Those words.

They were all I needed for the pressure to boil over. I groaned into her neck as her body shook against mine, both of us slick with sweat as we drifted into recovery.

I kissed her again, pulling up from her slowly and offering her my shirt.

"I'll get a towel, too," I said, my voice raspy. "Unless you just wanna shower?"

"Shower and a nap sounds good. I kind of like having some space to ourselves." An adorable shade of pink flooded her cheeks. "It sucks having to be quiet all the time."

I smirked. "You don't *have* to be quiet ."

"Have you met your roommates?" She laughed, patting my chest as she passed me on her way to the bathroom. I swallowed, admiring the sight of her naked in front of the mirror. She was beautiful, completely unaware that she made my heart want to pound out of my chest.

"It'll be worth it when we get our own place one day," I said. "You can be as loud as you want."

Her eyes met mine in the mirror.

Well, fuck.

Yup. I just said that.

A place we might have some day that I'd be at part-time. Unless she decided to pack up her life and move to California.

I gripped the top of the doorframe. "Mace, I have to tell you something."

She slowly turned around to face me, leaning her back against the sink and doing me no favors with covering herself.

"I have to go out of town for a few days, and I won't be here for Halloween weekend. I know it's still a month away, but my dad gave me that player out at FSU, and—" I hadn't realized I was rambling until her hands were on my chest.

She planted a soft kiss below my collarbone. "Did you butter me up with sex and that comment just to tell me you have a work trip?"

"Not intentionally, no," I admitted lamely.

Maci shook her head. "You don't have to always balance things out before you tell them to me. You have a great opportunity to work with your dad—build the business you've been telling me about since we met. I know how important this is to you."

"I just don't want you thinking that I don't want to be here with you. You were all excited—talking about costumes and shit."

"I mean it's going to suck not having you here." She reached behind the shower curtain and turned on the hot water. "But we can do our own celebrating when you get back."

"You say that now," I protested, wrapping my arms around her waist. "But when that weekend comes and everyone goes out and I'm not here"—I averted my gaze to the mirror—"this won't be the first time I miss something."

At this point I wasn't sure what I was doing. My girlfriend was telling me that what I thought was a problem was fine, and I was trying to talk her into seeing it as one.

"One day at a time, okay?" She grabbed my hand and stepped into the shower. "Let's talk about that place you plan on having with me."

I smiled. "One day at a time but you wanna talk house plans, huh?"

"Well *that* topic of conversation is fun. Imagining what we'll be doing together a few years from now doesn't drag me down on a Saturday afternoon."

I closed the curtain behind me and knew that one thing was certain.

Whatever house I had built for us in the future would have to have a bigger shower.

Chapter Twenty-Five

MACI

October 2016

There were many unpredictable weather transitions that happened in Ohio, but my least favorite was the one that lingered in the fall. As soon as October hit, summer wasn't sure if it was staying or if winter was going to make the strong strike and give us snow for Halloween.

It was the first day back after fall break, and Monday lunch with Katie and Spencer became an unexpected routine in my calendar. Even though Spencer and Jared refused to put an official label on their relationship, we could all see the adorable spark between them. She adored Jared's boyish charm and innocent smile, while Jared completely worshipped her literary brain and beyond perfect curves.

"There just isn't enough time." Katie slumped into her chair. "I love seeing my cousins when I'm home from break, but then I miss everything here. It sucks."

Spencer tossed her long blonde braid over her shoulder. "I think it's cool how close you are with your family. I couldn't imagine going back home just to remind me why I left in the first place."

I was beginning to think that Spencer and I might have more in common than I thought. "If my brother Chase wasn't home this weekend, I would've stayed and taken Jared up on his offer to crash your movie night."

Spencer narrowed her gaze. "He tried to call you during the opening scene. Something about Redbone being your origin story?"

I laughed. "Ah, yes. 'Come and Get Your Love.'"

"Have you guys decided—" Katie caught herself mid-sentence and shifted her question to Spencer. "Have you and Jared decided on your costumes yet?"

"Ohhh-kay," I exclaimed. "Just because I will be riding solo for Halloween, doesn't make me unavailable for prep. We've always gone shopping for costumes together!"

"I wasn't trying to rub salt in the wound!" Katie protested. "Every time I scroll past the Fred and Wilma option on the couples costume page my hearts dips a little bit for you."

I still had the skimpy white dress and red hair dye all set in my cart. As much as I didn't *want* Jaxon to be right about his prediction of me being disappointed that he was leaving, unfortunately I was letting him win.

Bryson would be the only other person in our friend group who didn't have someone they were dressing up with, and even he had some sort of "situationship" with Jared's sister, Elle. At least that's what I was calling it. Bryson was semi-interested in the mouthy sophomore and Elle wasn't having it. It was absolutely *fantastic* to watch.

"Listen, as much as you're acting like Jaxon missing your first holiday together isn't bothering you, I know it is," Katie stated confidently.

"It won't be our *first* holiday together." I took another bite of sushi. "We spent the Fourth of July together, and it was fabulous."

Spencer raised a suggestive eyebrow. "Fireworks?"

"Oh, honey, there were *lots* of fireworks," Katie answered proudly before I could get a word out.

She wasn't wrong. Jaxon and I spent the entire night on his balcony with me bent over the railing.

"I'm just saying," Katie started while Spencer and I laughed into our smoothies. "It has to suck, that's all. I know you're playing the role of the supportive girlfriend, but you're still allowed to be mad about it."

"Even if being mad is just being disappointed," Spencer added before murmuring to Katie, "I think we're going to go tomorrow after Jared's last class."

And just like that, I was back to being the spooky third wheel.

While Katie and Spencer talked, I pulled out my phone to check the time. I expected to see something from Jaxon, but instead I had a missed call and two text messages from Chase.

Chase

> Mom just called me. I wanted to make sure you were okay.

> I think we both saw this coming.

My mind began to spiral.

Maci

> Mom didn't call me . . . summary please? I'm about to go to class.

It wasn't a complete lie. While I still had some time before I had to walk across campus, I didn't have the energy for one of Chase's dramatic retellings. I had just spent the weekend with him and our parents. What could have possibly happened in that short amount of time?

Chase responded before I could exit out of our thread.

They're separating, Mace.

Fuck. Mom told me she was calling you!

Katie and Spencer paused their conversation to look at me. Apparently I shared my response out loud instead of internalizing my confusion.

After a painfully long moment of silence, Katie broke the tension by asking, "Who is separating?"

"My parents," I deadpanned. I knew Katie didn't need a follow up explanation, but I noticed Spencer trying to read between the lines. "Chase just texted me and said my mom was supposed to call me, but—"

Katie reached across the table and grabbed my hand. "What can I do? What do you need?"

I waited for the shock to take over my system, but nothing came. Every emotion I had regarding my parents came back empty.

"That's the thing. I don't feel . . . *anything*. Is that weird? Does it sound fucked up that I was more disappointed when Jaxon told me he was missing Halloween?" I lowered my phone to the table. "What do I do?"

Katie shrugged. "What do you want to do?"

An exasperated laugh escaped my pent up chest. "I want to call my mom and ask her why she didn't say anything to me. My missed call from Chase was from over an *hour ago*. What the fuck has she been doing?"

Another moment of silence passed around the table.

"You could call and ask her why she didn't reach out to you?" Spencer suggested. "But that is coming from someone who has an incredibly shitty relationship with her mom."

I gathered up my trash and added it to Katie's tray. "My mother isn't exactly what you would call maternal. She has never been easy to talk to. I had to learn on my own that I could pee with a tampon in."

Spencer winced. "Oh my god. Seriously?"

I sighed. "Seriously."

"You poor thing." Spencer looked to Katie to see if I was bluffing. When she didn't let up, she asked, "How old were you when you discovered the truth?"

I laughed. "Does it matter?"

"I mean kind of," Katie chimed in. "How long were you in the dark with it?"

I threw up my hands so I wouldn't burst into hysterics. Or maybe it was tears. I couldn't decide.

I just knew I hated the fact that I wasn't going to be Wilma for Halloween.

Chapter Twenty-Six

JAXON

October 2016

"Now, I don't know about you, but I always take a bourbon at dinner after a meeting goes well." Dad smiled at me from across the table and handed me the drink menu. "No pressure."

I took the leatherbound book from his hand and flipped through the options. If I were back in Bowling Green, I would have something bottled from the first page. Instead, I was deciding between an Old Fashion and a Cosmopolitan at a five-star restaurant because I was about to have my first client at Hayes Sports and Entertainment.

I never thought I'd consider a Cosmopolitan, but I was drawn to the drink that all of the characters in Maci's TV shows seemed to order.

"I'll have a Cosmopolitan and an Old Fashion, please," I told the waitress.

Dad raised a suggestive eyebrow before asking the waitress to add a Cosmo to his order too.

"The last time I had a Cosmo was with your mother in New York," he explained as the waitress placed our waters on the table. "We did a long weekend trip shortly after I graduated."

New York. I pictured Maci there next fall and slipped off my suit jacket. Suddenly, it was incredibly hot in here.

Dad studied me from across the table. We just hit a monumental milestone, and I was being a buzzkill.

"Maci is always talking about how good they are," I admitted, my smile shifting from forced to genuine. "She'll get a kick out of me having one while I'm here."

After our waitress returned with our drinks and took our orders, Dad raised his Old Fashion and suggested I do the same.

"Here's to a successful weekend and getting to spend some time together. I'm proud of you, son."

I clinked my glass to his, and felt the air shift between us. There had been so many moments in my life when my dad said he was proud of me, but this was different.

I was one step closer to the endgame.

I was finally giving back to the man who gave me everything.

"Thank you for trusting me with this," I said. "Ever since you gave me Drake's file in June I've looked at it at least twice a week."

"I know you have." Dad shifted slightly in his seat and leaned his elbows on the table. I recognized the position and braced myself for what he said next. "J, there's something I wanna talk to you about, and I want to get it out of the way."

I smirked. "Is it *you* wanting to bring it up? Or is this inquiry coming from someone else?"

"Orders from the queen, I'm afraid," he said through a hefty sigh. "The letter you received from John . . . I haven't said anything about it because I was giving you time to process." His tone took a serious shift. "He wrote to me, too."

I slowly lowered my Old Fashion to the table. "What?"

"Your mother doesn't know"—he shot me a warning glare—"and you know I don't keep anything from her. But there was no point in stirring a pot that I wasn't sure you wanted to tend."

"What did he say to you?"

"He said he wrote to you." His voice was calm, comforting almost. But the slight shift in his gaze told me there was more.

Even though there were dozens of conversations happening around me, the room went quiet. Eerily quiet. The kind of quiet that forced you to think about all of the thoughts you were trying to forget.

"Just tell me, Dad," I prompted.

"I'm going to say something to you, and then I promise we can move on. Sometimes we have ties from our past that we would do anything to break free from. Choices we aren't proud of, people we wish we never invested in . . . shame and the desire to forget have a way of tethering themselves to our future without us even noticing. They can impact every decision we make for our future, and we don't even realize it." He brought his drink to his lips before slowly lowering it again. "You have to *choose* to see yourself differently. It's the only way you can untie the baggage from your past so you can move forward."

I exhaled slowly through my nose. "You think I should go see him."

"I think you have the right to set boundaries for people who have made no effort to be in your life. You don't owe him a damn thing, son," he said sternly. "You owe yourself the closure that you think will help you move forward. *Not* the decision that you think will be seen as the right one."

Closure.

Just like Maci mentioned when I told her. I never considered finding closure in silence—in leaving loose threads behind where it wasn't worth tying.

I guess a thread couldn't be loose if you weren't planning on completing the project in the first place. I knew nothing about sewing and shit, but I did know one thing. Hearing my dad tell me it was okay to do nothing and accept that as a chapter ending brought me a feeling I was still getting used to.

It brought me peace.

I relaxed my shoulders. "There was nothing else he mentioned?"

His mouth curved into a slight grin. "That's for me to hold onto while you decide if you want to know more."

With one silent exchange, we both knew the conversation was over.

I picked up my Cosmopolitan and took a sip. The cranberry and lime hit the back of my throat, and I pursed my lips as the familiar warmth made its way down my chest. Dad noticed my facial expression and chuckled into his drink, following my example of switching from bourbon to vodka.

"Why did I think this would be mostly cranberry juice?" I laughed, having to take a break from the burn in my throat. "Damn."

"Oh, the Cosmos get you!" Dad exclaimed as the waitress dropped off our food. "Has Maci heard back about any of her internships? She applied to one in New York, right?"

"NYU," I answered proudly. I cut into my steak and shook my head. "So many of the shows she watches happen in New York. I love how excited she gets when she talks to me about locations and spots she could go to while she's there."

"You love how excited she gets, huh?" Dad shot me a cocky grin as he stuck his fork through this asparagus. "Did you ever think you might just love that girl?"

I almost spit out the last sip of my Cosmo. Another brief moment of silence passed between us before he switched up the conversation and asked how my classes were going.

As his question sank in, I wasn't sure what was more concerning—that I didn't argue against his assumption or that I said nothing at all.

Chapter Twenty-Seven

MACI

October 2016

After rummaging through the bars on Friday, we decided to take our crew through the rows of house parties that lined the streets of Bowling Green. The weather was decent, the drinks were calling, and I was thriving as a solo artist in my Black Widow costume.

What could I say? I couldn't part with the fabulous red wig I found at the store.

"Do you need another drink?" Bryson asked, taking a break from his winning streak at beer pong.

I looked down at the beer can I was nursing. It was almost one in the morning, and I had no intentions of getting a buzz.

"I'm going to call it a night!" I yelled over the music.

Bryson's disappointment was plastered all over his face.

"Ask Elle to play!" I teased, gripping Bryson's shoulder.

His eyes narrowed. "Go upstairs and see if you can find Katie. If you can't, come back down here, and I'll walk you home."

I nodded, knowing there was no point in arguing with his instructions. He had been checking in with me all weekend—ensuring that I had drinks and that I was always with the group when we left for the next bar. They were very out-of-character gestures for Bryson, but I didn't want to rain on our newfound friendship parade by asking questions.

When I got upstairs, I had the unpleasant pleasure of running into a familiar face I left behind sophomore year. My ex-boyfriend Isaac stood behind the kitchen counter in a poorly put together Jack Sparrow costume, his dark blue eyes burrowing holes into the chest of my Black Widow suit.

I should've just told the captain that I had my period. He'd go rushing back to the depths of the ocean because he'd find me disgusting and untouchable.

God. It sounded worse when I replayed it in my head.

Why did we allow the lowest forms of humans the highest impact on how we saw ourselves? Thirty seconds ago, I was a sexy superhero planning my exit. Now, I was recalling the version of myself who switched birth controls to become more available.

"Maci." My name slurred off his tongue. "Black Widow? You don't like superheroes."

Not the "Even after all this time, I'm going to remind you how well I know you!" bit.

"I do, actually," I stated before brushing past him.

He grabbed my hand to stop me from going any further. "Where are you heading after this? Wanna head to The Attic?"

"There you are!" Katie's drunken squeal rose effortlessly over the other sounds in the house. She linked her arm through mine, and I reached across her to adjust her Minnie Mouse ears. They were falling toward the back of her head, but the gloss in her eyes made it apparent that she hadn't noticed.

"I'm heading back to my boyfriend's place," I lied. "Bye, Isaac."

Isaac pressed his lips into a firm line and moved aside so we could head back downstairs. If Katie hadn't inserted herself into the conversation, he might've shared whatever rebuttal was hiding up his tattered pirate sleeve.

Katie presented a hurdle, and Isaac had no intentions of jumping when there were paths he could walk on.

It was wild how much could change in such a short amount of time. A year ago, I ran into Bryson, and now he was expecting me to let him know if I needed someone to walk me home. A year ago, I was waiting to hear back from Jaxon after he stopped us from hooking up, and now I was excited to see him when he came home tomorrow morning.

Yes. A year really could make all the difference.

Bryson was waiting for us at the bottom of the stairs. We arrived just in time to see a handsy Popeye and Olive Oyl slip into one of the open bedrooms, and I never felt more like a third wheel. I didn't even know them, and I was rooting for their happy ending from the other side of the wall.

Bryson snuck a peek over his shoulder, and I pretended not to notice. Behind him, Elle was sitting on a couch next to a good-looking guy dressed as a baseball player. When Bryson looked back at me, he had a cocky grin plastered on his face. "Let's go find Connor and head out."

We were halfway down Main when Bryson and I decided to give Mickey and Minnie Mouse some space to walk ahead of us. I was happy to see the couple on solid ground again, but everything they were murmuring back and forth to one another was the exact opposite of what should be written into a Disney movie.

I decided to add to the comfortable silence. "I could've walked home with them, you know."

"Ehhh." Bryson shrugged. "I was ready to leave anyway."

"Bryson Kennedy walking the streets of BG alone on Halloween," I teased, getting a laugh out of him. "What a haunting sight."

"Elle will hit me up later. I didn't want to leave with her when Jared was upstairs."

"I'm pretty sure Jared wouldn't have noticed," I said, recalling how cozy he was with Spencer all evening. "Wait, you're still seeing Elle even though Jared told you not to? Fuck, Bryson."

"Relax." He rolled his golden-brown eyes. "Jared said he doesn't want to see it. It's an easy workaround."

"An easy workaround for *who*?" I challenged. "You or Elle?"

Bryson furrowed his brow. "What do you mean?"

"I mean—" I broke into a chuckle. Black Widow and a gladiator were having a personal conversation behind a canoodling Mickey and Minnie Mouse. I found the entire situation comical. "How do you know that Elle isn't enjoying this arrangement? You say that you'll meet up later like you're the only one this workaround benefits."

"I'm not sure I get what you're saying," Bryson stated arrogantly.

He knew exactly what I was saying, he just didn't like the answer. He ran an anxious hand through his hair, and since I swore to only use my superpowers for good, I pretended like he and Jaxon didn't share the nervous tick.

"What I'm *saying*," I said, stifling a smug grin, "is that this whole thing might be benefitting Elle the same way it's benefitting you. Let's be real; she isn't the only girl you're seeing, and you might not be the only guy she's seeing. I think you finally met a female who can go toe-to-toe with your way of thinking."

Bryson narrowed his gaze and kept his focus in front of him. "Elle *is* the only girl I'm seeing."

I almost had to bend down so I could pick up my mouth from the sidewalk. Since Bryson refused to look at me, I kept my eyes on Mickey and Minnie. There was no reason to give Bryson shit when this might be the first time he was choosing honesty over lying through his perfectly straight teeth.

"Hmm." My voice wavered between two octaves. "Okay."

He scowled and I looked away to keep from laughing. "*Okay?*"

"Okay," I echoed.

A private conversation with a gladiator, a pirate ex-boyfriend, and Micky and Minnie Mouse falling into my boyfriend's stairwell.

What a terrifying treat.

Chapter Twenty-Eight

JAXON

October 2016

As I drove through the open roads that led into Bowling Green's campus, corn fields and wheat grass didn't seem so terrible. There was something beautiful about crops in front of a pink sky. I was excited to arrive at my home away from home, and I loved knowing that Maci was in my bed waiting for me.

Did you ever think you might just love that girl?

I turned up "Cake By the Ocean" by DNCE and hummed along to the chorus. Because of Maci and Katie's love for a boyband that broke up three years ago, I had the perfect segway into a topic that didn't always require emotions—sex.

Sundays were reserved for food, fucking, and finishing assignments. It was one of my favorite days of the week.

The living room was quiet, with lingering evidence that pregaming had taken place here the night before. Empty cans and bottles littered the counter, while a gladiator sword rested on the coffee table, and Micky Mouse ears hung from the corner of the TV. It was also fucking freezing since someone decided to leave a window open last night, and by someone, I meant Bryson.

Ohio's season of fall weather was over, and winter had officially arrived. It was only a matter of time before classes were being canceled due to snow and cold temperatures.

A thick wave of hot air hit my face when I opened my bedroom door. The ceiling fan was off, and the small space heater on the floor next to my desk read seventy degrees.

"Mace," I groaned, dropping my bag on the floor. I closed the door behind me and fell onto the blankets next to her. She was fast asleep and didn't even acknowledge that there was someone lying beside her.

I tucked her hair behind her ear and stroked her cheek with my thumb. Her face was clean of any makeup she wore yesterday, and her Black Widow costume was draped over my desk chair. Her hair had a slight curl from the night before, and her perfume lingered in both comforters she had pulled up to her chin.

"Mace," I whispered, moving my mouth closer to her ear. I kissed her temple and repeated her name. "Good morning."

She rolled so she was pressed against my chest. "Hi," she murmured. She brushed her nose against mine and kissed my cheek. "I missed you."

"I missed *you*, baby."

I cupped the back of her head and kissed her. She hesitated at first, probably thinking about how she hadn't brushed her teeth yet. I rolled on top of her, lifting up on my arms to keep my weight off of her tiny frame. When she finally brushed my tongue with hers, I grinded my erection between her legs, and a pained groan left her lips.

"Jaxon, I'm sorry, I can't. It's the last day, but still."

I was halfway down her neck when I shifted so I could look at her. "Last day of what?"

"My period."

I almost laughed, but her timid expression made me realize she wasn't joking. I rolled back on my side so I was laying

next to her and waited until she was looking at me to continue. "Wait . . . are you being serious? Why—"

"Trust me," she said with a nervous giggle that twisted
my stomach. "You want no parts of me right now. I'm
disgusting."

"Where is this coming from? I've never thought you
were—" My mind wandered back to the conversation we had
in Loco Lovers, and I knew there was something she wasn't
saying.

She shook her head as an embarrassed smile dug into her
cheeks. "It's fine. Forget I even said anything."

I grabbed her hand before she could stand up. "The guy
who told you that . . . was it the same asshole who made you
feel a certain type of way about coming?"

She looked like a deer in headlights, only with cherry-red
cheeks and bright blue eyes. "What?"

I took a deep breath to ensure my tone didn't suggest that I
found anything about this funny. "The first time I made you
come, I made a comment about you being a—" I raised an
eyebrow, remembering all of the times she made the sheets
wet. "Mace you looked nervous that I even said something
about it."

"Of course I was nervous!" She threw her hands toward
the ceiling, her voice drifting into a high-pitched ramble.
"I didn't even know I could do that and then right after it
happened, the guy I liked told me he couldn't sleep with me."

"Wait, that was the first time you—"

"Yes," she snapped, hoisting herself up from the bed. "And
so I don't have to see that cocky smirk of yours twice, it's only
ever happened with you."

Nothing about this conversation made me feel cocky. I ran my hand through my hair and exhaled slowly. "Fuck, and then I said—"

"Jaxon"—she closed her eyes and tilted her head toward the ceiling—"I can take an asshole telling me he doesn't want me. But I'm not sure I could hear it from you. You've never had to work around a . . . *schedule* before, and—"

I grabbed at her exposed hips and pulled her closer. When she finally looked at me with tears in the corners of her eyes, she might as well have dragged my heart across the fucking bedroom floor.

"Sweetheart," I said softly. "There hasn't been a moment since I met you, that I haven't wanted you. You're . . . everything, honestly. You're beautiful and sexy and fuck any guy who has ever made you feel otherwise."

She chuckled softly. "This is so stupid."

"It's not stupid, and I want you to hear me. I never push sex with you when I know you're on your period because if you're not enjoying it, then I don't want it. But it's *not* because I don't want you."

"It doesn't turn you off?"

"That you're a female?" I laughed. "No, it doesn't turn me off."

She offered me a small smile. "It happens once a month, you know."

"I'm aware how the calendar works, yes," I whispered against her lips before I kissed her again. "Do you need a good cry?"

She nodded as a few tears slipped down her cheeks.

I reached for the laptop in her bookbag. "Do you want *P.S. I Love You* or *Homeward Bound*?"

The dams finally broke, and she covered her face to try and muffle her sobs. "I just don't understand why Shadow has to fall into that pit."

I adjusted us so we were propped up against my headboard. "C'mere."

Maci settled into the nook of my arm and rested her hand on my chest. We sunk further into the pillows as the opening credits began for *Homeward Bound*. By the final scene of the movie, my shirt was wet, and she was completely out of tears to cry. Her rollercoaster of emotions was heading uphill again, and when she started to kiss up my neck, I knew where the track was heading.

Yeah, Sundays were for food, fucking, and finishing assignments. But after being away from Maci for a long weekend, a soaked shirt was just as good as having soaked sheets.

Chapter Twenty-Nine

MACI

After my first month of having to attend my placement school for student teaching, I was ready to wind down and take off my Miss. Lawson persona. Eighth graders were frantic puzzle pieces who didn't know where they fit. While the job left me exhausted, the work was worth it. It made me feel like I belonged in the world of education.

November went by fast, and it seemed like only yesterday that Katie and I were planning our big Friendsgiving dinner. Well, Katie was planning out the menu. I just suggested recipes I found on Pinterest.

Before I knew it, our day to host had finally arrived. I settled into my usual seat on the couch, glass of wine in hand, trying not to laugh as both Jaxon and Bryson fought the urge to make a comment about how hot it was in the apartment. We were a few minutes away from it being seven o'clock, and Katie was prepping the sweet potatoes in a kitchen that could've posed as the cover for a cookbook. Smells of cinnamon, turkey gravy, and fried onion strings blended seamlessly with the candle flickering next to the TV. The only things missing were Jared and Spencer with the pie Spencer promised to bake.

I said a silent prayer for Spencer and her baking skills. Katie couldn't fit dessert into the tiny Easy-Bake oven that came with our apartment, and Spencer bravely volunteered to provide the missing necessities. It was rare Katie gave up such a power.

"Happy Thanksgiving, ya'll!" Jared shouted, leading the way with a case of beer.

We all echoed his greeting.

"And we have the pie." Spencer smiled, showing off her contribution. "I brought apple and chocolate."

I felt Katie's shoulders relax all the way from the living room couch. "They smell amazing!"

"This entire apartment smells amazing," Spencer gushed. "The last time I—"

"Is the food not ready?" Jared whined. "It's seven o'clock"—he checked his phone and flipped it so Katie could see the screen—"on the dot!"

Katie's soft gaze shifted quickly as she stared into Jared's soul. "Go grab a GameCube controller and sit in the living room with the rest of the people who haven't had to help."

I scoffed, looking to both Jaxon and Bryson for some sort of backup. They appeared baffled by Katie's comment, channeling all of their focus into the final lap of their race.

Just as Bryson crossed the Rainbow Road finish line with Wario and Toad, Connor came scurrying in front of the TV.

"Kennedy, can you set the table?" he said, running a hand through his long blond hair.

Bryson shoved his controller into Connor's chest. "Nice apron, man."

"Keep it up," Connor threatened. "I'll fuck around and tell Katie you insulted her cooking."

Jaxon pulled me closer and we watched from the couch as everyone settled into their final positions before dinner. Bryson was putting the final touches on the table settings. Spencer and Jared sat across the counter with bottles of beer, laughing at something Jared just said. Katie was admiring the turkey, sneaking smiles at Connor as he filled the water glasses.

I wanted to take a picture, frame it, and tuck it away. It was a memory I knew I'd want to remember when we were having Thanksgiving in someone's first house instead of a crammed Bowling Green apartment.

"Katie gives Evelyn Hayes a run for her money," Jaxon murmured against my temple.

"I know," I said, admiring the work of my best friend. She had no idea how much I appreciated her effort since I would be spending Thanksgiving with my mom, who would likely order a pizza and serve it with cheap red wine.

Just my mom. Dad sent his apologies when he decided to stay in Georgia instead of visiting Chase in Pittsburgh. Even though the separation officially made us a divided family, a bittersweet feeling came with the change. For the first time since I was in middle school, I felt . . . *okay* with going home.

"Dinner's ready!" Katie announced, unable to contain her smile as everyone took their seats.

We were packed like sardines around our plates, but no one complained. My heart swelled as Katie lifted her wine glass with glossy eyes.

"To friends and found family," she said.

We all raised our glasses and beer cans, echoing her toast before we all clinked our drinks.

With our Hallmark couple at the head of the table, we drifted into what seemed like a scene from a movie. There was bickering and laughing and effortless conversation. The food was amazing, and after everyone had their fill, we watched Jared and Bryson pull the wishbone. It was an epic battle, but once Jaxon dropped the solo cup on the table giving them the okay to pull, Bryson sauntered around the living room with his winning piece. Spencer served her pie to anyone who had room, and by ten, everyone was beat and ready for bed.

"Beautiful job, chef," I whispered to Katie.

She raised her empty wine glass over Connor's sleeping head, and I returned the gesture. There was a silent exchange between us as we sunk into the realization of it being our last Bowling Green Thanksgiving.

Friends, found family, and an endless list of things we had to be thankful for.

Chapter Thirty

Jaxon

For as long as I could remember, Bella spent the long Thanksgiving weekend with me and my family. Mom would cook a massive dinner, we'd all eat until we couldn't budge, and then my parents would retire to the patio while me, Alex, and Bella all watched a movie in the living room.

As Bella climbed into Alex's lap on the couch across from me, I wondered if all those Thanksgiving nights I spent hooking up with random broads gave them the privacy they both craved. All those times Bella scolded me for being a manwhore, when really I was doing her a service.

I chuckled into my tumbler, letting the smooth liquor past my lips so it could warm the pit in my stomach. I missed having Maci here to share a comment like that with. A year ago, I was waking up across town in someone else's bed. Now, I was just a lonely trial boyfriend on the couch.

Ehhh, fuck the trial. I was done playing into Maci's terminology and making it sound like I was satisfied with a subscription.

As soon as the movie ended, Alex slowly rose from the couch. He did a dramatic stretch, reaching for the empty wine glass Bella was handing him.

He raised a suggestive eyebrow. "More?"

She smiled sweetly up at him, her hand grazing his side as he passed her. The gesture brought my attention to her ring finger. The light from the fireplace glinted off the stones and highlighted just how much shine actually came from a bright blue box topped with a white bow.

"Just a few more weeks, Bells," I teased, prompting a sleepy giggle out of her. "Still feeling good about it?"

"Yes." She scowled, sinking further into the couch. "It feels good to slow down, though. We've been nonstop with planning and figuring things out for December. It's just a lot."

It was hard to believe how much they managed in just a few short months. People took years to pull together their big day. Perhaps some things really were meant to be.

"Alex told me you decided not to go see John," she prompted gently. "How are you doing with that?"

Knowing Bella, that question was really difficult for her to ask. Regardless of how long we knew each other, it was never easy for her to ask Alex and I about our lives before Reed married Evelyn.

"I'm good, actually." I gave her a reassuring grin. "I think some doors are better kept closed."

"Oh, god." She winced. "You sound just like your dad."

I laughed into my drink, lowering it onto the coffee table so I wouldn't spill it.

The two of us were still laughing when Alex returned with the wine. "Maci still coming to the wedding?" he asked. "Or did she come to her senses and dump your ass."

Bella swatted his arm. "Shut up, Alex."

"You know you talk a big game for someone who hasn't gotten an *I do* yet," I murmured, ducking out of the line of attack from a pillow Bella chucked at my head.

"I hate both of you." She stood up, her wrinkles of frustration delving deeper into her forehead. "I need more pie."

Alex's eyes never left her as she walked across the room. He smiled slightly, his blue eyes softening at the sight of his fiancée. It was the look of a man who had all of the words but couldn't string them together to describe the way she made him feel. Words weren't enough. She was every emotion, every happy moment, and every piece of his future as he embraced a moment in the present.

I waited for my internal dialogue to chime in, to ask what the fuck I was talking about or where that line even came from.

I couldn't stand up fast enough. "Is Dad still outside?"

Alex looked taken aback by my sudden movement. "Yeah, I think so."

When I opened the patio door, I found my parents sitting in the loveseat near the brick-oven fireplace. It was quiet, with only the crackle of the fire interrupting their comfortable silence. They both looked up when I shut the door, eyeing me cautiously since it was out of character for me to still be home at this hour.

"Everything okay, baby?" Mom shifted slightly so she was sitting up.

I rubbed my hands together, mimicking Alex's expression from before and realizing that the words really did hide when you needed them most. "I want to thank you guys for everything you've done for me. You—"

I paused, noticing the gloss in my mom's gaze. The last thing I wanted was tears, so I decided that surface level was better. Dad cocked his head, prompting me to continue with what I had to say.

"I'm just really thankful to have you both as parents," I added softly. "I'm proud to be a part of this family, and I'm grateful to have two parents who have shown me that you can chase your dreams and build with your best friend."

Since my mom was close to combusting, I stopped there.

I wanted to thank my dad for allowing me to follow in his footsteps and for shielding me from parts of my past so I wouldn't have to fight them. I wanted to tell my mom that I admired how many sacrifices she made so he could do it all in the first place.

I wanted to thank them for believing in each other, and for giving me hope that regardless of where Maci ended up, we could work if we wanted it to. Because that was what you did when you found someone worth keeping. You held on for dear life and hoped with everything you had that they didn't let go.

I needed Maci in a way that was so unfamiliar, I knew it could only be one thing. There were no words because she was every emotion, every happy moment, and every piece I wanted in my future.

I needed Maci because she was my best friend.

I needed Maci because I was in love with her.

Chapter Thirty-One

MACI

December 2016

I was afraid that if I spoke too much while I was home for Thanksgiving, I would ruin the tiny moments between my mom and me.

I couldn't remember the last time we had a conversation where she didn't throw negative outcomes in my face or remind me that most things were only temporary. But when I told her I hoped to get an opportunity in Santa Barbara or New York in the fall, she smiled and wished me luck.

Maybe she was finally on the path of positivity. All it took was a "For Sale" sign in the front yard and a meeting with a divorce lawyer.

We spent Thanksgiving with delivery pizza, gas station wine, and my contribution of Campus Pollyeyes breadsticks. The beautiful thing about Campus Pollyeyes breadsticks? I could order them frozen and bake them from the comfort of my own childhood home.

While it was uneventful, it was the first time I wasn't counting down the minutes until I could pack up my car and head back to Bowling Green. My mom seemed happy. Even if that meant she was moving to Nevada after I graduated college.

Everyone I loved was heading in different directions. I was checking my inbox every day for internship follow-up emails. It wouldn't be long until I placed my pin on the map and joined the great divide between the East and West coast.

Two weeks had passed since Thanksgiving, and I was struggling to pretend that I was more interested in grammar instead of the catchy "679" by Fetty Wap that my students loved to sing. Last week, I was dancing with Katie near a stripper pole at The Attic to the same song. Now, I was rolling up the sleeves of my cardigan getting ready to write on the whiteboard with my favorite dry-erase marker.

What was happening to me? I didn't have to accept the nerdy light my students saw me in because I passed over the dreaded teacher line. I was still cool, I just got excited about classroom organization and English-inspired Pinterest boards. They were minor things.

I'd draw the line when one of these kids brought me a fucking apple.

"Now I won't see you all until after winter break," I said, pausing for the small little groans that made my heart flutter. "But we have some exciting new texts to dive into when we get back."

"Can we like, not do journaling when we come back?" Aubrey prompted. Seeing her smirk with a handful of books made me nostalgic for my middle school self. None of them were assigned by me, which meant she was utilizing the school library on her own.

I smiled. "Maybe some silent reading time."

The bell rang, and everyone flew from their desks to funnel out the door.

"Have a great break, Miss Lawson," Aubrey shouted over the hustle and bustle.

When the classroom was empty, and only dropped pencils and scraps of paper were left behind, I joined my mentor teacher, Tess, at the desk in the back of the room.

"Your first semester of teaching is done!" Tess beamed from behind her laptop. "It always goes so fast with a student teacher."

"It did go by fast," I said, slumping into the desk chair beside her. My phone buzzed in my purse, but ignored it. I wasn't ready to turn off my teacher brain yet. "Have you ever considered going for an administration role?"

"And be a principal?" Tess scoffed playfully. "I could never. Working with students is the passion piece for me. Once you step into admin, you deal too much with adults and their bullshit."

I was relieved we entered the safe space for cursing. I always waited for Tess to throw the first line before I let a few fun words slip.

"Part of me feels bad for wanting to move into higher education," I admitted. I knew there was no reason to feel guilty about wanting to make a difference from a higher tier, but interacting with students like Aubrey made it hard to ignore the impact one could have from the front lines.

"The best part about the chapter you're in," Tess offered with a smile, "is you don't have a deadline to decide by. You can teach for a few years and go back for your Masters if you want to!"

"But the internships—"

"Are internships. Not a life sentence. I firmly believe you will snag one of them, but it doesn't mean you have to give up this part of the career to hop into the next one."

I pondered her advice, watching her input grades into the gradebook. We were approaching the end of the semester, and decisions would be made in the next few weeks about the second rounds. They would determine if I was applying to teaching jobs or considering apartments in other states.

Images of a bustling Manhattan took over my headspace. Bright lights, hot dog stands, and skyscrapers created a vision board I wanted to dive into head first. Car horns, angry business folks, and the songs of Times Square were a soundtrack I wanted to listen to on repeat. Butterflies fluttered from the base of my stomach to my chest. It was hard to ignore where I wanted my next setting to be.

"Could you imagine living in a place where it's nice outside all the time?" Tess said, staring dreamily out the window. Snow started to fall, and an unfriendly wind shook the tree branches outside. "The weather in Santa Barbara today is seventy degrees!"

"You looked!" I laughed, wincing as I asked, "What's the weather like in New York City?"

"Of course, I looked!" she exclaimed. "I'm living vicariously through the opportunities you're applying for. Those weren't offered when I graduated." She clicked a few items on the screen and scrunched her nose. "Meanwhile, in New York, they already have two inches of snow."

I rolled my eyes. "The sacrifices we make to live a fabulous city lifestyle."

She chuckled, gesturing again to the windows. "Get out of here and enjoy the rest of your day. Be careful driving."

I gathered up my teaching tote, flung my hood over my head, and made the trek out to my car. It hadn't snowed enough to coat my windshield, but it was cold enough for me to crank the heat for a few minutes before I left the parking lot.

My phone buzzed in my purse, and I smiled at Katie's name. "Yes, Katie?"

"Just making sure you're not dead in a ditch somewhere," she shouted. "When will you be back? Can we go for a run?"

My face deadpanned in my rearview. "Katie we only go running for two reasons. You're either stressed about a grade or trying to work through what seems like an impossible choice."

"I mean . . ." Her voice went up two octaves. "Jogging helps me think! It calms me."

"You know what else is calming? A Harry Potter marathon."

"I got a job offer in Chicago," she said.

"What!" I screamed, suddenly very uninterested in the snowflakes hitting my windshield. "Katie, that's amazing!"

Her hefty sigh came through the phone, and my smile faded. "When do I tell Connor that I'm staying in Chicago?"

"Ah," I said, understanding the predicament now.

She hummed suggestively. "Glad we're on the same page now."

I could already feel another cloud brewing above Connor and Katie's relationship. The dust had just settled, and Katie's medical career was sending it flying into a shitstorm again.

"Don't simmer," I urged her calmly. "I'll be there in twenty minutes with Moscato and Pollyeye's breadsticks because we are not fucking running in the snow."

Chapter Thirty-Two

JAXON

December 2016

Alex was getting married in a week, and he seemed to be the only one who wasn't stressed out.

Since Monday, Bella had called me three times. The first call was to make sure I went and got my measurements done for my tux. The second call was to let me know that I would be walking down the aisle with her maid of honor. When I told her I wasn't an idiot and I already knew that's how a wedding party worked, she reminded me that her maid of honor was her best friend Jess, the girl I lost my virginity to the summer before high school.

The third and final call was to threaten me to be nice to Jess because she still hadn't forgiven me for ghosting her after.

Mom was running around like a madwoman trying to find more "perfect touches" for the venue, even though Alex and Bella's event planner had already taken care of the decorations. Dad was stressed about his flight being on time for the rehearsal dinner and somehow Maci, who wasn't even in the wedding, got roped into having opinions on the centerpiece placements.

I completely understood why people eloped. This shit was maddening.

"Just bring me, J," Bryson offered through a cocky grin. "That Jess broad won't want anything to do with you."

Bryson talked a big game, but I had confirmation from Maci that he was still exclusively seeing Elle.

I laughed, zipping up the last of my luggage. "I'm not worried about Jess."

My phone buzzed on the coffee table, and Maci's contact photo lit up the screen.

"If this is another call to see if one shade of green is too close to another shade of green, I might just bring you to this wedding," I said, waiting until Bryson was done cackling until I answered the phone. "What's up, baby?"

"Hey," she muttered, completely out of breath. "I'm heading to my last final now. Can you do me a favor? I left my charger in my room and my computer is about to die."

"Need me to run it to campus?"

"Please?" she begged through a whine. "The document is on my computer so I can't—"

"Mace, it's fine. Katie hasn't left yet, has she? Do I need to swing by and get your key from you?"

"Katie's there. I'm in the education building." There was a muffled sound against the speaker, and then she quickly said, "I gotta go. Thank you!"

The complex was quiet when I got to Maci's apartment, and the parking lot was empty except for a few cars. I did a double-take when I saw Connor's car parked next to Katie's. He said he was heading out a few hours ago. The last thing I wanted was to walk into the living room and be greeted by a scene I'd never rid my mind of. Three weeks was a long time, and from my understanding, Connor and Katie didn't have plans to see each other over break.

Once I reached the second floor, the calm and quiet ambiance of a deserted campus was replaced with muffled yelling and a loud banging. I stopped in front of Maci's font door, only to realize the yelling wasn't coming from the neighbor across the hall or a building across the street.

It was coming from the apartment.

The door was unlocked, and when I peered inside, Katie stood behind the kitchen counter while Connor paced near the couch. Connor didn't acknowledge my presence, but when Katie turned her head and I noticed the tears rolling down her cheeks, I crossed the room and turned him so he had to look at me.

I raised a suggestive eyebrow. "Go take a walk."

Connor's angry scowl fell when he realized I was standing in front of him. He didn't fight me, and a few seconds later he was out the door.

The room was quiet, and even though Connor was gone, an uncomfortable tension took over the space. I decided to break the silence first. "Are you okay?"

Katie nodded, swiping away the evidence on her cheeks.

I hated asking the question, but after what Katie went through last year I had to know. "Did he—"

"Don't." Katie met me with a hard gaze. "We were yelling and when I slammed a cabinet door, one of the frames fell from behind the TV. Connor isn't Tyler."

"I know he's not," I said calmly, taking a seat across the counter from her. "I'm sorry for interrupting. I'm just here to grab Maci's charger."

"She said you were stopping by. Connor should've left an hour ago." She sniffed, clearing the counter of the dishes that littered it. She struggled to keep it together as she stacked the cups so they fit into the cabinet. "I do love him, Jaxon."

"I know you do." I rested my elbows on the counter. "It's been a weird year."

"It hasn't been weird for you and Maci."

"Did Maci tell you anything about my birth parents?"

Katie winced, slowly shifting back into her regular state. "It was a high-level summary."

"Okay then." I laughed, prompting her to join me. "It's a fucking weird year."

"I was more so talking about you guys as a couple. You're looking at opportunities on opposite sides of the country, and neither of you brought up the idea of breaking up or not working out. He won't even consider sharing a state line."

"I mean *technically* Indiana sits between you guys."

Katie rolled her eyes. "Michigan and Illinois share a fucking lake. That's close enough."

I tried not to laugh, but the clouds of anger rolling in her eyes made it hard not to.

"All I'm saying is he's not giving me a choice," she said through a breathy laugh. "You never made Maci choose, and that's the difference."

"I could never expect her to choose me over an opportunity when I can't choose her over mine," I muttered. "Shit, that probably sounds terrible."

"It's not," Katie assured me, shaking her head. "It's just . . . a weird year."

"A weird year," I echoed, reaching over the counter to squeeze her hand. "You guys will figure it out. I know everyone keeps saying that, but—"

"What do you *mean* everyone keeps saying that?" Her eyes narrowed, and she drew back her hand. "What the hell?"

I shrugged, making a breakaway for Maci's charger that was sitting on the coffee table. "You guys are the Hallmark couple, remember? If you want my honest opinion, which I know you always appreciate, Connor will come to his senses and realize he's being a jackass. Just wait him out."

Katie scoffed. "When do men stop acting like children?"

I opened the front door and smiled. "My brother is getting married in a week. I'll let you know if that helps."

She laughed, throwing a rag across the room and hitting the back of the door as I shut it behind me. I turned to leave, only to find Connor standing against the wall across from me.

"I heard laughing," he said, sounding like his regular self. "Is it safe for me to go back in?"

"Depends. You done being a dick?"

He opened his mouth to respond, but I held up my hand to stop him.

"I just came to get Maci's charger. I'm gonna say this once, and then I'm officially butting out. She's not asking you to move to another country. She's asking you to live four hours away so she can start her career. You have the chance to be with the girl you love after you graduate, and you're blowing it. I don't have that choice, and if I did I wouldn't hesitate to make it."

His eyes softened, and I watched the tailwind of my advice overrule anything he was overthinking about regarding Katie.

Connor nodded slowly. All of the stress drained from his face, and a giant smile dug into his cheeks before he left me alone in the hallway.

Chapter Thirty-Three

MACI

December 2016

The first time Chase told me what Dad was doing for Christmas, I thought he was joking.

The second time, I chuckled at the alliteration.

The third time? I started overthinking a casual trip to see his college roommate in Georgia.

George from Georgia. Just sign me up for the CW episode of whatever sitcom I was starring in. His name couldn't be something else like Stan or Patrick?

Needless to say, our family wasn't getting together for the Christmas holiday this year. Chase was staying in Pittsburgh, where he was eagerly waiting to unwrap whatever surprise Trey had waiting for him under the tree. Images of a half-naked Trey and kinky foreplay weren't on my Christmas list, but I was happy everyone was settling into the holiday.

Jaxon and I crossed the Ohio border, and I knew I was pushing my luck with the comfortable silence that hung in the cabin between us. His Jeep was one of my favorite places to vibe out, but it was also a place that held some of our most intimate conversations.

"What's in your head, pretty girl?" he prompted gently.

I sipped my iced coffee and eyed him suspiciously. "I'm not sure what you mean."

Jaxon turned up the playlist he made for me. "You have until this song is over."

His playful threat made me smile as I looked out the window. "Hey Pretty Girl" by Kip Moore ended as quickly as it started, and I knew there was no reason to overthink my response.

He slid his hand over my thigh and squeezed. "Parents?"

"You're pretty good at guessing for only being a trial boyfriend," I teased.

Jaxon did a double-take as he struggled to keep his focus on the road. "Call me a trial *anything* again and we're not stopping to refill your coffee."

"Those are fighting words, Jaxon Hayes."

"Might be. But if you haven't realized by now that I actually *like* being your boyfriend, then maybe I'm doing something wrong."

"Nah, no complaints here." I sighed, placing my drink in the cup holder. I fought the urge to pull my legs to my chest since Jaxon's hand was on my thigh. His touch kept me grounded when I couldn't control the staggering thoughts. "It's our first Christmas in different places. My mom is selling our house in Columbus, and my dad . . . well, Dad is with George in Georgia—"

Jaxon stifled a smile.

I chuckled. "Don't ask."

"Are they like, together?"

"Who?"

"Your dad and George from Georgia."

I gave him all the credit for keeping a straight face with that answer. I couldn't, so I laughed for us both. "Honestly? I'm not sure. I just care that he's happy."

"The house thing sucks," Jaxon said, shifting our focus. "I know what it's like to have a place that holds most of your childhood memories. I'd be a little upset if my parents sold our house in Charlotte."

When we crossed the North Carolina border, Jaxon stopped so we could get refills on our coffee. He stood behind me in line and wrapped his arms around my shoulders, pulling me close to his chest.

As I rested my hands on his, he brushed his lips against my temple and whispered how excited he was to have a Maci in Manhattan. I laughed, knowing he probably rode the last few hours with that line in his head only to deliver it at this moment. He knew it would make me laugh. Jaxon always made me laugh.

Jaxon Hayes was never a trial. Being with Jaxon felt like I was going ten miles over the speed limit because the sun was shining. He was staying out late even though I had a test the next day. He was a Sunday movie marathon and a good blanket. He was the barista sliding the perfect color coffee across the counter.

He was my best friend, and the most glorious and unexpected natural kind of high.

Chapter Thirty-Four

JAXON

WHEN THE LIVING ROOM didn't look like the cover of a Christmas card, I tried not to look too thrown off. It was eating at my mom how we were already two weeks into December and there wasn't a single strand of garland or light hanging from the fireplace.

According to her, having Christmas decorations in the background of rehearsal dinner photos would clash with the overall wedding theme. When I mentioned that green was one of their wedding colors, Bella, Maci, and my mom looked at me like I had an extra head. Apparently, sage green wasn't even in the same category as pine green. We were three days away from the wedding, and I never wanted to talk about a color palette ever again.

With the girls out shopping for cocktail dresses, Alex and I took advantage of having the house to ourselves. Dad was scheduled to arrive any minute, and the space around me wasn't crowded with wedding chatter or a gasp when Bella or Mom came up with a "great idea."

"Beer?" Alex asked, setting his controller down.

I let out a long exhale. "Yes."

He laughed at my eager reply and placed two bottles on the coffee table. We rolled into our next game of Madden, with only the soft cheering of the imaginary crowd to accompany us.

After the start of the second quarter, Alex broke the silence. "Did you ever—"

"If this question has anything to do with your wedding, I will chuck this bottle at your head," I threatened.

Alex threw a touchdown pass and leaned back into the couch. "I was curious if you went with the green or black bowtie."

"Maci said the black looked sharper."

He smiled into his beer and nodded. "I thought so too."

I raised an eyebrow in question.

He gave me an innocent shrug, and his smile grew even wider. "What?"

"Why you smiling like that, bro?"

"I'm just happy!" he exclaimed. "I'm just excited for the day to be here, that's all. Mom and Dad are happy, you're happy, you have a *girl* who makes you happy . . . I'm just thankful for you, man."

As soon as I opened my mouth to reply, our focus shifted to the front door, where Dad made an unusual amount of noise with his luggage and coat. I peered back at Alex, and when our eyes met, I knew we were sharing the same internal thoughts.

Listening closely but only hearing Dad's work shoes on the hardwood.

Keys dropping in the bowl next to the stovetop.

Luggage hitting the side of the counter.

No "Hello!" or "I'm home ya'll!"

Alex widened his gaze and I mouthed, "I didn't do shit!"

He shook his head and fell back onto the couch. He was getting married in three days. Dad wasn't about to come home for the wedding pissed about something work-related when it could wait until after Christmas.

This left one option, only I had no idea what the fuck I did.

Dad appeared in the archway of the living room, still dressed in work clothes with no glass of whiskey to accompany them. His lips formed a hard line as he closed his eyes. When he opened them, they settled uncomfortably on me.

Fuck.

"The name Tyler Dukes," Dad stated calmly. "Does it ring any bells?"

I only knew one Tyler, and the last I heard he was . . . *ah fuck.*

I quietly cleared my throat and placed my beer on the coffee table. The sound of the bottle hitting the coaster was deafening. "I only know one Tyler."

"You need to tell me what happened right now," he demanded, eliminating the space between us. "And you better make sure you don't leave anything out. What the hell gave you the right to go throwing punches in a bar?"

I stood up when he planted himself on the other side of the coffee table while Alex remained seated. A pressure I hadn't felt in a while entered my chest at an unforgiving speed. Heat rose up my neck and settled in my throat.

"I got a call from my lawyer today. That kid's family is pressing charges against you."

My eyes narrowed. "He deserved it."

"That's a shitty answer, Jaxon." Dad shook his head, his chuckle void of any humor. "You put him in the hospital for God's sake."

His stern gaze dragged me back to every single time I disappointed him in the past. He looked at me like I wasn't worth figuring out—like I wasn't worth the trouble.

As a kid, I wondered every time I got in trouble if it would be my last day as a Hayes. I waited for Reed and Evelyn to realize that they could cut me out if they wanted to. As an adult, I held onto the simple fact that I could relieve Reed from the legacy that provided for his family but also kept him from us.

"He put his hands on Maci and one of her friends," I snapped. Images of Katie's face when Tyler approached her flooded my head. "The fucker busted Maci's lip open and would've decked her had I not gotten there when I did! I'll deal with the charges. But Tyler deserved what he got."

"I can get the charges dropped—" Dad took a deep breath to keep his voice from escalating even more. "That's not the issue here. If my lawyer hadn't already drawn up the paperwork . . . Jaxon do you know what a charge like this could do to you as an *agent?*"

Now it was my turn to laugh. I felt the asshole side of me creeping out, and when my first instinct was to smile, I knew I already opened the door. "Don't talk to me about what charges can do to someone."

Alex cleared his throat. "Go take a walk, J."

It wasn't a suggestion, but I was already heading in the opposite direction. Before I made it to the kitchen, the front door opened, and immediately Mom knew something was wrong. Her smile faltered, and the laughter shared between Maci and Bella came to a screeching halt.

Maci's blue eyes found mine, and I recognized the look on her face. It was the same worried expression she wore the night I got into the fight that caused this conversation in the first place.

Dad sighed, pulling everyone's attention back to the living room. His voice returned to his usual calm and steady tone. "I want you to run my agency someday, son. Think about that next time."

The room divided quickly. Mom rushed to Dad's side, muttering words I couldn't understand. Alex met Bella by the door, pulling her upstairs and pretending to be interested in everything she had in her armfuls of shopping bags. Lucy made a beeline for the den, quickly excusing herself from what was clearly a family matter.

"Let's go outside," Maci said, pulling me toward the deck.

Even though it was warmer here than it was in Bowling Green, I knew she'd still be cold. I grabbed my hoodie from the kitchen table, and she pulled it over her head.

As we walked past the pool, I replayed the conversation over again in my head. The anger won and I said shit I shouldn't have. I wasn't sure why I fed into the reasons why someone might shut me out. All I did was pour gasoline on fires I didn't start, and when I didn't start them, I handed people the fucking match.

Regardless of how I unwillingly learned it, my past taught me two things. People couldn't leave if you didn't let them in, and they couldn't let you go if you gave them a reason to keep hanging on.

Chapter Thirty-Five

MACI

December 2016

THE MORNING OF THE rehearsal dinner had finally arrived. After two days of navigating the aftermath that happened between Jaxon and Reed, everyone was happy the focus shifted to something else.

When I found out that Tyler was the reason for the argument, I felt guilty. I replayed the night at The Attic, and the look on Katie's face alone was enough to make me tear up. It was a moment I looked back on and hated myself for not making a better choice. If I hadn't provoked Tyler, he might not have lashed out the way he did. Jaxon wouldn't have stepped in.

Sunlight poured into the four-seasons room off of Reed and Evelyn's bedroom, and I tried not to ogle at the countless photographs that covered the walls of their space. As intimate as it was to walk through the bedroom of your boyfriend's parents, the decor made it feel warm and welcoming. The way Bella was leaned back in one of the hanging chairs made it clear that she had been out here plenty of times. I followed her lead and made myself useful when Evelyn arrived with the supplies for the centerpieces.

"We should've just used the decor for the wedding." Bella groaned, plucking a white rose from the pile of flowers. "Isn't the rehearsal dinner supposed to be relaxing?"

"Oh, sweetie." Evelyn chuckled slyly as she plugged in her hot glue gun. "You won't be relaxed until you're on your honeymoon."

Bella rolled her eyes, and I giggled at the childish response. I adored the relationship she had with Jaxon's mother. She was already part of the family.

Bella slid her first completed centerpiece to the side of the table. "I need a mimosa. Anyone else?"

"Sure!" Evelyn and I said together.

Evelyn smiled reassuringly, and when Bella was out of earshot she said, "I remember how flustered I was the night before mine and Reed's wedding. I was nervous about everything but the *actual* getting married part."

I smiled back. "Why is that?"

"Because even though the day is supposed to be about you and your spouse, you still manage to think about everyone else. And if you haven't noticed, none of the men involved seemed bothered by anything going on."

"Nice to know that doesn't change as they get older," I added getting a laugh from her. A comfortable silence fell between us, but I couldn't shake the nagging feeling in my chest. "I want to apologize for what happened between Jaxon and Tyler."

"I'm not following, hun." Evelyn softened her gaze, and her term of endearment made me love her even more.

"The charges . . . if I hadn't provoked Tyler the way I did—"

"Sweetheart, I'm gonna stop you there. Jaxon told me *exactly* what happened that night. If there's one thing I know about my son, it's that he doesn't do anything he doesn't want to do. It sounds like an entitled prick put his hands on you and your friend, and his privileged parents don't want to accept the real story."

"I know how much taking over Reed's business means to him."

Evelyn arranged a few more roses and shook her head. "Reed wasn't supposed to talk to Jaxon until after *we* talked about what happened. The man got ahead of himself and let his anger drive the conversation. He probably spent the entire flight on edge, came home, and exploded. He knows better. While Reed was focused on the legal jargon of the aftermath, I couldn't have been prouder for how Jaxon chose to act in the present. Sounds like the kid deserved what he got."

"You raised a good man," I admitted softly. "Jaxon's been an amazing friend to my best friend Katie, too.

"Ah, yes, I've heard about Katie," she said with a chuckle. "He's always taken his time to open up to people, well . . . *emotionally* that is." She waved a hand in my direction and rolled her eyes. "You know."

A playful smirk dug into my cheeks. Talking about my boyfriend's sexual history with his mom wasn't in my plans today.

Her eyes softened again. "I told that boy I loved him *months* before he ever said it back."

I wanted to raise my imaginary mimosa and tell her to join the fucking club.

"I even waited some extra time because he was so young, and we had just finalized his adoption. As soon as I saw him—" She shook her head fondly. "I loved him the same way I loved Alex."

"Jaxon's middle name," I prompted cautiously. "Is that a coincidence or . . ."

"He asked to have it changed." There was a slight gloss to her eyes as she said, "He wanted everyone to know who his real dad was. Reed was beside himself. He talked about it for months."

The pressure behind my eyes threatened to ruin this moment with tears. I swallowed to keep them at bay. "I love that."

"Lucy and I had to run to the store for more champagne," Bella announced as she reunited with the seat at the head of the table. Lucy followed behind her with a tray of champagne flutes and a jug of orange juice.

"When are the bridesmaids getting here?" Lucy asked.

"Now that the guys are gone they can come whenever," Bella said as she passed out the drinks.

"You mean Jaxon?" Evelyn raised a brow as she sipped her mimosa.

I pretended to have a sudden interest in the floating candles. Jaxon told me all about his past with Bella's maid of honor, Jess. He was the asshole freshman looking for sex, and she was the heartbroken junior when he didn't call the next day.

"Just wait until I tell Jess she has to compare her speech to Jaxon's so we can make sure they are under five minutes." Bella let out a hefty sigh. "I'm just over it. I get that what Jaxon did sucked, but Jess is bringing *her boyfriend* to the wedding. It's not like it happened yesterday, and it's prevented her from moving on." She gasped and her hand flew to her chest. "Do I sound like a bitchy bride right now?"

Evelyn burst into hysterics, and we all joined in. Throughout the entire wedding process, Bella had been the exact opposite of bitchy. We knew she wasn't downplaying her best friend's feelings. She was frustrated with having to accommodate a situation she didn't think she'd have to hear about again.

"On a positive note, I've heard Jaxon's speech and it's pretty good," Lucy added. "It doesn't even sound like Maci helped him with it."

"We wanted to make sure his original thoughts were there." I giggled, thinking back to how many crossed-out drafts littered his bedroom a few nights ago. "I mostly helped with the organization."

"Jaxon *did* mention how he's prepared to help you with numbers for the rest of his life as long as you help him with words," Evelyn added. She winced, looking at Bella for confirmation. "I probably shouldn't have said that. Let's all forget I said that last part."

I masked my reaction with another sip of mimosa, acting like her words hadn't just placed my heart at the starting line.

Chapter Thirty-Six

JAXON

December 2016

If there were one voice I could forget from my past, it would be Jess Hampton's.

I imagined that this was how one of the rings of hell felt like. The punishment was having to sit across from every person you didn't call after they convinced themselves that they were in love with you. There was another hour added to your reunion if you slept with that person and pretended that they didn't exist.

My parent's office was getting smaller and smaller by the second.

As Jess rambled on and on about how Bella and her met in some safety class in preschool, I tried not to drain the rest of my whiskey. Regardless of our little argument the other day, I'd have to thank Dad for encouraging an open bar.

"And then I try not to cry." Jess chuckled nervously. Her entire demeanor made me uncomfortable. She kept playing with her hands and inching closer to my chair. All that was left was for her to try and lace her fingers with mine and ask me again why I never called.

"So we're good then," I said, eager to get back to Maci.

Her face fell. "Mine is so much longer than yours. Maybe I should—"

"You do that," I countered. "It'll be great."

I almost made it to the door when she stopped me. "Jaxon?"

Fucking A. I turned to face her, unable to hide my irritation.

Jess stood up and took a few steps toward me. Her eyes lingered on my chest, slowly making their way to my mouth. "I'm sorry I've been weird. I really don't mean to be." She crossed her arms in front of her chest. "You're the first boy who broke my heart."

I lied. *This* was one of the rings of hell. No part of me wanted to have this conversation, but I was trying to be better—I wanted to be someone who Maci had no reason to be ashamed of.

"I was *fourteen*, Jess," I stressed with a small smile. "I wish I could say I knew better, but until a few months ago I was an asshole with no filter and one thing on my mind. I'm sorry for how I treated you. You didn't deserve it then, and you don't deserve it now."

She looked shocked by my apology. "A few months ago, huh? You know, Cora called me after she slept with you last year."

Cora, Rachel, Violet, Missy . . . all girls in Jess and Bella's friend group from high school, and not a single one of them would give me a positive review in the follow-up category. The truth was rough when I looked back at the receipts.

"Mace and I have been together since March," I explained. "She knows everything about me—how I used to be and who I am now. She's important to me."

"I never thought you'd change," she admitted through a breathy laugh. "*Not* being an asshole . . . it looks good on you."

I chuckled at her honesty and opened the door so she could pass me.

We rejoined the party, and I was happy to see everyone moving around the house. I was too antsy to sit, and it was too fucking hot for me inside with all of these people. While Jess rejoined her boyfriend and a few bridesmaids near the bar, I surveyed the crowd for a pair of blue eyes and a smile I couldn't wait to kiss. I found her with my mom in the kitchen, and when I saw the tight black material of her dress hugging her ass as she leaned over the counter with a glass of wine, I needed a breath of fresh air.

I slipped my hand around her waist and lowered my mouth to her ear. "Come with me."

The gesture caught her by surprise, but Maci didn't skip a beat. I led her through the dining room and out the den. She giggled behind me as we crossed the deck, the only sounds around us being the music coming from inside and our feet brushing over the grass.

"Jax, where are we going?" she whispered as if we were interrupting the party.

"Somewhere we won't be missed," I said over my shoulder as I did one final look behind us. I tugged lightly on her hand, pulling her into my mom's rose garden. We followed the winding hedges until we closed in on the fountain. "I've talked to more family members than I can count tonight, and all I wanna do is get you out of this dress."

"Here?" she exclaimed, stealing a glance at my bedroom window. "What if someone sees?"

"My room is the only view, remember? No one is coming over here."

Her lips slowly curved into a smile. She was nervous, and it made her even more adorable.

I dropped in front of her, pressing her back against the wooden bench. "Eyes on me, Mace."

Her lips parted as I lifted her leg over my shoulder. I trailed my fingers up her inner thigh, trying to keep myself together as she steadied herself with her hands on my shoulders. With a hooded gaze, she watched as I disappeared under her dress. My tongue swept over he clit in soft strokes, moving slowly and keeping up with the sweet sounds she was making. Her hand moved instinctually to my hair, settling on my head. Last night she had curls to hold onto.

"Fuck, Jaxon," she murmured, using her other hand to hold onto the bench.

I spread her legs wider, giving me more access and the room to slip my hand between them. Quickening the movements of my tongue, I slid two fingers inside her, curling them and moving them back and forth until the grip on my head was so tight I knew she was close. Her sighs turned to moans as she bucked her hips, and when I peered up at her one last time, she threw her head back and screamed my name.

As confident as I was that no one would see us, I couldn't guarantee that no one would hear us. She was riding the high, a track I could listen to on fucking repeat. Once her body stilled, I stood up and started on the buckle of my belt.

"Slide this up," I commanded, nodding to the hem of her dress. "I don't wanna use my hands."

She followed my lead, pulling up her dress so she could kneel on the bench in front of me. Her hands rested on the back as she looked over her shoulder. Her jaw went slack, curving into a devious smile. It was the only prompting I needed to ease myself inside her, slow at first to give her time to adjust to the position. She groaned, leaning forward as far as she could so I could go deeper.

"Fuck, baby." My voice raspy from the pressure already building at the base of my spine. No matter how many times I had her, I couldn't get enough. I wrapped my hand around her throat and leaned forward, bucking my hips harder and tightening my grip on her waist.

She cried out, and my hand quickly moved to her mouth. I rested my forehead on her neck, hating the fact that I couldn't kiss down her bare back or feel her skin on mine. I needed the contact. I wanted the intimacy of touching her even more than I already was.

I gathered up her hair and angled her chin so she could see me. I kissed her, keeping my hips steady as they worked to hit her sweet spot over and over again. She kissed me back, nipping lightly at my bottom lip and prompting my tongue into her mouth. Her walls began to tighten around me, and when our mouths couldn't muffle out her pleasure, I couldn't take it anymore. I groaned into the crook of her neck, gripping her hips and steadying myself so we wouldn't fall over.

Our breathing slowed, and I knew her legs had to be sore from kneeling on the bench. I slid out of her slowly, doing my best to keep the mess contained and away from our clothes.

She sat up and adjusted her dress. "Shit. Do you have anything?" She chuckled at my smirk, gesturing to the dress pants that were around my ankles. "I wasn't sure what you had in those."

I laughed. "I got you sweetheart, don't worry." I fastened my belt and offered her a cocktail napkin from the pocket of my pants.

"Such a gentleman," she teased.

I used my thumb to fix the lipstick she had smeared onto her cheek. "Minimum resources out here, pretty girl. I can push you in the fountain if you want."

She glared at me, tucking the used napkin into the pocket of my pants. "I think we've tainted this garden enough for one night, don't you think?"

I stared down at my grandmother's name on the bench Maci had just occupied. I never got the chance to know my grandmother well, but I liked to think she supported the first relationship I ever had.

Maci shook her head. "On your grandmother's bench."

"Says the girl who just came twice on it," I murmured, quickly turning away so she couldn't smack me.

When we rejoined the party, I felt my mom staring from across the room. Maci squeezed my hand before she left to get us drinks from the bar, and I answered the silent call from Mom behind the counter.

She softened her gaze and offered me a pepperoni roll.

"What?" I smiled, taking the food from her.

She took a deep breath and sighed. "I don't wanna know. You look too happy for me to ask questions I probably don't wanna hear the answer to."

Jess had been wrong before. It wasn't the "not being an asshole" part that looked good on me. It was the fact that I was in love with Maci Lawson, and it felt pretty damn good.

Chapter Thirty-Seven

MACI

"My veil!" Bella's screech echoed through the halls of the Welsh Estate. The beautiful white brick mansion sat on acres of manicured land, and the neighbors down the road probably still heard her. "I need my veil for the entrance!"

The room spun into chaos. Evelyn rummaged through the piles of bags by the door, while bridesmaids and the photographer scoured every inch of the floor. I made myself useful by checking the drawers of the vanity and rifling through the closet. The only white article of clothing was the beautiful strapless gown Bella was losing her mind in.

"We took those candid photos on the staircase," Jess offered, shifting her focus to me. She looked gorgeous with her golden hair styled in a twisty bun and makeup that made her green eyes pop. "Could you check there?"

While everyone was involved with the veil crisis, I knew her maid of honor energy dwindled the longer the bride-to-be was upset. I nodded, giving her a reassuring pat on the shoulder as I passed.

Doing the best I could in my heels, I ran down the hall and made my way to the staircase. My hand glided down the railing as I guided myself downstairs, scanning the floor for anything white. I reached the bottom step and adjusted my dress. The material left very little room for bending and snapping, but the rouching accentuated my ass and hugged my hips to perfection. Evelyn truly had an eye for classy and sexy, and she was even more impressive when she suggested that I get the dress in black instead of burgundy.

"Black is timeless," she had stated to me in the store. With a few nods from the bridesmaids and a smile from Bella, I was sold.

I checked the floor on both sides of the staircase and let out a frustrated groan. "Fuck!"

"Fuck, huh?"

When I looked to my left, my mouth went dry at the sight walking toward me.

Jaxon skimmed his thumb across his bottom lip, raising his eyebrows and slipping his other hand into the pocket of his dress pants. His shoulders pulled at his black dress shirt, the material clinging to his chest. His green eyes darkened as he got within arms-length, the smell of his cologne flooding my senses.

I wanted to tear off his bowtie and work down the buttons of his shirt.

Sure, black was timeless. But it also looked sexy as fuck on the man that you loved.

"I think it's bad luck for us to see each other before the wedding," he said with a smile that made me go weak in the knees.

I tilted my head. "I think that's more of a bride thing."

He shrugged, slipping his arm around my waist and kissing my forehead. "You look beautiful."

"And you look . . ." My eyes traveled down his chest, and I resisted skimming my fingers over the bulge in his pants.

"We found the veil!" Evelyn's voice echoed in the upstairs hall.

"Thank god," I murmured, giving Jaxon a quick kiss on the cheek. "I'll see you soon. I—" I froze a few steps up the staircase. All of this wedding energy was giving me false confidence. I almost blurted out "I love you" on a grand staircase like I was staring in a romantic comedy. "I'm really happy I'm here, Jax."

He flashed me a cocky grin. "Wouldn't want anyone else, pretty girl."

I always ugly cried at weddings. I couldn't contain myself when the music started, sending the beautiful bride down the aisle. Her father would hand her off to the groom, and the soon-to-be Mr. and Mrs. would look at each other as if they were in awe that it was actually happening.

This was a normal reaction. But when Reed handed Bella off to Alex at the alter, I turned into an embarrassed puffy-eyed audience member. Jaxon smiled through their vows and whooped and hollered with the rest of the crowd when Alex finally kissed his bride. With a dramatic Hollywood style kiss, Alex and Bella officially became husband and wife. As Jaxon walked back down the aisle with Jess, he reached for my hand to give it a quick kiss before continuing his duties as best man.

Cocktail hour couldn't go by any faster. With every video and picture Jaxon sent me from the party bus, my need to have him in front of me grew more intense. A simple touch of his hand was all it took to send my urges into overdrive. There was something so naughty about being wet and ready with no panties around your boyfriend's family. It was like my dirty little secret, and I was dying to to share it.

I pulled out my phone to text Katie. Maybe my slick situation would get a chuckle out of her now that she and Connor were officially back on track.

He was moving and she was elated. All was well in the world.

I was so focused on sharing my story, I almost dropped my third plate of bacon-wrapped shrimp when Evelyn approached me at the bar.

"Need another?" She placed her empty wine glass on the bar and nodded when the bartender prompted her with a refill.

My watered down cranberry and vodka looked sad next to her white wine. "Yes, please."

While the bartender went to work on my drink, Evelyn shifted so she faced me. Her dimples cut deep into her cheeks, and her green eyes had a slight gloss to them. She looked like she hadn't had a single negative thought all day, and now that her wedding duties were over, she was ready to party.

"I'm already emotional because of today, so forgive me when I say this," she said, taking a deep breath.

I tried not to stiffen as the bartender placed my drink in front of me. Could the woman read minds? Could she sense I had no panties on? I wouldn't put the super power past her.

"Thank you for loving my son, Maci." Her once glossy gaze prompted a tear to slide down her right cheek. She swiped it away before anyone could notice. "Watching him give his heart to someone else . . . he's never leaned into someone the way he does with you. He's careful, but sometimes I fear he's *too* careful. I was afraid he'd miss out on having someone he could be happy with."

I nodded, unable to form a simple sentence.

She pulled me in for a hug, squeezing her tiny frame against mine and putting parts of me back together that I didn't know were cracking. It felt good to be hugged and accepted.

It felt good to be hugged and accepted by a *mom*.

She chuckled when we parted, her bright smile returning as I echoed her carefree response.

"They should be back soon from pictures," Evelyn said, clearing her throat before breaking the grip on our clasped hands. "Grab your drink and let's find our seats."

I followed her to a small table near the front, where Reed stood proudly as his wife closed the space between them. Just as he pulled out Evelyn's chair for her to sit, the music started, letting everyone know that the wedding party was ready to be announced.

The venue exploded as the DJ made his enthusiastic introductions, going couple by couple as they danced their way to the head table. I laughed as Jaxon and Jess took on a playful photographer bit for their entrance—with Jess striking various poses and Jaxon creatively capturing her every move. He shot me a wink before he stood in front of his seat. I returned the exchange, quickly shifting my focus as Alex and Bella entered the room as Mr. and Mrs. Hayes.

Once Alex and Bella took their seats, everyone but Jaxon followed their lead. He pulled a microphone from under the table, his sexy smile capturing every set of eyes in the room. I caught Evelyn's warning glance and stifled a laugh. With a slight nod, he reassured her that he would be on his best behavior. He scanned the crowd, acknowledging the room until his eyes locked with mine.

"When Alex told me he was proposing to Bella, he made everything sound so simple. Meet the girl, fall in love, and make her yours."

We exchanged a small smile at the snippet of our breakfast conversation that made it into his speech. Still reeling from Evelyn's admission, I struggled to keep the tears at bay.

Jaxon shifted his focus to the head table and said, "Since middle school, I've been watching Alex and Bella try to ignore the fact that they were meant to be together. I'm glad they both came to their senses so we all could be here today." A few chuckles floated from the crowd. "Bella, for years you've been like the sister I never had and didn't know I wanted. Today, I feel extremely lucky to officially call you family, because I couldn't imagine mine, my parents', or Alex's life without you."

"I told you not to make me cry you jackass," Bella murmured, dabbing her eyes with a napkin.

Jaxon moved the microphone away from his mouth so he could laugh with the rest of the room.

"Alex, I promised you no sappy shit, but I just want to say that I'm thankful everyday we grew up together. You've been my role model, my partner in crime, and my best friend. I'm so proud of everything you've accomplished and who you've become. I love you, man, and I could not be happier for you guys." Jaxon raised his glass. "To simple."

The room echoed Jaxon's toast, and even through his sip of champagne, his eyes never left mine.

No matter how many barriers I presented him with, Jaxon saw me. He saw me through the stress of what would happen after gradation. He saw me through balancing student teaching, school, and the time we had left to spend together. He saw me through my new family dynamic.

Even when I wasn't in his line of vision, he saw me as someone who was important to him. It was one thing for someone to tell you that you were important to them, but it was another thing when they actually made you feel that way.

Chapter Thirty-Eight

JAXON

DECEMBER 2016

MACI HAD NO IDEA how much I wanted to ditch the plans I made for us tomorrow so I could tell her I loved her right now.

While the Welsh Estate was home to acres of polished landscaping and gorgeous gardens, there was also a lake that had a breathtaking view of the sunset. I rented a boat from Mr. Welsh and planned a picnic for us tomorrow night. She didn't know that we'd be spending two nights here instead of one, but I wanted to do something special since Dad and I were flying back to California on Monday.

I'd be missing Christmas with her after I invited her to stay. I felt like an asshole for letting her down, and the more she reassured me that it wasn't a problem, the worse I felt. I didn't want our relationship to be filled with her compromises and my excuses as to why I had to work or leave.

Jess raised her glass of champagne, pulling my focus back to the reception. Dinner was served first to the head table, and as soon as the bar opened up to invite people out of their seats, I made my way over to where Maci was sitting with my parents.

I approached her from behind and rested my hands on either side of her plate. She was halfway through a bite of mashed potatoes when I kissed her temple and whispered, "Hey, pretty girl."

"Hey!" She angled my face so she could give me a kiss. "I was just telling your mom I need more wine. Wanna get a drink?"

I raised a brow in my mom's direction. "Four glasses in, Ma?"

"My job is done, sweetheart. I've got a room upstairs and my husband home for the night. Let me have my wine." Mom stood up and dragged my Dad across the dance floor. His goofy grin made me wince. The thought of my parents having a wild night in the room down the hall left a bad taste in my mouth.

The lights dimmed above the dance floor, and the slow and steady intro of "All My Life" by K-Ci & JoJo encouraged people to find their partners.

Partner. For the first time in my life, I had a *partner*. I had someone to pull to the dance floor when a slow song made it's way into the mix at a wedding.

I dipped my mouth back down to Maci's ear. "Dance with me."

"Dance with you?" She turned around in her chair to look at me. "Can you dance?"

"Can I *dance*?" I shrugged off my jacket and offered Maci my hand. "Come here."

With Alex and Bella stationed in the middle of the dance floor, almost every couple decided to join them. I stopped us at the edge, unwilling to go any further because I craved the intimate space. I spent the entire day a part from her and surrounded by friends and family. I wanted her to myself for a few minutes, even if it was just for a song.

I softly sang the intro, inviting her closer with a smile and an exaggerated point of my finger.

She looked me up and down before tucking a curl behind her ear. The lights above us caught the light shade of blue that settled at the edge of her irises.

Beautiful.

"I'm like waiting for you to bow to me." She chuckled. "That's how awkward this is."

"It's not awkward. Nothing you do with me will ever be awkward."

She rolled her eyes, allowing herself to be pulled to my chest until her free hand rested on my shoulder.

We spent the rest of the song in a comfortable silence. I'd hum a bar of the song near the sensitive spot under her ear, and she would giggle into my chest. The sound would send goosebumps up my neck, eliminating the people, chatter, and movements around us. It was just me and her.

It reminded me of the first night we slept together—the first time either of us showed any vulnerability toward what we were or what we could be. I used to be afraid of unknown territory. Now I didn't even care if I had a fucking map.

"I think I was in middle school the last time I danced to this song," Maci said, looking up at me through dark lashes.

"Am I a better dance partner at least?"

"Oh, absolutely," she answered quickly. She smoothed out the lines in her forehead and smiled. "I've always loved this song. I always wanted to dance with someone—"

While her words halted, I knew what she was saying. The unfinished sentence sat in the beautiful pair of blue eyes staring back at me. I knew what she wanted to say to me. I knew what she was holding back. I was robbing myself of the one sentence I wanted to hear her say more than anything.

"I know," I murmured softly. "Me too."

Chapter Thirty-Nine

MACI

December 2016

Me too.

Jaxon might as well have taken the last breath from my chest and bottled it.

As I grabbed my clutch from the table, I felt all of my drink choices rush to my head. I had made the cardinal mistake of mixing wine, beer, and liquor. This was the start of the headache I signed up for.

I groaned, using my thumbs to rub my throbbing temples. Some ibuprofen and water were a necessity at this point, especially since an unexpected rush of emotion decided to join the sugar gathering in my system.

What the fuck was happening?

We were at the end of the wedding. The emotional scenes were done and over with. We were at the happily-ever-after part of the film where the couple rode off into the sunset.

So why did it feel like I was suffocating?

I steadied myself on a chair and took a deep breath. It wasn't long before I felt a warm hand on my lower back.

The subtle notes of Jaxon's cologne grew stronger as he leaned in to whisper, "Let's go upstairs."

We walked hand in hand up the staircase, following the high-ceiling corridor that led to our suite at the end of the hallway. Between each of the white doors that led to other rooms, the walls were decorated with brightly colored photographs of the grounds and past events that were hosted at the Welsh Estate. It was subtle yet beautiful decor that added even more charm to the warm and inviting space.

Jaxon took the key from his pocket and unlocked our door. He ushered me in gently, closing the door behind him as I walked a few steps toward the bed. I crossed my arms, slowly lowering myself down on the comforter as Jaxon kneeled in front of me. He hadn't said a word the entire walk up here, but he knew something had shifted since our last dance.

It was the Cha Cha Slide. No one was upset when they were doing the Cha Cha Slide.

"Talk to me, please," he said, tossing his jacket and phone on the loveseat near the door. He rested his hands on my knees, stroking them with his thumbs. "What's going through your head?"

"It's something your mom did tonight," I said, drawing in a shaky breath. "She came up to me and thanked me."

Jaxon's brows pulled together in concern as a few tears gathered in the corners of my eyes.

"She thanked me for loving you." I cleared my throat, determined to sound like I had it semi-put together. "And I was so caught off guard that I couldn't tell her that it's the easiest thing I've ever done. That I adore every single part of the man she's raised, and that when I imagine my future he's in it."

The tension left his face as my admission once again filled the space between us. His shoulders relaxed, and his dimples fought against the grin he was trying to hide.

He sighed, his eyes flicking down to his hands before they looked up at me. "Sweetheart—"

I cleared my throat. "It's not a wedding without a few tears, right?"

His mouth curved into a slight smile, like he had just lost an internal battle with himself and he wasn't mad about it. "I love you, Mace, and I'm sorry it's taken me so long to say that to you. I was just—it's something I never thought I would say to someone. I think I've loved you for a long time, I just didn't know what it was. There are only a few things in this world that make me nervous, but you . . . you, Maci Lawson, scare the shit out of me. You're the first thing in my life that I'm scared of not being enough for."

I wanted to savor this moment—bottle it up, and pull it out later so I could remember it over and over again. For nine months I imagined what this would feel like. All of the reactions and responses I let play out in my head didn't matter.

Jaxon Hayes loved me.

And I wanted to hear him say it again.

"What was that thing you said earlier?" I prompted, repeating his phrase from the night I told him that I loved him.

He followed my lead by repeating my reply. "I don't know. I said so many things."

I traced the curve of his cheek with my finger, drawing him closer to me. "I need you to say it."

"I love you." His voice softened as he searched my face and kissed my hand. "I love you and if you promise me that those are happy tears, I'd like to show you."

"Oh, they're happy," I pleaded as he made his way from the floor to the bed.

His lips skimmed up the side of my neck. "They're happy?"

"Yes." I chuckled impatiently before he pressed his mouth to mine.

He kissed me slowly as he wrapped his arm around my waist so he could pull me on top of him. He sat up, keeping a hand on my lower back while his other fisted the hair at the base of my neck. I trailed my fingers down his dress shirt, working the buttons and helping him shrug out of the sleeves. My hands pressed against his skin, warm and waiting to be explored like I had done so many times before.

In one smooth motion, Jaxon gathered the fabric of my dress at my hips, pulling it up and over my head before tossing it to the side. His mouth moved to my neck, peppering me with kisses until his lips wrapped around my nipple. He sucked softly, making me arch my back as his fingers trailed over the sensitive skin above my panty line.

"You've had nothing under your dress this entire time?" His green gaze darkened as my fingers ran through his hair.

"I've wanted you since you ran into me on the stairs this morning," I murmured against his lips. I rocked my hips, using the friction of his erection to drive my body into a frenzy.

He groaned, causing me to move a little faster. I loved to hear how much he wanted me. I loved every sound Jaxon made when he was turned on.

My forehead fell to his as Jaxon's thumb made slow circles against my clit. His breathing quickened as he guided my hips to match the movements of his fingers. I kissed him harder, tugging on his bottom lip with my teeth and moving quickly against his hand. I was close, but I wanted more of him. I wanted *all* of him, and he wasn't in the teasing mood tonight.

Thank *god* for that.

With a few pumps of his fingers, I felt the pleasure make its familiar sweep. My thighs gripped his hips as his name fell from my mouth. I threw my head back, digging my nails into his shoulders as he let me ride out the high of his touch.

His pants were wet from my arousal, and with a satisfied grin, he rolled us again so he was on top of me. "Fuck, I love when you do that."

Jaxon's eyes traveled down my naked body as he stepped out of his pants. His boxer briefs fell to the floor, and he began to stroke himself. I watched him closely as he crawled over top of me, his hand still at work while his other skimmed the line of freckles that spread from my stomach to my hip.

I shuddered at his touch. Closing my eyes, I sank further into the mattress as the velvet skin of his cock dragged over my core. My body begged for more, my hips instinctually grinding against his erection as he continued his teasing movements.

"Mace, look at me," he said, his voice raspy.

His demand had my full attention. Our eyes locked, and I felt the familiar pull in my chest.

Jaxon laced his fingers with mine and drew my arms over my head. He kissed me softly, his teeth gently tugging on my bottom lip before I realized I couldn't go another moment without saying it back.

"I love you too," I whispered past the small lump in my throat.

Jaxon smiled against my lips before he kissed me again, easing himself inside me as if he were filling me for the first time.

My head fell back into the mattress with the movements of his hips, his pelvis hitting my swollen clit in a rhythm that pushed me closer to the edge. He kissed up my neck, peppering my jawline as his hands held me in place. His hips rolled to hit the spot inside of me that was on fire, over and over again until the sensation threatened to make me explode.

He reached down and lightly flicked his thumb across my clit, coaxing my orgasm out in one full sweep.

"Jaxon," I whimpered, my sighs turning to moans as I rode out the pleasure. My walls gripped him over and over again as his mouth moved down to my chest, leaving a warm trail of "I love yous" as his lips brushed against my skin.

I wrapped my legs around his waist, allowing him to turn us without breaking our rhythm. I spread my legs wide, reaching behind me and gripping his legs so I could take him deeper.

"Fuck, Mace." He groaned, running his hands up my inner thighs. I watched him struggle to keep his eyes open, every part of him wanting to throw his head back and fuck me harder.

I knew he was trying to hold onto this moment. I knew he was trying to make it last.

So I did it for him.

I lifted my hips, slamming down on him over and over again until he met me with a primal gaze. He quirked a brow, daring me to continue if I wanted him to go harder. My tongue grazed my bottom lip as I nodded, egging him forward to wrap his arms around my back so he could pull me close.

He kissed me, slowly until his hands gripped my ass and he pressed into me with quick, hard thrusts. I grabbed his neck, trembling into his chest as his mouth collided with mine and he found his release.

We fell into a lazy rhythm of soft kisses. The heat and eagerness of before was gone, and an irreplaceable calm settled over me as Jaxon's heartbeat slowed under the gentle touch of my hand. I would've sat there for hours just to memorize the feeling, but the unforgiving cold from the AC unit had other plans.

Jaxon noticed the goosebumps on my arms and leaned us back onto the bed. He covered us with the comforter while I snuggled into the crook of his neck. My body relaxed into his as he wrapped his arms around me.

Everything else in the world seemed to drift away. It was only me and Jaxon, and nothing else mattered.

Chapter Forty

JAXON

January 2017

It was every guy's dream to spend Christmas with their dad in a hotel, especially when their girlfriend was still at your house celebrating with your mom, brother, and his new wife.

Fuck that. I felt like shit for leaving Maci only a few days after I told her I loved her.

When my dad's appointment was moved from the day after Christmas to the day before, I had to make a choice. It was a meeting regarding my first client, and I had to get used to dropping things no matter how important they were.

Correction. I had to get used to disappointing Maci even though she would never tell me she was disappointed.

Halloween *and* Christmas? I felt like I was heading back into boyfriend trial territory.

The New Year announced itself with the same energy as the holiday season. After Christmas, Maci spent the remainder of winter break with Chase. We chatted a few times on the phone with some text messages in between. She was over-the-moon excited to share that Chase and Trey were moving to Europe thanks to an opportunity Trey received from his firm. Even though she was happy for them, I heard the undertones of sadness in her voice. Her parents were seperating, and her brother was jumping continents.

I wanted to be there for her in person. Instead, I had to settle for being supportive through a phone screen. It was our first taste of seperation since summer break, and it fucking sucked.

Before I knew it, I was driving back to Bowling Green's campus for my last semester before graduation. It was the last time I'd make this journey in my Jeep. While I wouldn't miss the winding mountains of West Virginia or the boring-ass two-lane highways, I would miss the feeling of seeing the exit sign for BGSU and passing the giant falcon statue that greeted me home.

When I pulled into the Falcon's Pointe parking lot, I was surprised with how empty it was. It was later in the day, and most students would be back on campus by now. Maci, Katie, and Connor all arrived this morning, and Jared and Spencer returned a few hours ago from some winter book festival.

Bryson had been pretty quiet during the break. I wasn't sure if I should be concerned or grateful that he didn't have a lot going on. To my pleasant surprise, his giant cocky grin greeted me as soon as I walked through the door of our apartment.

"Well, welcome back," he said, placing a tray of pizza rolls in the oven. A case of beer sat on the counter and one of his playlists played on the TV. He rolled me a drink and set the timer. "Wanna play a game of Madden once you settle in? I can move the music to the speakers."

His agenda sounded perfect, so perfect, that I dropped my bags on the floor of the living room so I could grab the beer before it tipped over the edge of the counter.

I popped the tab and took my favorite corner seat on the couch. "Where have you been, man? You disappeared over break."

"Had stuff going on." He shrugged, taking the spot next to me. "What do you think about a beach trip for spring break?"

I chuckled into my beer. "Spring break? That's like two months away."

"So!" His contagious laugh filled the room. "You know that people need time to book shit. What does your schedule look like? I saw you went to Cali again for Christmas."

"Wasn't my first choice," I murmured, selecting heads for our coin toss. The referee deemed my team the winner, and I chose to start with the ball. "I didn't go to Cali for Christmas. I *missed* Christmas."

"You didn't *miss* Christmas, bro." He scoffed, taking advantage of my wandering mind to throw a touchdown pass. He set his controller down on his lap, allowing his player the time to enjoy his victory dance. "You had to travel for work, and it happened to be on a holiday."

"Doesn't erase the fact that I wasn't there. How's Elle?"

Bryson laughed. "She's good. A little wild, but good. I actually saw her for New Year's."

I paused the game. "Hold on. What?"

It was clear by his smirk that he wasn't sure if he should talk about it.

Since we had small windows of opportunity when Jared wasn't around, I scanned the area to check that it was just the two of us in the apartment. "You can't say that and not say anything else. Since when do *you* make plans to see someone on New Year's? I was wondering why I didn't get a morning-after photo—"

"Because I couldn't send you a topless photo of Jared's sister. Plus, how would your girl feel about something like that showing up in your inbox?"

My girl.

I blew out an exaggerated breath. "I told her that I loved her."

"Well, fuck," Bryson stated, placing his controller on the coffee table. "Imma need something stronger than beer to process that. Fuck. You *what*?"

Bryson looked like I just admitted to having a contagious disease. He went into the kitchen and took a bottle of vodka from the freezer.

"So that's why you *missed* Christmas." He raised his eyebrows as he said "missed." "Fuck, man. You're completely gone."

I didn't know what to say. In a matter of nine months, I went from being the guy who was browsing bars for broads with my best friend to the guy who cared about missing holidays.

Maybe I wasn't gone. Maybe I was growing the fuck up. Either way, it felt like the most natural thing in the world.

I sat across the counter at one of the bar stools. "Don't make it sound like some devastating life sentence."

"Isn't it, though?" Bryson free-poured some vodka into a solo cup and filled the rest with lemonade. "You just erased a lot of possible trips to California for me."

"You can still come to California!"

He scoffed. "I'm not flying from New York to Cali for you not to take one for the team. What if I need a buffer for a leech?"

A leech. It was a disgusting term we used for girls who couldn't take the hint. A buffer might have been worse. It was the role Bryson or I stepped into when one of us wanted to sleep with a girl but her friend wouldn't back off.

"Well, I couldn't sleep with the girl who tagged along, but I could put a movie on for her," I offered lamely.

"Get the fuck outta here." Bryson burst into hysterics, and I joined him.

"Would Elle even let you come visit me once you move to New York?" I prompted once we both caught our breath. "She's what, a freshman?"

"Sophomore. She'd technically be a junior, but she took a year off after high school."

"Hmm." I drained the rest of my beer and threw the can in the trash. "Interesting."

Bryson raised a brow in question.

"You didn't argue when I asked if she'd let you," I stated.

"She's cool, okay. She calls me on my shit, and she's not clingy. Elle's just easy."

"I wouldn't include *easy* in that description once Jared gets back."

Bryson smiled. "Easy in the sense that she doesn't give me a headache or ask what I'm up to all the time."

"It kind of sounds like you ran into the perfect broad to finish out your college days," I said, throwing in "broad" to see how he'd respond.

The small quirk of his lip answered the question I didn't ask.

Chapter Forty-One

MACI

January 2017

No matter how many sips I took of sweet red wine, nothing could relieve my mouth of Katie's new muffin recipe. While the peanut butter and banana combination was to die for, the texture, well, the texture was a wild ride.

"They are a tad dense," Katie declared, her mouth struggling to keep up with the muffin that wasn't breaking down.

I couldn't cover mine fast enough, sending pieces of muffin flying across the counter. Katie recoiled from my disgusting overshare.

"Dense!" I exclaimed, worried my breathy reaction was going to cause this muffin to be my last meal. "Katie, I am *trying* here!"

"You just have to take smaller bites!"

I swallowed the last bit of muffin, happy to know that I would live another day. "These muffins should come with a warning label."

Katie had never been able to handle constructive criticism over her food. Her apparent scowl and eye roll let me know that I was already on thin ice. "I bake you muffins and this is the thanks I get!"

I fell back on the couch, putting as much space possible between myself and the killer muffins. "Did you and Connor look at any apartments?"

"We did! We are between a one-bedroom and a two-bedroom. It's just so expensive compared to what we pay here."

I threw my hands up and surveyed the living room. "You mean you can't get all of this for the steal of six hundred dollars in Chicago?"

"I mean you can," Katie said with a suggestive laugh. "But I'm trying to find a place that doesn't scream undergrad. Have you even *considered* what you're going to pay for an apartment in New York?"

"New York," I said dreamily. "I should hear back from them by the end of March."

Katie took her usual seat in the recliner and tossed me a muffin. I wasn't sure why or how, but she read my mind. For some reason, I wanted another one.

"I've heard California has nice apartments too?" she offered with a shrug of her shoulder. She bit into her dry-ass baked good, and I knew I had a few moments to answer while we both chewed for our lives.

During my Christmas morning bliss with Evelyn, Alex, and Bella, I realized something. Even if I got denied my internship in New York and got accepted into Santa Barbara, there was no guarantee that Jaxon and I would have a ton of time for each other. Sure, we would be in the same state. But Santa Barbara was still two hours away from his soon-to-be office.

Regardless of the outcome, it wouldn't be the same. I wouldn't be sitting in my apartment down the street waiting for Jaxon to arrive for our first Thursday dinner of the semester. It would be like the summer long-distance all over again.

"Simmering?" Katie prompted.

I swallowed my last bit of muffin. "No."

"Actually, I take that back," Katie murmured quickly, sitting up in her seat. She pointed at me with her glass of wine. "Jaxon has now missed three holidays with you because of work and you haven't said a damn thing about it. I'm giving you permission to bitch about your boyfriend—*no judgment*—before he gets here."

I chuckled. "What is there to say, Katie?"

She sighed through a hefty eye roll. "That you're disappointed."

I sure as shit was, but I wasn't starting our first dinner of the semester with a negative attitude. "Yeah, I am, but these are little things compared to what he's doing to prepare for his future. We have plenty of Halloweens, Christmases, and New Years ahead of us." I gestured to her with my wine. "You'll even have an extra bedroom for us to crash in when we visit."

"Fine." Katie fell back into the recliner. "If you wanna stick to the overly supportive girlfriend role, go for it. Just know I'm here if you start to boil."

"You know you make a lot of cooking comparisons for someone who can't bake some muffins," I snapped, shielding myself from the pillow she whipped at my head.

I appreciated Katie's concern, but right now my answers would just lead to roundabout conversations. Jaxon knew where he was going after graduation. My plans were still pending. It wasn't worth stressing about since I didn't have the answers.

Holy shit. Had I just talked myself *out* of overthinking?

Look at you, bitch, growing and shit.

As soon as the clock on our microwave read five o'clock, two knocks sounded on our front door. Connor and Jaxon immediately let themselves in, both of them invested in their riveting conversation about hockey.

Jaxon broke in the middle of his sentence to greet me with a long, much-needed kiss. Even though it was below freezing outside, his lips met mine in a warm and familiar embrace. I had to place my wine on the coffee table so I didn't fall off the couch. It had only been a day since I last saw him, but my body was acting like it had been weeks.

Jaxon eyed me playfully as he shifted his weight to the back of the couch cushion. "You okay?"

My enthusiastic nod didn't have him convinced.

"You'll just have to see the Red Wings in action," Connor exclaimed, clearly not through with the topic of hockey. "You guys can fly out to Chicago for a Blackhawks game, and you'll see what I'm talking about!"

I admired Katie's adoring gaze from across the living room. She offered Connor one of her risky yet oddly satisfying muffins before pouring herself more wine. It was nice to hear Connor embracing their plans in Chicago, and I loved the idea of the four of us hanging out after college.

Maybe it didn't have to be the end of an era but the beginning of one.

"Bryson brought up spring break today," Jaxon announced. I stifled a grin as he bit into one of Katie's muffins.

Katie leaned over the counter slowly, shooting daggers at Jaxon as she watched him process the baked good. Her eyes never left his face, but Jaxon wasn't making it easy as he tried to look anywhere but back at her.

"*Thoughts?*" she pressed.

Connor turned on his heels and headed for the safety of the recliner.

"Sorry," Jaxon muffled through a mouthful of muffin. "It might take me twenty minutes to give you a full review. They're like *really* fucking chewy."

"Dense!" Katie countered, sending Connor and me into a fit of laughter. "Whatever. Whatever to all of you. You'll all be wanting another one in the next fifteen minutes I'm calling it—"

"So spring break," Connor interjected. "What did Bryson say?"

"He—fuck." Jaxon cracked open a beer and took a giant swig. "Girl, you almost took me out," he said, laughing as I fell into his chest to hide more of mine. "Bryson said he wants to go to the beach."

Katie raised a brow. "Doesn't he *live* in Florida?"

"Yes," Jaxon replied sweetly. "But he wants all of *us* to go to the beach."

"Not *everyone* from last time, right? Or would the fan club you and Bryson created be joining us too?" Katie's dig was a direct hit at Jaxon for insulting her muffins. She shot him an innocent smirk as she lowered herself onto Connor's lap.

Jaxon backed down and let her have the upper hand. "Just couples."

"But wouldn't that require Bryson to—" Katie shot up, almost knocking Connor out with the dense muffin in her hand. She locked eyes with me, and at the same time we screamed, "NOOOO!"

"Elle?" I exclaimed.

"She's not . . . no . . . they aren't officially . . ." Jaxon stammered. His arms shot out in front of him as he tried to regain control. "No one ask about Elle, okay? They aren't together, but he's asking her to go. She might not even come."

I shook my empty wine glass, standing up as soon as the oven timer alerted us that Katie's Kickin' Chicken was done.

I held up a hand when I saw her preparing to leave Connor's lap. "I'll get it."

I pulled the tray of chicken from the rack. "Fifteen more minutes?" I suggested, turning the tray so Katie could see.

She scrunched her nose. "I would do ten."

After I adjusted the timer, I rounded the counter and plucked a muffin from the plate. I paused halfway through the wrapping. "Why the fuck do I keep eating these muffins?"

Jaxon tipped his head and held out his beer can. "Can you bring me one? And a beer?" He cracked an adorable grin as I reached into the fridge. "I love you."

It was a muffin he wanted, correct? Not the Oreo-stuffed chocolate chip cookies from The Cookie Jar that were a few streets over?

Because even in these negative temperatures, I would've brought him those too.

Chapter Forty-Two

JAXON

February 2017

While it was a new year with new beginnings, it was the same old winter weather in Bowling Green, Ohio. It was fucking cold and it fucking sucked.

I wasn't anticipating so much negativity in the month of love when I was officially in it, but as I drove over to Maci's apartment so we could do some homework and watch a show called *New Girl*, my dad reminded me again of choices I'd have to make once I took over his company.

"It's a lot to ask, son." Dad's hefty sigh filled the speakers of my Jeep, his voice laced with sympathy. "But it is the only flight I could find that is direct from Seattle back to Toledo."

"And there's nothing that leaves late that night? The earliest option is the fifteenth?"

As in, the fifteenth of February.

As in, the day *after* Valentine's Day.

As in, I wouldn't be present for yet another fucking holiday.

Yesterday I was worried about what to get Maci for Valentine's Day. Now none of my ideas mattered. Flowers, candy, jewelry, a night out, it was all irrelevant.

I wouldn't be there.

"I'm afraid not, J," Dad said disheartedly. "I can always fax the paperwork over for you to sign electronically, but—"

"But it leaves a window for the client to change their mind," I repeated his words from my first day in his office. This client would be one of the first tied to my name instead of my dad's book of business. "Book the flight please and text me the information."

"If you change your mind, Jaxon, there's no hard feelings here," he stated firmly. "I know you've had to make some sacrifices already. I don't want you giving up what is important to you right now—"

"I'm not giving anything up," I said a little too harshly. I closed my eyes, taking a deep breath as I pulled into my usual parking spot in Maci's lot. "I'm sorry. I just hate feeling like I'm choosing my future over Maci when I want her in it."

Dad's light chuckle made me realize that I must've said something right. "Then make sure she knows that. I love you, J. I'm heading into a meeting, but I'll have Helen email you the flight information."

With how many times I ran my hand through my hair going up the stairs of Maci's building, I had to look stressed. I couldn't even hide my curls with a beanie or a hat. I knocked on the door twice before letting myself in.

Maci furrowed her brow. "Everything okay?"

My chest felt incredibly heavy as I stripped off my hoodie. It was fucking hot in here, but the two blankets hanging over Maci's legs confirmed that it wasn't the apartment. It was just me panicking.

I slumped down on the couch beside her. "I have to go to Seattle."

"Seattle?" Her eyes widened as she shifted beside me. A slight smile curved into her cheek. "I've heard Seattle is gorgeous!"

Her attempt to create a positive spin-off of my news made my next line even harder. "I have to leave next Saturday."

Her focus drifted to the blanket that covered her legs. She knew what was coming, and it made me feel even shittier.

No, correction. What made me feel even shittier than shittier was that she was trying not to look upset about it.

She smiled weakly. "For how long?"

"I won't be back until the fifteenth." I pulled her legs into my lap before I eagerly added, "Any chance you could come with me? Maybe we could do Valentine's Day in—"

"I have student teaching, Jaxon," she said through a frustrated sigh. She quickly lightened her tone. "I can't just take two days off, and I'm not sure if flying out for one day would be worth it with the time difference."

Without meaning to, I filed her answer into my memory bank. It sounded uncomfortably familiar to the answers my mom used to give to my dad when he'd try to make a work trip into a mini getaway. The time difference alone would cause us to miss half our day.

"I'm sorry, Mace." The words were painful leaving my mouth. They were coated in a saying that eventually lost its meaning the more you used it. "Fuck, I should just tell my dad I can't make it. I had to leave you for Christmas and we missed New Year's and—"

"First of all, you didn't leave me during Christmas. I got to spend it with your family. I had a great time, and you knew I was going to see Chase for New Year's."

"That's not the point," I snapped, dragging my hands down my face. "All I've done so far this year is spring things on you. It's just been a preview of what next year is going to be like, and the year after that."

Maci threw the blanket off of her legs and stood up. I watched her walk to the fridge and pull out a bottle of water. With her hand on her forehead, she paced behind the counter, and I knew better than to poke her before she was ready.

"You were incredibly clear when you mentioned taking over your dad's business," she said, her voice laced with frustration. "I feel like you keep waiting for me to tell you not to go, that I'm going to lose my mind because you're actually doing what you said you would have to do. Can you *please* just stop?"

Her pained admission forced me out of my seat. I crossed the living room and wrapped my arms around her, pulling her to my chest. Her breathing steadied, and I felt my heart rate return to normal as the two of us stood there in the kitchen.

Since I stepped back on campus in August, I couldn't grasp the time as it passed by. Weekends turned to months and months turned to the end of the fall semester. Weddings and holidays ate up winter break.

I felt like I couldn't stop and enjoy the moments that mattered. The moments that I would want to remember when this chapter of life seemed like volumes ago.

"I'm not *waiting* for you to tell me not to go," I admitted with her head still pressed against my chest. "I'm waiting for you to get tired of feeling like you can't. I already know that you support me, and I love you even more for that. But I don't want you to think that I'm taking this for granted—that I'm taking *you* for granted."

She rested her chin on my chest. "Things were a lot simpler when it was just a trial, huh?"

"Nah, they weren't simpler." I took her face in my hands. "Things just got a little harder when I had to adjust the plan I made back in high school."

"And what exactly are you adjusting?"

"It might sound a little cheesy."

"Oh, I *love* cheesy," she said with pleading eyes and a wide grin. "Please continue."

I blew out an exaggerated breath. "I adjusted the space in my . . . no that's not what I want to say. My heart is . . . nah."

She giggled as I struggled to make my thought an actual sentence.

"What I'm trying to say is that I wasn't expecting to fall in love with you, Maci Lawson. But I'm really glad I did. It just—"

She pressed her index finger to my lips. "Please don't continue anymore. You'll ruin it."

I laughed as she wrapped her arms around her neck and kissed me. Her tongue grazed my bottom lip and she stood on her toes so I could pull her closer. My hands grabbed the backs of her thighs so I could place her on the counter. Her legs wrapped around my waist, opening herself up so I could slip my fingers up her shorts and past her panties. They slid effortlessly over her clit—wet and ready from her arousal as her nails dug into the back of my neck.

She groaned. "Here?"

"It can be here," I murmured as I moved my mouth down her jawline. "It can be on your couch." I kissed her collarbone. "It can be in your room." I trailed my tongue back up her neck and kissed her softly on the mouth. "It can be anywhere you want. I just want you."

Her hand wrapped around my cock, giving me my answer. My knees threatened to buckle when she started her slow strokes, my hips moving instinctually to the movement of her hand.

I removed my hand from her pussy so I could take off her shorts, giving me the space I needed to tease her properly. I pushed two fingers inside her, keeping my thumb on her clit as I paid close attention to the sweet spot I knew would push her over the edge. Her strokes began to quicken, and I knew if she kept going at this pace I would finish before I even got inside her.

She was too wet, too needy for me to be this far apart from her. Even though I stood between her legs with my fingers at work and her hand on my cock, it wasn't close enough. I needed to be closer.

I shifted my hands and a pained chuckle fell from her lips.

"Give me a second, sweetheart." I pulled her from the counter and placed her back on the floor.

As if she read my mind, she turned around so her back was toward me. She gripped the counter in front of her, dropped her hips, and looked over her shoulder. That look alone threatened all of my self-control.

I dropped my pants to my knees and lined myself up with her entrance.

"Jaxon, please," she begged.

I eased myself inside her, gentle at first so she could adjust to the angle before I slammed my hips into her backside. Her hands gripped the counter in front of her and her arms struggled to keep her at the angle I needed to hit her right where she wanted me, but she didn't let go. My girl hung on as if her life depended on it, as if she needed me as much as I needed her.

My nails dug into her soft skin, pushing me to go faster as I chased the high our bodies created. I wrapped an arm across her chest and dipped her lower, alleviating some of the pain I knew her arms were feeling. She gripped my forearm, her sighs turning to moans as my skin slapped repeatedly against hers.

"Fuck, Jaxon." She cried out as her body shook underneath me. The walls of her pussy pulsed against my cock, making it impossible to fight the pressure building at the base of my spine.

I groaned into the back of her neck, keeping her close as I gave into the pleasure and spilled myself inside her. It was the kind of intimacy I wanted to give into over and over again. It was a feeling I didn't know I wanted until I thought about all of the ways it could be taken away.

The shallow sounds of our breathing provided a peaceful contrast to the sounds we made only a few minutes ago.

"Here." She sighed, wincing as her hips adjusted to standing upright. "Yeah, here is good."

I grabbed the towel from the handle of the stove so I could catch the mess before it fell onto the floor.

She gasped. "Katie's *Gilmore Girls* towel?"

I handled the towel carefully so I could look closer. The quote, "This is a jumbo-coffee morning" and a giant cup of coffee were both sewn into the fluffy material.

"I don't know this show or these people," I joked. "I can barely keep up with yours."

Maci snatched the towel from my hands. "Just add it to our list of things to watch, Jaxon Hayes. Even though at this point our list is going to take us at least five years."

I pulled up my sweatpants and slipped my arms around her waist. "What'll it take to get me a ten-year list?"

I finally understood the dangers of mixing sex and emotions. Getting laid gave me the confidence to say the most unfiltered shit.

An adorable shade of pink flooded her cheeks. "Ten years is a long time."

It was a long-ass time. Would we both be in California? Would Maci have a career in New York? Would I have someone else running the office in LA so I could live permanently on the East Coast?

Logistics didn't scare me—what scared me was a version of my future that didn't have Maci in it.

I gently pressed my lips to hers as she ran her fingers through my hair.

"Five years, ten years, it doesn't matter," I murmured, giving into more unfiltered thoughts. "As long as you promise me that we'll always have a list."

Chapter Forty-Three

MACI

"KATIE, IT'S ALREADY SEVEN o'clock you better move your ass!" I shouted over a pot of boiling noodles.

My prompt was meant to be a loving reminder that Connor should've been here five minutes ago to pick her up, and she was already pushing her luck. Instead, I sounded like a bitter girlfriend whose boyfriend was at a business dinner in Seattle.

Katie strutted into the living room in black heels and a rich red dress. The material hugged her curves, and the straps accentuated her shoulders. It looked amazing paired with her choices of dangly necklaces and matching earrings.

"Ugh!" I swooned, losing my stirring spoon to the boiling water. "You look gorgeous!"

"Thank you." Katie smiled sweetly and peered over the counter. "Are you sure you don't want to just order something? I knew I should have cooked for you. Just because you're celebrating Valentine's Day when Jaxon gets back doesn't mean you should spend the real day hungry and alone."

"I'm *not* hungry and alone," I said defensively, gesturing to my noodles and then the TV. I caught my spoon before it did another lap around the pot. "I have Alfredo and *New Girl*, and I have Cookie Jar being delivered in a half hour. What more do I need?"

The knock on our front door made her switch gears. Katie pointed at me from across the room as she grabbed her coat from the hook. "Save me a cookie."

"Please." I scoffed right as Connor opened the door. "Act like you're coming back here tonight."

Connor's eyes practically bulged out of his sockets as he caught a glimpse of Katie's dress under her jacket. He shook his head. "Yeah, she's not coming home."

Katie giggled as he pulled her in for a kiss and waved to me over her shoulder.

I listened as their laughter disappeared down the hall. It warmed my heart to see Connor and Katie in full swing again. Tonight wasn't just about Valentine's Day. The happy Hallmark couple was also celebrating their new apartment—which they officially signed for last night. The paperwork had been approved this morning, and come June, Connor and Katie would be the official renters of a two-bedroom apartment in Chicago.

My phone buzzed on the counter.

Jared

> Wanna come get food with me and Spencer? Last chance!

I smiled at Jared's sweet offer.

Maci

> I'm okay! Have a good night and let me know how it goes!!

Jared replied with a meme of Robert Downey Jr. rolling his eyes. I had official word from Jaxon that Jared was planning on asking Spencer to be his girlfriend tonight. I was just waiting on the "Oh my god!" text from Spencer to confirm the title change.

After ten minutes of scraping dried noodles from the bottom of the pot, I was alone with Jess, Nick, Schmidt, and Winston.

It was a quiet and uneventful way to end my early evening, but I didn't care. I'd see Jaxon tomorrow and we'd celebrate the day like we originally planned to—with wings and cheap beer at Carl's Corner, just like we did a year ago from today.

I twirled noodles onto my fork and watched the guys of *New Girl* try to help Jess with her latest problem. Who needed one man when you could have three through the TV screen?

***

I had never been one who could wake up and recall my dreams. I had a short, thirty-second window where my mind did it's best to recall what was happening in my sleep.

Something pulled the blankets down my body, and I felt a weight hovering over my chest. The familiar scent of Jaxon's cologne entered the scene, and I was convinced that this was one of those moments where I knew I was dreaming and in control.

When the throbbing started between my legs, I knew I wasn't dreaming.

It was Jaxon, and his hips were settled between my legs and his hands were working on the sleeves of my T-shirt.

"Jaxon, what are you doing here?" I murmured.

"I went to the airport early to see if I could fly standby home," he whispered, trailing kisses down my neck.

I squinted as my eyes struggled to adjust to the darkness. "How did you get in?"

He leaned back and smiled. "Stop asking me questions and let me make love to you, baby."

I threaded my fingers through his hair as his mouth moved across my stomach. "Mhm."

He chuckled, his warm breaths dancing over my belly button. He lifted my hips to slide off my shorts, spreading my legs so he could dip in between them. His tongue swept slowly over my clit, and I tugged on his hair, barely recognizing the moan that fell from my lips.

His movements were soft, allowing me to grind my hips to find the rhythm I needed. The pressure began to build, and I appreciated how quickly my body responded to his touch this early in the morning. I had woken up to Jaxon wanting sex multiple times in the morning, but this was different. The room was dark, and the outside world was still quiet. I was ending and starting my day with Jaxon between my legs—completely and captivatingly consumed by him.

I clutched the pillow behind me and bit my bottom lip, keeping my whimpers to a minimum when every fiber in my being exploded. I sank further into the mattress as I watched Jaxon remove his dress pants.

He pressed his mouth to mine as he slid himself inside me. "Morning, Mace."

"Morning," I breathed, closing my eyes again as he repeated the motion.

He kissed me slowly, taking his time and matching the rhythm of his hips. With every thrust, I moaned into his mouth, and with every kiss, I wanted more of him. I slid my hands over his shoulders and around his neck, pressing my nails into his skin as the pressure began to build again.

"You feel so fuckin' good, baby," he whispered, sending sender a shiver down my spine. "Give me your hands."

Pinning my hands above my head, he dipped his free hand between my legs. Only when I expected to feel his fingers I was met with a stream of vibrations. I gasped at the familiar sensation of The Red Bullet, a breathy laugh taking over my groan as I watched Jaxon's mouth go slack.

Jaxon pumped his hips harder, keeping his strokes slow but hitting the spot that was going to put me over the edge. The combination of everything was too much for me to take. I was going to boil over, and since he had my hands, I couldn't stop it. I arched my back as the trembling began in my thighs and worked its way up to my shoulders. My walls pulsed against him, gripping him as I fought against the implosion.

"Come for me, pretty girl."

I cried out as the release rippled through my body. With every wave, the pleasure grew more intense, and I knew Jaxon was seconds away from losing it. He released my hands and gripped my hips, pressing his chest against mine as a satisfied groan vibrated from the back of his throat.

Jaxon rolled onto his side and turned me with him. I trailed my fingers down his chest, admiring the layer of sweat that had built up between us. His lips brushed against my temple, and I angled my mouth so he could kiss me.

"I love you," he whispered, kissing me again.

The familiar lump formed in my throat. I brushed my thumb across his cheek as my mouth unwillingly lifted into a slight smile. "I love you, too."

Chapter Forty-Four

JAXON

February 2017

One thing they don't tell you about attending a college in Ohio in February? Prepare to have the temperatures drop so low that it is deemed unsafe to go outside.

When Maci and I woke up this morning, her room was so cold that even I was wrapped in the extra comforter she slept with. Frost coated her windows, emphasizing the age and condition of her apartment building, and her furnace struggled to keep up with the chill.

"Mace if you keep digging your toes into my thigh you're going to break the skin," I murmured with my eyes still closed.

We shifted our lounging into the living room where the space heater was working at full power. Even with all of our layers and blankets, Maci was still acting as if we were camped outside in the frozen field of BG.

"Aww, look!" Maci flashed her phone in my face. It was a text thread between her and Jared. "Jared asked Spencer to be his girlfriend last night."

"I still can't believe they met because she hit his car."

Maci's teeth began to chatter, and I pulled her closer. "At least we have plenty of themed movies to keep us busy today. *Frozen, Ice Age*, and—"

"*Hairspray*," I cheerfully finished the sentence for her. "Because this movie just *screams* winter chill."

"No," she said calmly as if I still had time to change my statement. Her blue eyes were void of any humor, and I couldn't determine if it was from her being cold or if she was starting to get stir-crazy from being stuck inside. "It reminds me of the warmth of your love. That's why this choice makes sense."

I scoffed, laughing at the transparent shift in her face as a guy named Link Larkin appeared on the screen. "You like this movie because of that man right there."

"I have loved Zac Efron since he was in *Summerland*, okay! I have seen every movie he's been in, and I know every song from his musicals. He's an amazing talent!"

"Yeah, he's amazing," I murmured.

"He has another musical coming out this December so buckle down." She patted my stomach playfully and peered over the couch so she could see the stove. "Five minutes!" Her smile reached the corners of her eyes. "Are you ready?"

She practically ran into the kitchen. I planned to take us to Carl's Corner for wings like we did last year, but with the weather and a text from Katie to say she was just staying with Connor, we were left to fend for ourselves.

I made it sound like I was left with nothing to eat but bread and butter. I wasn't complaining, but I had never eaten anything Maci made before. I wasn't even aware that she *could* cook. As I leaned over the counter and watched her pull her homemade lasagna out of the oven with a giant grin, I couldn't help but smile appreciatively at her effort.

Even if she couldn't cook, she looked fucking adorable in an apron.

Maci placed the steaming platter of lasagna on the counter between us. "It looks good, right?"

"It looks amazing," I said, echoing her excited tone. "I'll get the plates."

As I moved around the tiny kitchen assembling our dinnerware, a rewarding sense of peace drifted over me. By some miracle, I was able to get a flight back last night, and because of that miracle, I was able to spend the entire day with Maci uninterrupted by school, friends, or work.

I thought that last year would be the best Valentine's Day I ever had. I got to have beer and wings with the girl I fell for, and today I was having lasagna with the girl I wanted to love for the rest of my life.

Jesus Christ, Jaxon. I couldn't even blame getting laid for that one.

Her spatula hovered nervously over her creation, surveying the best part to cut first. Her eyes flicked up to mine. "Do you want a big piece?"

I scoffed. "Yeah, baby. You're starving me over here."

"I believe I just fed you an hour ago," she murmured, lining up her spatula.

She wasn't wrong. I could still taste her on my tongue. "And I'd like another serving of that in about"—I looked around her to check the time on the microwave—"an hour if that's okay."

Maci was halfway through her eye roll when her spatula met the top of the corner piece with a tough thump. She tapped it again as if her plastic serving ware would break through her uncooked top layer.

I covered my mouth with my hand, knowing I was screwed either way. If I laughed I was a jackass, but if I encouraged her to keep trying to break through the hard exterior of her cooking I was still a jackass.

So I laughed. If I didn't laugh, Maci would start to question if she ruined this day with her first try at cooking for me, and that simply wasn't an option.

Growing up with Evelyn Hayes, I knew exactly what went wrong here. I took note of the unopened jar of red sauce on the counter behind her.

"Mace, how many jars of sauce did you use?" I asked cautiously, keeping my tone light.

She placed her hand on her popped hip and stared down at the lasagna with a bewildered gaze. "I used the one we had in the cabinet! I didn't want it to be too saucy!"

"Hmm." I cocked my head and gestured to the dish. "Seems a little ironic to have thought that now, huh?"

"The box said the noodles were oven-ready! I thought that meant they just cooked in the oven!"

I no longer held back my laughter. "Sweetheart, it does mean that. But it's the sauce that cooks the noodles."

"Great." Her giant grin fell to a disappointed smirk. "My first time cooking dinner for us and we can't even eat it."

"That's not true!" I said quickly, grabbing the spatula from her hand. I used it to peel off the top layer of uncooked pasta and slip it into the trashcan. "We just have to dig a little bit, that's all."

She chuckled weakly at my attempt to brighten her mood. "Now it just looks like slop. I love you for trying to save this, but we don't have to eat it."

"Baby, it's *fine*." I reached across the counter and grabbed her hand. "We just know now moving forward that you'll help the kids with their English homework, and I'll make the lasagna."

With a quick quirk of her lip, she said, "What made you say that?"

"Because I meant it," I admitted, her shy smile digging into her cheeks. "I always saw myself with boys, but I think my karma will throw me a girl."

"I think your karma might have changed, Jaxon Hayes. You're not the same guy you were when we first met."

"Shit, I hope so," I said, taking a bite of lasagna. It tasted incredible. "Fuck, this is really good."

"It should be." She leaned forward to blow on her fork. "It's your mom's recipe."

I paused mid-bite, slowly lowering my fork to my plate. "My mom gave you one of her recipes?"

She looked taken aback by my response. "Yeah. Is that weird?"

Evelyn Hayes never gave recipes out to anyone. There were family members who weren't even worthy of the information.

The rewarding sense of peace returned, and even though I was only four bites into my lasagna, I felt comfortably full.

Chapter Forty-Five

Jaxon

March 2017

It was another spring break road trip and another year when no one was on time.

"Just grab your keys, Jared!" Spencer screeched with one foot out the door. If there was one thing they didn't handle well as a couple, it was chaos.

Katie, Maci and Connor all sat at the breakfast bar, sipping coffee while Jared fought for his life at the coat hangers. He struggled to identify his BGSU lanyard in the tangles of coats, keys, and scarves that had made a home there over the last month.

"Here!" Jared held up his prize. "See! I told you they were—"

Spencer grabbed him by the hoodie and pulled him out into the hall.

"Ugh, I love her so much," Katie swooned while Maci nodded approvingly. They both sat there in hoodies—Katie in Connor's and Maci in mine—looking like the co-hosts of a snarky talk show. "Do we have anything to make this coffee a little less . . . *dry?*"

I poured myself what was left of the coffee, looking over my shoulder and doing a double-take when I realized Katie was talking to me.

"She means do you have anything to spike it," Maci whispered, trying to stifle her grin as I smiled lovingly at her best friend from across the counter.

Before I could even add creamer to my coffee, the front door burst open. Elle stormed into the living room, practically knocking Connor to the couch while she peered down the hall. "Is my brother here?"

We all shook our heads.

"Ugh! Fucking Bryson." She crossed her arms and made a beeline into the kitchen.

I ducked out of the way so she could grab a bottle of water from the fridge, joining Connor in the living room to give the girls some space.

The co-hosts shared a look before the two of them rose slowly from their barstools.

"What happened?" Maci prompted gently.

"He's just an idiot, that's what happened," Elle answered sternly.

"Sweetie, let's pause for a moment, okay?" Katie offered. "You're still wearing the man's shirt."

Elle glanced down at the same Tampa Bay Lightning shirt I saw Maci in over a year ago. While I tried to push away the memory of Maci standing in my doorway in my best friend's shirt, the three of them exploded into a fit of giggles.

It was wild how much could change in just a year.

Maci peered over her shoulder, cocking her head slightly to ask me if I'd mind leaving. She smiled appreciatively when I suggested to Connor that we should start packing up the car.

While the two of us hauled snacks and drinks to our rental, I tried to ignore the snippets of conversation that I caught coming from the episode of *Maci & Katie* happening on our couch. When I heard Elle mutter something about how men will say anything to convince themselves that women actually need them, I decided it wasn't worth trying to guess what she was upset about.

Meanwhile, Bryson was stepping out of his car like nothing was wrong at all.

"Is Jared here?" he asked.

I slid the final bag into the trunk and slammed it shut. "Did you fuck up?"

Bryson scoffed. "No, I didn't fuck up. I actually thought I was doing a *good* thing for once." He pointed to the staircase. "This is why I don't do that shit. She's in there bitching, isn't she?"

I shook my head, reading a missed text message from Maci. "Wouldn't know. Maci said they'll be downstairs in a few minutes."

I scrolled past Maci's name and realized I had a missed text message from Alex.

Alex

> You'll be in Florida until Friday, correct?

I didn't like where this was going, but typed back that I would be. I barely took a step forward before I felt another vibration.

Alex

> You can say no because you're on break. But is there any chance you could do dinner with one of our investors?

> Just dinner.

> But the dinner is in Jacksonville.

> So dinner and a night in Jacksonville.

The request grew more annoying with every text that came through. Jacksonville was on the other side of the state, which made it at least a four hour drive from where we would be staying.

Alex

> Dad said if he asked you that you would say yes. He didn't want you taking time away from your trip so I'm asking for him.

I sighed as another text from Alex slid into our thread. I already knew what was coming.

Alex

> It's mom's birthday on Monday, J.

My answer determined if my parents would be able to spend my mom's birthday together. It determined if my mom would have to sacrifice another night my dad probably promised her would happen.

Jaxon

> It better be a nice fucking hotel room.

Alex typed back a hand clapping and thumbs up emoji to express his gratitude.

I rounded the car to see Maci walking toward me with her phone in her hands. Her steps continued their slow pace across the lot while her focus remained glued to her screen. She waited until she was a few feet in front of me to look up, meeting me with glossy blue eyes and tear stained cheeks.

I closed the space between us. "Baby, what's the matter?"

A slight smile replaced her stoic expression as she softly said, "I got the internship."

I eyed her playfully. "You *what?*"

"I got the internship!" she squealed, jumping into my arms.

I spun her around the parking lot, completely unaware of anything else happening around us. I didn't have to ask which one she heard back from. I could tell from the stars in her eyes and the light in her smile.

My girl was heading to New York City in the fall, and my heart understood what it felt like to love and break at the same time.

Chapter Forty-Six

MACI

March 2017

New York City.

In just a few short months, I'd be in New York, working on my masters in a city that never sleeps and writing the next chapter of my life. It would be my way with no apologies, and I could barely contain my excitement.

It was the best news I could've received before having to sit in a car for sixteen hours. Yet, as soon as Jaxon told me about his investor dinner in Jacksonville, the last sip of my iced hazelnut coffee left a bad taste in my mouth.

And my coffee *never* did that.

Part of me shouldn't have been shocked when the words left his perfect lips. His dad knew he was off of school this week. I wasn't sure why I expected to have some uninterrupted time with my boyfriend and our friends.

Valentine's Day had been a fluke. The only reason we saw each other was because Jaxon fought to be there.

So why did it feel like he wasn't fighting now?

I knew I was getting into my head. This was just another preview of what was to come. My internship email only confirmed what our reality would be once Jaxon moved to California.

I'd be in one time zone, and he'd be in another. I'd be working toward my dream while he worked toward his. I couldn't complain about it. I wasn't *allowed* to complain about it. It was the only scenario where we stayed together after graduation . . . together while being on the opposite ends of the country.

The irony drove me fucking insane.

The tension was high in our hotel room as Jaxon and I both unpacked into our dresser.

He sighed behind me, unable to stand the silence any longer. "Mace, the timing is shitty. But if I didn't tell you today, I'd be telling you the morning I had to leave—"

"You couldn't even wait a day?" I snapped, my reaction surprising us both.

Welp. So much for I couldn't complain about it. I should've just waved goodbye to that option as it flew out our balcony door.

It was devastating how all of your growth could be eliminated with one shitty question. I watched as the gears began to turn behind Jaxon's dark green eyes. His mouth fell into a cocky grin, but when his lips curved into a dismissive smirk, I braced myself for the worst.

"Alex texted me right before you told me about New York," he muttered. "I'm sorry but it's one night—"

"And you couldn't even *consider* saying no?" I shook my head, pacing along my side of the bed. "I tell you that I am moving across the country from you this fall, and your instinctual response is to jump at the chance to get a work dinner in?"

"I didn't *jump* at anything," he said, taking a defensive step toward me. "If I go, then my dad doesn't have to miss my mom's birthday. For once he can take a step back and—" He took a deep breath to recollect himself. "Do you understand how amazing it is that my dad was even *okay* with sending me instead of coming himself?"

"Do I *understand?*" A condescending laugh fell from my lips. "Of course, I understand! I'm not dismissing how important this job is to you. I'm not ignoring the fact that your family will always be your first priority."

That seemed to strike a nerve. His eyes narrowed and he laced his fingers, placing them behind his head.

I swallowed around the lump in my throat. I tried Katie's method of not simmering. I tried to be flexible. But all of the words I wanted to say in moments when I felt like I was coming in second place boiled over without warning.

"Please don't say it like that," Jaxon pleaded in a much calmer tone. He shook his head. "Don't make it sound like I don't give a shit about us."

I blew out a frustrated breath. "I didn't say you didn't. It's just been hard."

"Yeah, Mace, it's gonna be fucking hard." His tone drifted dangerously into his I-don't-give-a-fuck territory, immediately setting me on edge. "But you have to be willing to work with me."

"*I* have to be willing to work with *you.*"

"Okay, clearly I said the wrong thing just now," he muttered, rounding the corner of the bed.

The wall I was trying to build between us crumbled helplessly before me. He stepped right through it, rubbing his hands down my arms, trying to determine if he could get closer.

"I'm scared," I whispered, my voice catching at the end of my admission.

His eyes softened. "About what?"

I took in a staggering breath as his fingers continued their agonizing trail against my skin. "I'm scared because you've had this hold on me since I met you and—I can't compromise the last piece of myself. The piece that I saved in case I have to put myself back together again. If this doesn't work out or if it's only temporary—" I shook my head. "I've given you all of the others, but I can't *give* you this one—"

A few months worth of tears broke free when he pulled me to his chest. His lips grazed my hairline as he whispered, "You're allowed to be scared, you know. You can keep that piece for as long as you want, but I'm gonna be here to put all of the other ones back together when you can't, Mace." He held my face in his hands and smiled lazily down at me. "We were never a trial period to me, baby. We were never temporary. You make me say shit I never thought I'd say. You make me wanna talk about living together and babies and where we'll spend Christmas. You . . . *fuck* you make me wanna be the best version of myself because you deserve that."

Since I couldn't formulate a response fast enough, I angled my face to his and kissed him, soft and slow until he parted his lips and grasped the hair at the base of my neck. His tongue danced cautiously with mine, aware that with just one swift move he could have us on the bed behind me. My hands wandered up his T-shirt, tracing lines along his abdomen and finding a place on his chest so I could feel his heartbeat.

"Have I mentioned that I also pick fights when I'm scared?" I added through another round of breathy kisses.

"You don't have to tell me that," he muttered as his lips moved down my jawline. He smiled against my skin. "*That* I already knew." He pulled away, leaving me practically panting and wanting more. "I'll cancel Jacksonville. I'll tell my dad I can't go."

I was shaking my head before he even finished the sentence. "No. You're going and I'll be mad at you and it'll be just fine."

His thumbs pulled at the waistband of my leggings as his cocky grin deepened into his dimple. "At least you're giving me the heads up, right?"

"And a raincheck." I smirked, pulling down on his hands. "Let's go down to the beach before people think we went missing."

He whined as I walked around him to my duffle bag. "What's another twenty minutes?"

I sifted through my belongings, realizing I left my only hoodie in the rental car. "Twenty minutes? You're being pretty optimistic today."

I giggled as his arms wrapped around my waist, squeezing me until I thought I would implode.

"Don't play with me," he said, the warning loaded with his obvious need to prove me wrong. "Just put my hoodie on. It doesn't smell too much like me so you'll be fine. Since, you know, you're all mad at me and shit."

⁂

It wasn't on my senior-year bucket list to find out from Chase that my parent's divorce would be final in thirty days.

For as big of a bombshell it was to drop, neither Chase nor I seemed bothered by the life change. It was a little weird to see our childhood home up for sale, but it was comforting to know that another family would hopefully fill it with growth and opportunity.

An ending wasn't always a bad thing, not when it made room for better beginnings.

While Jaxon was halfway to Jacksonville in our rental car, I was taking my moment of solitude to reflect on the beach with the waves. With every crash, a thick gust of ocean air sent a fresh poof of Jaxon's cologne from his hoodie straight to my nostrils.

Who was it that said the best smell in the world was the man you loved? Was it the queen, Jennifer Aniston? She must've never sulked in his cologne-infused hoodie.

I was thankful that today's weather was breezy with overcast. My sensitive skin wasn't ready for the sun when Ohio wasn't scheduled to receive it for another few months, and it guaranteed me an almost empty beach until midday. Since the rest of our friends were having brunch in the hotel lobby, I had at least another hour to myself before my negative energy became noticeable.

I rolled my eyes at the familiar whistle that was approaching me from behind. "Katie, I told you I'm—"

I turned around, and instead of being met with Katie's obnoxious grin, I was met with Jared's. I should've known when the whistling sounded identical to Redbone's "Come and Get Your Love."

"Good thing I'm not Katie, then, huh?" Jared sank into the sand next to me and rested his arms on his knees. He nudged me playfully with his shoulder. "If I'm being honest, I'm not being nosey. I needed a moment away from Spencer, and you seemed like a good out."

I scrunched up my nose. "You're using me to avoid a conversation with your girlfriend?"

Jared quirked an innocent brow. "I didn't say it was a conversation."

"It's you . . . and words." I pulled down my hood to see him better. "I know it's a conversation."

"Ehh," he whined. "Maybe a few words."

"Nice to know you aren't denying that you're using me, though," I mumbled pathetically.

"Nah, I could never use you." Jared smiled reassuringly. "I just sensed that you were doing some thinking, and I needed to do some of my own. Thinking loves company."

I laughed. "I think you mean misery. What's the reason for *your* thinking?"

"I'm scared she doesn't feel the same way," he admitted quickly. "We want different things, and since I'm unsure, I'm scared I'm going to turn my feelings off."

I raised my eyebrows. "Damn. You had no problem spilling to me. Now why can't you do that to Spencer?"

He cocked his head back and forth to weigh his answer. "Bigger risk."

"I don't think it works like that. *Feelings*, that is."

"They do, actually. Turning the feelings off is easy. It's turning them back on that doesn't always work. Once I get too much distance . . . that's usually it."

It was as if Jared overheard my most recent argument with Jaxon. While Jared's distance wasn't measured in miles, it still carried the same importance. He felt distant from Spencer while he was sitting across from her at brunch, and that seemed worse.

"And you think you'll be able to do that with Spencer?" I prompted gently. "All because you guys want different things?"

"I don't know." He stared longingly at the water as if the answer to his dilemma would wash up on the shore. "She doesn't want to"—he chuckled—"God, I feel like an idiot saying it. She doesn't want to get married, like, *ever*." A light shade of pink flooded his cheeks. "And I do."

"You do?" I swooned while Jared tried to play it off with a laugh, making him even more adorable. "Has she said why?"

"She said she's never pictured it. She wants a career in writing and the freedom to do what she wants without having to explain herself." He ran a hand through his shaggy blond hair. "Fuck, what are they putting in the water at Bowling Green? First Connor gets together with Katie, then Jaxon makes it official with you . . . now I can't shake this idea of a future without Spencer. What happened to Fun Dip?"

"Ha!" I exclaimed, falling into his side so I didn't faceplant into the sand. "How dare you bring up the embarrassing ambitions of my past. Speaking of, don't forget about Bryson."

Jared scoffed. "Oh, yeah. Don't forget about Bryson fucking my sister. Thank you so much for that."

Now I was clutching my stomach, belly laughing at Jared's super short paragraph summary of our senior year. He chuckled alongside me, unable to keep a straight face.

"I know I need to talk to her," Jared added while I regained my composure. "Saying it to you made that part even clearer. I'm just afraid she'll tell me she's done with me, and in the past it's always been easier for me to distance myself before the other person can cause any damage."

"You're not the only one who is scared about what happens next, you know. You should talk to her."

"Does that mean you'll talk to J?" he challenged with a quirked brow.

"I did talk to Jaxon, but I think we've done all of the talking that we can do. No matter how many times we talk about how hard it's going to be, nothing is going to change our situation."

"You mad he left this morning?"

I smiled fondly to eliminate any doubt Jared might get from my answer. "Jaxon's family will always be his first love, and I'm okay with that."

"First love?" His eyebrows knit together. "I wouldn't say that."

"What would you say?"

"First obligation, maybe, but first love?" Jared shook his head. "Nah. You guys are on the endgame track."

"Endgame?" I echoed doubtfully.

"Yeah," he stated as if the definition was incredibly clear. "Endgame."

He slung his arm around my shoulder and gave me a playful squeeze. As soon as he started to sing "Come and Get Your Love" by Redbone, I followed his lead, allowing the layers of my stress to fall into the lyrics of our song and the crashing of the waves.

Chapter Forty-Seven

Jaxon

March 2017

I was so tired of feeling like I was living out of a suitcase.

I couldn't wait for the part of my job where I sat behind a desk. If I had to board one more plane or fill another tank with gas just to get to a work event I would lose my mind.

A year ago, I wouldn't have thought that. A year ago, I wasn't leaving someone behind every time I went.

I spent the evening having a few drinks with our investor who had nothing but amazing things to say about my dad and his firm.

But to hold a dinner at a five-star restaurant just to sign some papers? It was the perfect example of a This-Could've-And-Should've-Been-An-Email. I was in bed by ten o'clock, exhausted and counting the hours until I could drive back to Clearwater.

Even with the air turned all the way up, it was still stuffy in the cabin. The muggy Florida air clogged my ears and blurred my vision, making it hard to stay on track.

My mind kept taking wandering routes. One went down the path that showcased my life in California, with tons of traffic, suits, meetings, and a lofty apartment. Another took a leisurely ride to view all of the moments I would get to reunite with Maci for holidays, breaks, and anytime we both had the opportunity to take advantage of free time.

Then there was the view of Maci trying to navigate life in New York without Katie or the stability of her family. The home she grew up in would no longer be hers, her brother would be in Europe, and her parents in two separate states. With so many divides happening at the same time, I was worried she'd fall through the cracks.

It would be impossible to catch her if I wasn't there. No matter how well my words sounded through a speaker or a screen, I wouldn't be there to hold her hand. There would be moments when she'd need me not because she couldn't handle it, but because she shouldn't have to do it by herself.

My last route came full circle as I merged onto the final stretch of the highway. I couldn't rid myself from the anxiety that came with having to merge the most important pieces in my life. As much as I hated myself for having such an even split in my priorities, I worried that I wouldn't be able to balance both halves.

Two things I wasn't willing to give up—Maci and my family's legacy. I couldn't shake the unpleasant vision of having to choose one over the other. I could choose to work with her. I could choose to balance the job and my relationship.

But even if I gave it my all, would she continue to choose me?

I dragged a hand down my face. Maci insisted that coffee eased the traveling soul. I followed my instinct and pulled into the nearest Dunkin Donuts drive-through.

One sip of my iced hazelnut coffee sent a cool and calm energy into my system.

Maybe it wasn't the Florida air that was my problem, maybe it was just a lack of caffeine. Either way, I felt prepared to answer my dad's incoming phone call as I got back on the road.

"What's up, Dad?"

"Welp." His smile was apparent through his hefty sigh. "I woke up to a pretty damn good email."

"Yeah?" I smirked, taking another sip of coffee. "Good review then I'm guessing?"

Why are you asking?

The question slipped even though I already knew the answer. I killed it last night, so why was it getting harder and harder to accept my dad's compliments?

"He loved you, J. He's already booked another meeting with us next quarter. Helen just put it on your calendar."

My calendar—the thing that would run my life for the next few years.

"He vacations in March every year," Dad explained. "His schedule is a little wonky. He actually booked with you during St. Patrick's Day weekend—"

"Dad that won't work," I stated, surprised that it wasn't laced with hesitation. It had been the most confident I sounded regarding my leadership role in the company since my dad even brought up the opportunity. "That's my anniversary with Maci, and I know I'll want to see her."

Dad chuckled softly. "Then it sounds like you gotta have that meeting moved on your calendar."

I relaxed my shoulders, realizing I didn't have to brace myself for an argument. "Just like that?"

"Just like that," Dad echoed. "A year from now—" Another sigh came through the speakers as he processed the rest of his sentence. "It doesn't have to be in a year, Jaxon. Your role in our company doesn't have to be decided right after you graduate. It's not that I don't think you can do it. You're my son, I know you can. But I want you to be sure that this is what you want."

There were multiple times when Dad made it seem like my taking over was a choice. This was just the first time I heard it presented as something that I could decide.

"It is what I want," I reassured him. "I just can't let it take everything else from me. With Maci in New York, there will be certain things I don't want to miss. Our anniversary is one of them."

"Still see her in your future even a year from now, huh?"

I nodded even though he couldn't see me. "Is that dumb?"

He laughed again, only this time it delivered a different tone. It was the same laugh he had after I rode my bike for the first time without training wheels. The same one that floated from the stands after I had good play on the football field.

When he found out I changed my middle name to his, he responded with that laugh. Ever since that day, I never questioned what that sound meant.

"There is nothing dumb about prioritizing someone you want to keep in your life, Jaxon," he stated proudly. "It might just be the smartest thing you ever do."

Chapter Forty-Eight

MACI

March 2017

There was nothing like the calming sound of pins being knocked over to add some romance to an anniversary. It was St. Patrick's Day, and while people were already passed out around campus, Jaxon and I were pregaming for our last holiday in BG with some bowling at Al-Mar Lanes. It was also just the two of us, and I was soaking up every moment before we joined everyone else at the house party on Main Street.

Jaxon's bright pink bowling ball kept a steady roll down the middle of the lane, crashing into his pins perfectly for the fourth time in a row.

"Boom!" Jaxon's fist shot into the air, and he spun around to shoot me a cocky grin.

He was already torturing me in a backward hat and a flannel that showed off his forearms—seeing him in rented bowling shoes left me at a loss for words. I wasn't expecting my giddy reaction, but I wasn't mad about it either.

"When were you going to share that you were a closet bowler?" I shoved his shoulder and took my place at the top of the lane.

He chuckled. "I've never bowled before."

My jaw went slack. "You're lying."

He shook his head and took the bowling bowl from my hands. "Nope."

Before I could stop him, he took my turn for me, shifting from his spectacular aim to the gutter that ran along the right side of the lane.

"What the fuck!" I screeched as he ducked out of my reach. "*Now* you can't bowl?"

We watched on the scoreboard as two pins pretended to fight on the screen, lasting only a few seconds before a giant red banner flashed the words GUTTER BALL.

Jaxon lifted his beer to his lips and took a long swig, eyeing me playfully as he tried not to laugh.

I closed the space between us slowly, helping myself to the seat across from him. "Did you ever think you'd be here?"

He raised a brow in question. "Where?"

"Here." I gestured to the scene around me. "Bowling with me instead of doing Kegs and Eggs with the guys."

Jaxon leaned on his elbows and held my gaze. "I knew I was in trouble last Valentine's Day when I dropped you off. I didn't think I'd ever be here. I think there's a lot of things I didn't know I wanted until you gave them to me."

I sipped my drink before tipping it toward him. "Fuckin' feelings, huh?"

He chuckled and clinked his bottle to mine. "Fuckin' feelings."

I dragged my free hand over his exposed forearm. "Don't say I never gave you anything."

Jaxon sat up, eyes wide as he scanned the area around us. "Did you bring it here?"

"Wait, what?" My mouth fell open as I put together what he was referring to. "No!"

The Red Bullet had joined us in Tree Hill, both of our bedrooms, and even made a guest appearance in Jaxon's car a few times. I refused to bring it to Al-Mar Lanes.

Jaxon opened his mouth to speak, but we were interrupted when the familiar sounds of sirens erupted through the bowling alley.

One fantastic thing about attending a college that was surrounded by cornfields? Tornadoes. Well, at least tornado *warnings*. I was fortunate that I never experienced an *actual* tornado in BG.

"Fuck," Jaxon set his beer down and grabbed my hand. "We might as well head back to your place now. They aren't going to let us bowl."

I nodded, gathering my things from the table and leaving a ten-dollar bill in their place. It was plenty to cover the tip for our cheap beer and order of mozzarella sticks.

When we arrived at my apartment, the sirens were still going strong.

"You don't think they'll close the bars, do you?" I asked, looking up at the sky as if I were suddenly cast in *Twister*.

What the fuck did I know about funnel clouds or storms?

"I'm positive that a full-force flood could come through this town and they still wouldn't close these bars." Jaxon laughed, throwing his arm around me. "Text Katie and see if they're still at the house on Main or if they left for the bars."

My thumbs were already ahead of him. It was barely eight o'clock, and that only meant one thing on St. Patrick's Day. Either our group was ready to call it a night after partying for twelve hours or they were rallying for part two.

The old lady version of me would've been content with the first option. Spending the rest of our anniversary with a bottle of Moscato and my choice of movie? Sold.

However, the nostalgic side of me knew I would regret not going out for my last green holiday in college. So when Katie texted back to let us know that they were playing pong on the porch at the house on Main, I pointed over toward the train tracks to let Jaxon know where we were headed.

We had officially transitioned into a wet spring season. For those of us who loved a good crop top, we could finally throw on a jacket and be comfortable walking down the street. Every house with a porch on Main Street had some sort of gathering in the front yard. Music blended seamlessly together as we walked past house parties and cookouts all decorated in green, orange, and brown. It was one of those feelings you didn't want to end. It was a beautiful and natural high that came with the carefree college spirit.

Jaxon tightened his grip on my hand as he led me across the front yard. It was hard to miss Katie's cackling coming from the porch of our destination, and we arrived just in time to see her sink her pong ball into the cups across the table.

Connor paused his throw and turned to Jaxon. "Take this for me. Celeb shot!"

The crowd on the porch cheered as another gust of wind whipped down the street. It took a whole new level of skill to play beer pong in these conditions.

Someone turned up the music inside to try and drown out the sirens, and Asher Roth's "I Love College" came through the sound system. Everyone erupted into cheers and held up their drinks, prompting the usual reaction this song received whenever it came within fifteen miles of a college campus.

"Mace can take it." Jaxon turned and handed me the ball. He patted me playfully on the ass and urged me to the head of the table. "Let's go, pretty girl."

Bryson put his hands on his knees, glaring at me as I took my spot across from him. I sang along to the lyrics and took my shot, only instead of my usual shrug-it-off toss, I bounced it to the left side. Elle stretched across the table to try and deflect the ball, but when she missed and my bounce made it in, the crowd around us burst into applause.

"I believe that's a bounce." I checked the win off with a cocky grin and observed the penis-shaped cup arrangement in front of me. "And I believe they just won because you guys re-racked."

Bryson slung his arm around Elle's shoulders and pointed at me. "You got lucky."

"Nothing to do with luck." I leaned into Jaxon's chest. "Your shot is shit anyways."

Jared came barreling onto the patio with a tray of bright green shots. "Last call before the bar ya'll!"

We helped ourselves to the St. Patrick's Day send-off and embraced the moment of silence where everyone cringed at Jared's potent sip.

Jaxon winced. "What the *fuck* did you put in this?"

"It's my take on the green stoplight shot from Brathaus." Jared beamed, sending Spencer into a fit of giggles.

"Makes sense," Katie mumbled.

Jaxon laughed. "Girl, you have no room to talk."

Katie opened her mouth to speak, but I cut her off by yelling, "Blood Orange Sangria!"

As we revisited one of the first memories we shared together, Asher Roth's anthem came to an end, reminding me that in just a few short months, Bowling Green State University would no longer be home.

Jaxon grabbed my hand and we followed Katie and Connor to the sidewalk. With Bryson, Elle, Jared, and Spencer behind us, I closed my eyes and took a deep breath.

In June, Jaxon would move to California while Katie and Connor would head to Chicago.

In August, Bryson would start his firm down in Florida with hopes of moving to the big city. Jared, Spencer, and I were headed to The Big Apple.

All of us were on different paths, but one thing was certain. *Man*, did I love college.

Chapter Forty-Nine

JAXON

May 2017

IT WOULDN'T HAVE BEEN a typical Friday morning in BG without the loud-ass train running alongside Maci's apartment building. I considered it a parting ceremony.

One last train horn, one last goodbye.

The voice coming from the living room didn't see the sentimental value.

"Jesus!" Chase screamed. His complaint was followed up by Trey's nervous commentary.

Through the thin walls I could make out, "Is someone trying to break into this apartment again? I told you we shouldn't have stayed here."

Ahh, last year's memories.

While Maci's parents decided to drive in tomorrow for the ceremony and book hotels, Chase and Trey thought it would be better to come for the entire weekend. Chase was fine with the apartment situation. Trey . . . not so much.

I wasn't judging. My parents pretty much called me a caveman when I told them they could stay at my place for the weekend. Apparently, a four-star hotel a few cities over was a better option.

"I tried to tell Chase that Trey would do better in a hotel," Maci murmured into my chest. She sat up, groaning as she swung her legs over the bed. "I do *not* feel like packing all this shit up today."

I watched her look around her room as if she was trying to take in every chip of paint and uneven dip in the carpeting. The space contained so many of her little touches that made it home during the last two years. It had to feel weird knowing it was time to let it all go.

I rubbed her back, coaxing her to lean back so she was resting against my hip. "You okay?"

"Yeah." She sniffed, staring down at me with a glossy gaze. "It's just . . . *weird*, you know?"

It pulled on my heartstrings to know that she was struggling. It was a big change, and after everything that happened this year, I knew she was trying hard to be in the present.

"Yeah," I echoed softly. "I know."

With Chase and Trey camped out in the living room, the space was a little packed for breakfast. Katie navigated around the kitchen, frying up eggs, sausage, and bacon as a thank you for everyone coming to help her and Maci pack up their apartment.

It was cute for her to think that Connor and I had a choice. But when she slid a plate across the counter for me that was stacked with all of the fixings plus a few chocolate chip pancakes, I didn't question the gesture.

"Oh my god!" Trey shouted, practically throwing his eggs on the floor. "There's a giant-ass ant crawling across your carpet!"

Katie and Maci burst into hysterics while Connor took care of the bug with a napkin. He and I took turns plucking the tiny creatures off the floor whenever one was spotted.

"I'm curious, Trey," Maci prompted playfully. "If you had to rate our college apartment, how many stars has it earned?"

Trey glared at Maci from the couch while Chase looked away so he could laugh.

"Put it this way," Trey stated. "If it were me packing up this morning, I wouldn't miss a damn thing."

Maci scoffed. "Ever since you booked your ticket to Europe you've become such a snob."

"A snob"—Trey rose from the couch and planted a kiss on Maci's head—"or someone you're going to miss *terribly* when they are gone?"

"You can be both," she snapped, mimicking his scowl.

"Listen, you can say anything you want about this place, but we made a ton of memories here," Katie added, staring fondly at Maci. The two of them shared a silent exchange, and when I noticed Maci's cheeks getting pink, I rested my hand on her thigh.

As we packed the apartment away in boxes and totes, I was reminded of how much time I actually spent here—before and after Maci and I became official.

Time was lost in Thursday dinners, pregaming, movie marathons, and sleepovers. Levels were created in ex-boyfriends trying to break in, recovering from bar fights, and Blood Orange Sangria. Every tiny moment captured in this living room added to the bigger picture of my junior and senior years on campus.

I grabbed another handful of hoodies and tossed them on Maci's bed. I thought packing up the living room would be the most brutal part of the process, but nothing prepared me for this girl's closet.

"You're gonna have to make sure that cozy studio apartment in New York has a decent closet," I joked.

It was all I had been doing about New York. *Joking*. It was the only thing I could do so my heart didn't sink when I thought about her actually going. It was a wild reaction, being so incredibly happy for someone yet devastated at the same time. I was proud of her . . . *fuck*, I was proud of her. But that wouldn't replace the hole in my chest that started to form the moment my dad booked my ticket out to Los Angeles.

Maci shoved something into my back. "Do you want this?"

I turned around and was met with the birthday card that Maci gave me a few months ago.

"Of course, I want this." I took it from her hands and reunited with the words inside it. "How did it end up here?"

"Oh, sweetie." She tenderly patted my face and smiled. "You were so hammered that night."

"And then Katie made us all fill out our graduation applications the next morning," I groaned, dragging my hands down my face. "Yeah, that hangover was brutal."

"But the next night was fun." She wrapped her arms around my waist and drew me closer. Her fingers trailed under my shirt, making me forget all about the card and the sweet words she wrote inside it.

It was the first time I had the words "I love you" in writing from her, and the fact that she had to ask me if I wanted it was comical.

She worked her way up my back, turning me on with the simplest touch. I kissed her, keeping in mind that we agreed to go to Mister Spots in five minutes for one last round of chicken fingers and fries.

"It was very fun," I said, my voice raspy. I cleared my throat as Katie's voice rang through the apartment, letting everyone know that we were leaving as soon as Connor came back from the moving truck.

Maci took a deep breath, and I sensed she was starting to get in her head again. The slight curve of her smile was a sign that she needed a pick-me-up.

I lightly squeezed her hips. "I have something for you."

"We have five minutes, Jaxon," she murmured. "Let's just wait until tonight."

"Nope." I laughed, loving how her mind immediately went there. "Not talking about that." I leaned around her for my bookbag and pulled out my find from yesterday's last-minute run to Kroger.

She snatched it from me. "You did not."

"I did."

She tore open the package and put the stick of candy in her mouth. "You're a smartass." She coated the stick in the red sugar and offered me a taste. "Very clever, Jaxon Hayes."

The cherry left a sweet and sour taste on my tongue. "It wouldn't be the end of senior year without some Fun Dip."

"Fun Dip, a Red Bullet, and a trial," Maci said fondly. She shook her head and took another dip of powder. "Where did this year go?"

"I want that to be the last time you say trial," I warned her through a breathy laugh. She eyed me cautiously and I took her face in my hands, forcing her to pause her next lick of Fun Dip. "You're the best *trial* I ever signed up for Maci Lawson. But every time you say that it sounds like I haven't made room for you in my future. You take up the biggest part of it. Everything I do from here on out is going to be for us. If there ever comes a day when I'm not what's best for you—"

"Stop!" she exclaimed through a tear-filled chuckle. She gently pried my hands from her face but didn't let go. "I need you to stop because I don't have a version of my future that doesn't have you in it. I believe in this . . . in *us*. And I'm so proud of you for following your dream, no matter where it takes you."

I leaned forward to kiss her, and she pulled back so she could finish the bite I interrupted. I cupped the back of her head and pulled her to me, chasing the cherry flavor on her tongue and leaning her back on the bed. Her arms wrapped around my neck, and we fell effortlessly into this new adventure we were taking together after graduation.

It seemed like yesterday I was chasing Maci down the steps of The Attic. Fourteen months of a trial, and I was still chasing.

"I love you," I murmured right before I eased myself inside her.

Her fingers tugged on my hair, pulling me close to her again to muffle her moans into my mouth. She nipped at my bottom lip, smiling softly against our kiss as she said, "I love you too."

Mister Spots would have to wait. There was nowhere else I'd rather fucking be than here.

Epilogue

Maci

It was crisp and cool mornings like today that made me think back to all of the walks I took to class in BG. The air was calm, but there were hints of the seasons changing in the sounds of the leaves and the sudden need for a cardigan.

It was louder than I thought it would be in New York. I wasn't sure why that revelation shocked me. I should've known when I visited NYU's campus for the first time that I would get the full effect of city life. The streets were busier and much more chaotic, and sometimes I found myself nostalgic for the small-town vibe of Bowling Green.

Still, as I started my chapter at NYU, I couldn't help but be reminded of the one I just closed. Since I started my journey at Bowling Green State University with Katie, it seemed fitting for us to end it that way. The morning of our graduation, we sat on the floor of our empty apartment, drinking coffee from Grounds for Thought since we packed up our appliances and mugs.

We reminisced about just the two of us. We laughed. We cried. We hugged and we embraced the comfortable silence.

It felt like we were wrapping up the most crucial part of our lives when the most exciting parts were just beginning. One day we'd be reuniting in Katie and Connor's apartment, hosting the same shenanigans with adult responsibilities and hopefully better quality wine than gas station Moscato.

The ceremony went quickly for having hundreds of students all waiting to get a blank congratulatory piece of paper. My parents sat on opposite sides of Chase and Trey, leaving them humorously uncomfortable for the entire event. I considered it payback to Trey for disrespecting my apartment, but that didn't change the fact that I cried like a baby when he and Chase left for the airport to begin their European adventure.

Once I said goodbye to my parents, I found Jaxon and his family among the chaos of people crowding around the Stroh Center. While people waited in an endless line to take pictures with the falcon statue, I embraced my warm congratulations from the Hayes family, trying not to get emotional when Jaxon's parents told me how proud they were of me and my accomplishments.

Seriously. Like Jared mentioned on spring break, what the fuck are they putting in the water at Bowling Green? One moment you were chill as a cucumber. The next moment you were bawling over accomplishments.

After four years of classes and tuition, my eighty thousand dollar proof of education would be mailed to my house in a few weeks. Needless to say, I was sent into panic mode since I didn't officially have an address to my name. So I did what all sane girlfriends would do in a crisis. I vented to my boyfriend in hopes that he could fix it.

Jaxon received my diploma at his Los Angeles address about two months after graduation. He called me immediately and held it up to his. They both looked great against the fresh paint job in his office, and when he fell back in his desk chair and spun around, I couldn't wait to have my fun in the CEO's headquarters.

Well, in his home office headquarters. Jaxon wouldn't have the official title for at least another year or two at Hayes Sports & Entertainment, but that didn't take away the fact that he looked sexy as fuck in business attire.

"What is it about men and dress shirts?" Katie asked.

Every Monday morning, Katie and I chatted on my walk to get coffee. Somehow, I was able to get a studio apartment in Chelsea that my internship partially funded.

Heavy on the word partially. It covered at least half and allowed me to afford a safe space to live in by myself.

I pulled on the door of my favorite local coffee shop. "I think it has to do with them looking like grown men instead of college guys."

"Mhm," Katie agreed. "Yes. Yes, that is it! You know Connor might have to get *glasses*?"

I squinted at the menu in front of me even though I knew what I was getting. "Has he aged that much since I left him in BG?"

She laughed. "You're missing the point. Picture Jaxon right now in some glasses while you ride him on his desk chair."

It was always the sign of a great day when I remembered to keep Katie off speakerphone, especially since the pink in my cheeks would've alerted everyone around me that I was picturing exactly what she said. I crossed my ankles to try to ease the throbbing between my legs. It was way too early to be horny and hungry while I stood in line for overpriced coffee.

"Your silence says it all," Katie stated confidently. "Ugh, I miss you."

"It'll be Thanksgiving before we know it!" I reminded her, trying to stay positive about our long-distance friendship.

Long-distance boyfriend? Sucked ass.

Long-distance best friend? Sucked the life out of your soul.

"Just make sure Jaxon gives himself enough time for travel. I'm not convinced that boy understands the difference between West and East Coast."

"Definitely one of the tribulations of being on opposite ends of the country," I mumbled.

"Ohhh the trials and tribulations of Jaxon Hayes." Katie laughed. "Sounds like the next great American novel."

I chuckled halfway into ordering my iced hazelnut coffee. The barista shot me the same warm and inviting smile she gave me every Monday morning. As much as I would've loved to add her to my daily routine, my small compensation for interning wouldn't allow me to afford it.

It was either coffee or keeping my lights on. I'd be lying if sometimes I reminded myself how much I loved the dark.

My phone buzzed in my hand, and my headphones told me that "Jax" was calling.

"The main character in that novel is calling me now," I joked, taking my drink from the barista and bidding her a grateful nod. "I'll text you after class."

"Remember! Picture those glasses and his de—"

I was still laughing when I switched the line over to Jaxon. "Hello?"

"Hey, pretty girl." There was a loud buzzing near the speaker as Jaxon headed into the office. "What's so funny?"

I pushed the heavy door of the coffee shop and reunited with the busy streets of New York. "Oh, nothing. Katie is writing you into the next iconic piece of literature. Normal Monday morning shit."

"*Literature?*" He said the word like he was settling for coach airline seating.

"Yes, sir. *The Trials and Tribulations of Jaxon Hayes.*"

He laughed. "That sounds terrible."

"I know. Kind of creates unnecessary negative foreshadowing, doesn't it?"

"Makes me sound like I'm fighting for my life. How's your apartment?"

Part of me was surprised that wasn't his first question when he called. Jaxon asked about my apartment at least once a week. He hated how I was living by myself in such a big city, and when I told him he was doing the same thing, he always reassured me it was just because he worried about my safety.

Because if he could handle living by himself in a new setting, so could I.

"Apartment is good," I said, taking a much-needed sip of my coffee. "Have you ever considered glasses?"

"Glasses?" His voice shot up an octave before he greeted Helen in the background. "Why?"

We spiraled into a conversation about desk chairs as I made my way closer to campus.

"The things I could do to you in this office," Jaxon growled. He went silent as I pushed open the door to *my* office, keeping an erotic daydream to himself. "I have windows that overlook the city and—"

"I'm going to need you to pause for a moment as I get into my . . . *not*-so-massive office," I whispered, offering the secretary a friendly wave good morning.

While my office wasn't massive, I felt a flutter of pride as I took my space in the back. Surrounded by textbooks, a small window that overlooked part of campus, and a solid oak desk to set my belongings on, I didn't need anything else.

It hadn't taken long, but I was only a month into this internship and my office felt like a piece of home. It made moments like these harder, where I would do anything to have Jaxon in front of me. He'd play out what was happening in his head, and in an even more perfect world, Katie lived down the street so I could tell her all about the amazing experience after it happened.

"Okay." I sighed into my chair and braced myself for what came next. "Keep telling me about this sex we're having in your office."

"I wish I could, but I have a meeting in exactly three minutes," he grumbled.

"At six in the morning your time?"

"The trials and tribulations of working with a client in Florida." I heard him smile on the other end of the phone. "I'll call you when I get home, pretty girl. I love you."

My heart sank just a tad. I needed to start my day too, but I always hated getting off the phone with him. "I love you too, Jax."

"And tell Katie I'll figure out Thanksgiving," he added quickly. "I can't imagine going any longer without seeing you. I won't make it."

And just like that, my heart floated back to surface level.

We had a long road ahead of us, and we were just getting into the driver's seat. While there would be moments that were hard, it was times like these when I remained optimistic.

Trials and tribulations, none of them mattered. I wanted to believe that nothing mattered if the person was your endgame.

Author's Note

This is my third time writing an author's note, and I still cannot believe that the journey I started four years ago would bring me here. Who knew that Maci and Jaxon would come to life not just once, but twice! A story that began in my head made it to print, and I am so grateful.

If I am being honest, I struggled to write this sequel. I outlined the first draft before I began writing *The Trust Factor*, and I would be lying if I said that shifting from Deacon and Lyla back to Jaxon and Maci was easy. After feeling such a strong connection to *The Trust Factor*, a story that connected me with deep feelings of grief and the importance of mental health, it t seemed a little silly to reunite with messy characters who were just trying to figure it out in college.

But once I got back into Jaxon and Maci's journey through their senior year, I was reminded of one humbling fact. Their crazy, overdramatic and humorous world was why I started this all in the first place. Writing from a place that filled me with college nostalgia brought me back to a time in my life when everything seemed so complicated. We've all been put in a position where we have to choose, and I wanted to write two characters who tried to have it all.

I've read tons of romance books where one of the characters has to give something up to be with the other person. I didn't want that for Jaxon or Maci. Both characters were clear about what they wanted after graduation, and it was important to me that both of them stayed true to themselves and what they worked hard for.

I said I would have a third book in this series, and as of right now, I'm not sure if they necessarily need it! I have some options of where Jaxon and Maci could go, and believe me when I say it won't be what you expect! To make sure I do it to the best of my ability, I am going to hold off on a possible third book. The last four years have taught me a lot about my creative process, and when the time is right, I will know.

If you have made it this far, thank you so much for reading. If this is the third book you've read by me, I cannot thank you enough! With so many amazing stories and authors out there, I am honored to be included in your page reads and on your bookshelf.

Thank you to my husband, Noel. The amount of support and love you give me is unmatched, and I am so lucky that you ran into my table and asked me to arm wrestle.

Thank you to my friends and family who read my books, and thank you for not judging me for my spicy scenes (even though I know most of you secretly enjoy them).

Thank you to all of the incredible readers and authors who I have met through social media. I had no idea when I made that first TikTok that it would open so many doors for me. I am forever grateful for the amazing amount of support I have found. Thank you for loving my books and my stories.

Thank you to Sadie, at Dot The I Edit. You've been in my corner since we first chatted on Instagram, and I am lucky to not only have you as an amazing editor, but as a friend.

My last thank you is actually a shoutout to *One Tree Hill*. That show has gotten me through some dark times and the characters are unmatched. Brooke Davis is an inspiration and

Naley will forever be iconic. I hope my fellow OTH fans enjoyed reading those chapters as much as I enjoyed writing them.

With love,
Brittany

About the Author

Brittany Wilson is an author who writes romantic comedies and contemporary romance. She graduated from Bowling Green State University with a degree in education and the college serves as the setting for many of her books! Brittany has always had a love for writing and a passion for telling stories. Her books are available on all platforms! Make sure to follow Brittany on social media to stay updated on her author journey!

TikTok and Instagram – @brittanywilsonauthor
www.brittanywilsonauthor.com